THE NIGHTMARE CURSE

A CHRISTMAS CAROL RETELLING

THE NIGHTMARE CURSE

A CHRISTMAS CAROL RETELLING

KAYLA MCGRATH

CONTENT WARNINGS

This book includes content that may be disturbing to some readers, discretion is advised. Content includes graphic violence (blood, gore, body mutilation, decapitation, murder, death, death of family), sexually explicit scenes, vague suicidal ideation, depictions of demons/demonic influence, depictions of Hell, depictions of Heaven, and alcohol consumption.

*For my readers, my gift to you this season.
Merry Christmas!*

PROLOGUE

ADELAIDE KANE

DECEMBER 24, 1866

Vanity was the hardest sin to rid oneself of and such pride would be Adelaide Kane's demise. She was kind to a fault, but that, paired with her exquisite beauty, and miserly hands made her the perfect victim of jealousy. And the ruinous Nightmare Curse.

"Please," she begged the demon whose face was an abyss of stars beneath an ivory hood. "I repent, I truly do! I see the error of my ways, I will share my coin, donate to charity, I will live in a ramshackle hovel. Please, let me leave this dreaded nightmare with my life."

Someone had hated or envied her enough to cast a killing curse on her, willing to risk their own life in exchange for hers—should she succeed in change. The demons didn't care who lived or who died, they collected a soul either way.

"And what of your beauty? Would you forfeit that?" the demon asked in an echoing voice that prompted existential fear.

Adelaide pressed a dainty hand to her creamy cheek. Her fingers were slender, but not bony, her nails perfect, pink ovals. She felt the softness of her skin, the heat of her rosy cheeks. She was in her seventh decade, but due to having performed the Staying in her thirtieth year, she appeared not a day more.

"Would you still scorn those who do not possess the same radiance as you?" The demon drew closer and lifted a cosmic hand, its not-skin swirling as its eldritch fingers captured a golden ringlet and spun it. "Dedicate less to how you look? To let society judge you at your most natural?"

The horror that shivered through Adelaide was a physical thing and she couldn't help pulling away from the last demon. She couldn't lie to the demons who visited her, it was a compulsion of the curse. Even if she wanted to deny it, to lie to herself even, she could not. It was a physical impossibility and she couldn't force her tongue to move around the untruth.

Her eyes flickered to the frozen grave that yawned open from the snowy ground. They were in a cemetery past midnight and were utterly alone—not even a mouse scurried within the demon's presence. Wind howled through the skeletal branches of the dark trees and beneath the moonless night—not even shadows played upon the untouched snow. The edges of the grave had roots like corpse fingers, reaching up from the pits of Hell to drag her down. The hole was so deep she could not see the bottom. And she did not want to. What lurked below terrified her beyond measure.

"I—" she opened her mouth to answer the demon, but despite her fear, she could not.

Hellhounds of smoke and darkness paced by the demon, their eyes molten embers of red-hot flame. Lips pulled back from teeth with the promise to devour her if she threatened to run. She had been warned they would drag her to her demise, should she try to flee.

"You do not truly mean to change your ways, therefore I shall take your soul and feast on it."

The demon lifted its hands in summoning. Ghostly chains of black iron appeared from the ether, wreathed in deepest crimson light. The haunted chains danced in the air, puppets of the final demon's ministrations. Undulating like snakes, they slithered on the frosty air and slid around Adelaide.

Tears spilled and froze on Adelaide's cheeks as she subjected herself to the phantom links that would drag her to the underworld. The weight of her sins—pride and greed—bound the chains and pressed into her, crushing her, suffocating her. The dark magic forced itself into her mouth and down her throat, clogging her air and stealing her breath. She gorged herself on greed and squeezed her lungs with vanity.

The pain was excruciating, so much agony that she could not scream, could not plead, could not pray. She was jailed to her form without reprieve, suffused in endless suffering. It was endless and it was seconds. Time ceased to mean anything. All was pain.

The hellhounds yipped with excitement and anticipation, increasing their prancing and snarls.

Bones crunched, skin split, ivory protruding from the scarlet and viscera. Her once beautiful face purpled and bloated as the chains continued wrapping, compressing her skull.

The demon cast her into her oblivion-grave where her physical form finally gave way and she was nothing but mist and blood, gore and shards. Splatters of blood arced from the hole and scattered on the snow, leaving perfect frozen rubies in the glittering white.

Her soul screamed on the descent to Hell, as it would for all eternity until some beast swallowed the final morsel of her spirit. Divining on her agony like a delicacy.

The demon watched facelessly, and vanished with the hellhounds, concluding the night's end.

In the morning, the church bells unknowingly called out Adelaide Kane's death knell on Christmas Day, pronouncing her as the twenty-first victim of the Nightmare Curse.

STAVE ONE

DECEMBER 21, 1873

Azure light bled out from between Benedict's splayed fingers as he carved geometry through the air. It wasn't necessarily geometry, but rather sigils, summoned from his intrinsic ability borne of blood from his warlock status. His hands moved, pulling and knotting from the ether, twisting symbols and knitting them anew. He did this from halfway up his prison cell, floating cross-legged many feet above his old brass bed.

Levitating was virtually second nature to him now. It came with an ease from boredom, and necessity due to filth.

The prison was not known for its hygienic standards—personal standards which Benedict still held highly even after seven years of purgatory.

Seven fucking years.

How had it been so long? Yet how had time passed him by so quickly? Time held so little meaning when he was serving a one-hundred-year sentence and it passed in blinks and blurs, and startles and stops. It could drive a man to insanity.

How had he afforded a fate so like his own mother's?

The jingle of keys alerted him to a guard's approaching presence. Benedict gracefully descended from his lofty perch and balanced on his slipper-clad feet. Meeting the guard at the door, Benedict waited for the slot to open and food to arrive. When the slot opened, the guard casted a small sigil through it. Benedict held up a hand while the symbol emblazoned itself upon his palm, stifling his magic for three minutes.

Immediately, he felt hollowed out. Like his chest was carved open and left gaping and only he was privy to the horror of his evisceration. His magic had been stolen from him. Bled from his being. Pried out of his soul.

It made him feel like a eunuch.

To be cut off from the virtual lifeblood of his magic was like severing half his body. He was not whole without it. He was not him without it. It was the only thing that kept his sanity. Why he hadn't attempted something…drastic.

The feeling was as mystifying as it was horrifying and he was just grateful that the cantrip was temporary.

"Happy Solstice, Benedict," the guard, Klaus, announced once Benedict had assumed the spell. "It's a lovely one, the snowfall is light and well—magical, I dare say. You should see it."

"And how would you expect me to?" Benedict snapped.

Klaus glanced in his cell and noted the lack of a window as his face flushed with embarrassment. His entire pale face turned as crimson as holly berries, pressing into his fair hairline and down his weak neck.

The guard was young, perhaps freshly twenty at most, and he wore his youth like a shiny badge—it was hard to miss. His jawline was soft, as were his puppy-eyes, large and evergreen. His golden curls were cherubic, angelic even, worn in a fashionable coiffure that had just come into style the year Benedict was framed. His build was lean but he still retained some baby fat, the sort that would disappear within a few years. The boy still had much growing to do. Much maturing.

"I did not mean offense," Klaus said placatingly.

"You did not intend to point out a fact to me that I should not obviously know, nor will I be able to confirm, due to being imprisoned?"

Klaus sighed. "I was just making conversation."

"Make conversation elsewhere."

Klaus slid the metal tray of food through the slot and then shut the tiny door behind it. His footsteps retreated with the jangle of keys. Eventually, the sounds tapered off.

Benedict stared at the tray. A small tin of water. A hunk of sourdough bread, some gray gruel, boiled carrots that looked weeks past edibility, and some very dry mystery meat. A sad and bruised apple sat on the edge. There was even a small brown worm hole in the fruit.

Next door, Benedict's cell-neighbor began to cough. The previously dry sound had turned to wet hacks. It had been mild days ago, but with the cold settling in, his neighbor was not faring well. Benedict ignored the pang of pity and sorrow for the man. Besides, he didn't know why he was locked up— for all he knew he'd raped and pillaged a dozen villages.

"You know young Klaus was just trying to spread the Christmas spirit," the neighbor chided after his coughing fit subsided.

Benedict scoffed. "What spirit? The Ghosts of Christmas?"

When Benedict's neighbor gasped, it was like all the air in the jail was sucked out. Everything suddenly seized up with tension, as if even the stone walls drew and held breath. The wards strung tight, pulling tension through the structure.

"That is not something to jest about. Particularly now." His neighbor's voice was wound with anxiety. "The possibility of the Nightmare Curse approaches rapidly and you do not want to tempt the fires of Hell to choose you."

As his neighbor exhaled, the air seemed to relax too.

The Nightmare Curse held certain requirements, and as Benedict had been ensconced within these walls, he could not fulfill such specifications. His inaction wasn't leaving anyone to die, his less than desirable qualities were not being enabled by anyone, he did not have anyone still hoping for the best in him, and certainly no one was being undervalued by him. He did not let himself think about the stipulation that perfectly fit, especially on this very day.

"The curse can't touch me. I haven't fucked over enough people."

Benedict began picking over his sallow meal as his neighbor picked up a coughing attack that rivaled the first. His magic returned to him in a wave of relief, and though it filled a void, there was a worry in the pit of his stomach. He didn't know why, but something about it unsettled him deeply.

DECEMBER 22, 1873

The next day a rare letter arrived for Benedict. He tore open the envelope the moment Klaus handed it to him—moments after the magic-stealing sigil branded itself to his palm.

He thought he felt empty after his magic was struck from him. He hadn't known empty. Not until he read the contents of the letter and every last particle that made up everything he was sloughed away.

He was less than a skeleton. Less than the soul that made him who he was.

His best friend and mentor was dead.

The paper fell from his hand and innocently fluttered to the ground, heedless of the implosion it had just wreaked on his psyche. The name stared up at him as if it were shouting at him.

Nicholas Whitehill.

After having fought a decade long battle with one of the only immortal-afflicting diseases, he'd succumbed to the ail of the Wasting just yesterday. On the anniversary of her—

No. He didn't let himself think of her. Of that.

When a warlock completed the ritual of The Staying, they were frozen at the age of the rite's completion despite their true years. It was not without its risks, as the Staying could become fatal, but the benefits far outweighed the negatives. It was uncommon to find a warlock who had not, or would not, be performing the ritual.

Benedict had completed it at twenty-seven—just eight years ago. Nicholas had been a year shy of thirty, though his true age was more than three times that.

With the added blessing of eternal youth, warlocks were impervious to all human agues—no influenzas, poxes, or blights. What they were susceptible to, were three very specific diseases that only immortals could contract: Ember Fever, Midnight Malady, and the Wasting. All were fatal without treatment, but only one had a cure—to contract one of the others was a death sentence.

The Wasting in particular was a cruel beast. It was an ailment that slowly drained a person of their vitality. Shut down all the body's systems, sapped their strength, health, and energy, until all that was left to take was their personality, their drives, their morals—everything that made them, *them*.

Rage and grief suffocated him, everything within him rebelled at the restriction on his magic, the tethers on his emotions. He hung his head in his hands, pulling at his chestnut curls, wanting to rip them out. To tear. Destroy.

Finally, he felt the leash on his magic snap and he broke with a yell, falling to his knees, a blast of magic careening out of him. The blue waves crashed against the stone walls, shaking the corners of his cell. The stone was cold and hard against his knees, and they smarted from the impact, but he did not care. His mouth opened in a silent scream, wailing against injustice.

He was researching the cure when he was framed. He was so close to solving the puzzle that encompassed the Wasting. He was so close to a breakthrough after *she* discovered how to eliminate Ember Fever. But now…all that effort. All the research. For nothing. It was all for naught because his best friend, his mentor, was dead.

Ember Fever was a virulent illness that struck fast, but was short-lived. The fever boiled an individual from the inside out—melting organs, cooking blood—and caused exsanguination from orifices, as well as the melting of one's eyeballs. To contract it was a three-day countdown.

Tears slipped noiselessly down his face and plummeted to the freezing stone beneath. He stayed there, lost, until a voice broke through the gloom.

"Are you quite all right, Lord Edwards?"

Benedict lifted his head as he recognized the voice of his cell-neighbor, Christopher—he didn't know his surname. And of course, Christopher used his formal title. He hadn't been addressed as "lord" in years. It shocked him enough to draw his attention.

"I am not," Benedict finally responded after a round of quiet. He sat back on his haunches and leaned against the wall. "My dearest friend has passed away."

"I am sorry to hear that. Was it an accident?"

"The Wasting."

A quick inhalation of breath was Christopher's first answer. "That is truly terrible."

"It is." And for some reason Benedict wanted to say more. "The worst part is, I think I could have saved him." He began to ramble on a tangent, regardless of if his cell-neighbor was listening. "Before I was locked in here, I was a professor and a researcher. My studies brought me to immortal diseases because Nicholas was suffering from one. Myself and—" he cut himself off, "another professor, had made a breakthrough. She learned how to cure Ember Fever. We inquired if the Wasting could have the same application in theory. I was days away from solving the riddle of the illness—perhaps less. Maybe I know it now. Unfortunately, she died and all the secret research died with her. We never found out who killed her, but they all thought it was me."

"Which is why you're here."

"Which is why I'm here. And why two lives are gone when they should not be."

"But you think you could cure the Wasting?"

"I believe so. I've been able to magically treat other diseases with ease."

Benedict's eyesight was going gray and fuzzy, his limbs cold and non-compliant. He slouched down until he was completely leaning against the wall, his backside to the floor.

"I do not wish to upset you in your grief, but if you know how to help with the Wasting perhaps you can help me with…"

But Benedict had tuned Christopher out, staring blankly and endlessly at the stone wall before him as those very stones suffocated him in his darkness and loss, pulling him under.

That night, Benedict had slipped into his mind, behind the shroud of his intelligence and magic, into a space devoid of jail and misery. It was a room, like an alchemist's study, potions burbling and beakers trickling, complex tubes and ancient tomes. It was wizardry and science wrapped in one.

The study was his salvation, a secret area he constructed during his sentence. He'd built it up over the years, stored resources and memory, spells, enchantments, and most of all, research.

There, within his mind he researched and tested his theories and hypotheses. He linked the idea *she* had and the breakthrough *she* made, then applied it to the workings of the Wasting. There, in the false study, the magically preserved specimen of the Wasting reacted and then it began to turn, eating itself like an ouroboros before it coiled in on itself and devoured until it was dust. It became ash and then nothing. The Wasting was cured.

But Nicholas was still dead.

And everyone he'd ever loved had left him. It began with his parents, who'd sought to use him and dispose of him when need arose. Then others left by sickness and death, while others from lack of faith.

Benedict roared within his study, his magic smashing everything in its path. Potions shattered against the wall and rained glass and fluid over the shelves and books. The wooden desks and tables were smashed beneath the might of his fury, the magic throwing it all in an exploding orb against the walls.

He collapsed.

When he came to, his cell was also destroyed. His bed was crumpled against the wall, twisted and folded in on itself, the thin moth-eaten sheets shredded from the force of his power, moldy feather pillow obliterated. His metal tray was warped and dinged; the remnants of food spread around the room in infinitesimal particles. The bucket used for his eliminations was in splinters and he was just thankful that he regularly spelled-away any evidence every time.

He shivered, feeling the iced-over tears biting his cheeks, his numbed fingers cramped. It was always cold in the cell at night—worse so now that winter had fully descended. He climbed on the ruined mattress and wrapped the tatters of the blankets around him.

Shaking, he twisted his fingers and summoned a sphere of flame. It lit up his face in shades of blue—cerulean at the core, icy at the edges. He let it hover in front of him, providing warmth as he curled in on himself and tried to slip into oblivion.

DECEMBER 23, 1873

Dawn awoke with golden rays that Benedict could not see. He stayed wrapped in his ruined bed as Klaus came around with meals—soupy, gray gruel, a squishy clementine, hard bread, moldy cheese, and a questionable cup of milk with a regular tin of water. He ignored Klaus's footsteps.

"Good morning, Lord Edwards," Klaus proclaimed cheerfully.

Benedict wanted to throttle him in response. How dare he be so chipper when Benedict was doused in desolation? Not only was he wallowing in this shithole for a crime he didn't commit, he lost two of the most important people in his life, and no one gave a single damn.

The small metal slot opened and Klaus drew a large intake of breath.

"My Lord, what happened?"

Benedict scoffed. "You must not be a very adept warlock if you cannot recognize the aftermath of magic."

Klaus was visibly flustered and searched for words. Implying someone was a poorly trained or untalented warlock was one of the most insulting offenses one could offer. Benedict had never stooped to such a level before, but he was angry and hurt, and he wanted someone else angry and hurt, too.

"Of course, I'm familiar. But I do not understand why."

"That's none of your fucking concern."

"If I must rectify the room, it certainly is."

"With *your* paltry magic? What a show."

Klaus was taken aback. "Something bad happened."

Benedict gasped with mock surprise. "*No.* However could you tell?"

"Did you lose someone?"

"*Fuck. Off,*" Benedict said lowly. Lethally.

Klaus didn't bother with the spell and instead just shoved the metal tray through the slot. It teetered precariously before crashing to the ground. Benedict could have caught it with magic, but he did not. He would have been too late. Just like he was too late for Nicholas. Just like he was too late for *her.*

Benedict didn't acknowledge the mess and did not entertain the pleading questioning of his cell-neighbor either. Eventually, he crawled out from his ruined bed-nest and picked over the cheese. He tore off the unsalvageable bits and then nibbled on it. It was aged, and had it been served in its prime, it would have been delicious. He looked at the spilled milk and knew there was a joke in there somehow, but he did not deign to reach for it. The gruel was a loss, but he did pursue the orange and bread.

The rest of the day continued as such. Benedict wallowed, Christopher tried coaxing answers out of him, and Klaus had given up after his relentless kindness was finally and fully wasted on the former Lord Edwards. The trays were haphazardly pushed through the slot, again, one teetered. The dinner one did not. Benedict was more miserable and crueler than before.

It didn't give him any satisfaction, and with every passing second, he felt increasingly hollow and empty.

DECEMBER 24, 1873

Benedict was still in his fugue when a voice chimed outside his cell, arriving with the scent of vanilla cinnamon perfume. He stiffened, recognizing both before slowly turning to the source.

Sabine Van Arsdel stood just beyond the door of his cell, the warlock having casted a transparency charm against the interior-warded door. Her hands were still glowing with crimson light, a sharp sigil akin to a snowflake wavering in the air between them.

"I'm sorry about Nicholas," Sabine said, genuine sorrow painting her face.

She was dressed in a form-hugging gown of emerald velvet with a snowy cape of white wool cast over her shoulders. Ornate gold buttons followed the line of her sternum, a clasp of holly leaves holding the cloak at her throat, her décolletage low and bare of jewelry—likely confiscated by Klaus or another guard to prevent assisting an escape.

Benedict, unshaven, clad in dingy gray linen pants, a ragged beige sweater, and a pair of dark socks with a hole in the great toe felt horribly shamed and underdressed. Like a pauper in a princess's presence.

Assured that his attention was trained on her, she began speaking again—more formally.

"Hello Lord Edwards, it's been many months since we last exchanged words."

Benedict stared at her emotionlessly, so drained he couldn't muster even a petty quip, or a thank you, or an agreement. She was kind enough not to bring up the state of his ruined room.

Sabine twisted her dark gold hands in nervousness, the gesture not affecting the charm. "I meant to visit the other day, on the anniversary—"

"Did you ever settle down with someone?"

Sabine bit her tongue, surprise flooding her deep brown, nearly black doe eyes. She regained her composure, sharpening her plush features against his slight.

"No. I did not."

"Why?"

"Well, it wasn't because I still harbored feelings for you, my lord."

Once upon a time, many years ago—before *her*—they had been lovers. It had been casual and fun, purely of the flesh with no romantic entanglements or marital prospects between them. Benedict had been an awkward and scholarly professor, never having touched a woman, and Sabine was sick and tired of misogynistic men who could not get her to completion. They'd struck up a deal, because he was kind and wanted to learn, and she was eager to teach and be treated with respect.

Their affair was brief, but pleasant. It ended mutually when Sabine met Nicholas and introduced Benedict to *her* the very same night. He was unconditionally and singularly devoted ever since, and Sabine had become one of his dearest friends—until his sentencing when he pushed her away.

Sabine, meanwhile, had never gotten over Nicholas—to Benedict's knowledge. They had been star-crossed, he withholding his heart only because he knew he was dying of the Wasting and did not want to subject Sabine to his untimely demise.

Still, he knew it hurt her.

Sabine tucked a lock of darkest red hair behind her ear, the impossibly long fall of her tresses unbound—a norm here, unheard of in the Victorian women of Mortal London.

When magic became more mainstream, the power of the conduction of spells caused a rift in the mortal world. In doing that, it created a second plane of existence, a mirror to the city. When this happened, warlocks flocked to the new London—Vonor—through the portal of Blackfriars Bridge, and created their own new society—devoid of many mortal constraints. Vonor was the first of its kind, then Paris followed, then Cairo, New York, Beijing, and more.

"I just…now that Nicholas is gone too, I—" she broke off, swallowing. "I've just felt so alone."

Benedict clenched his teeth and an involuntary sound of pain left him. He was alone too. More than either of them had been. *They* could still see each other—before he'd died. He was separated by walls, and magic, and death.

But Sabine was not without her losses. She was a shell of who she once was, all her vivaciousness and fire was tamped down. No longer the sass and chide that was her norm carried her. She was formal, lacking all the warmth she'd always had.

It just made him angrier and sadder.

"You wish to wax poetic about your losses? To me? Of all people?"

Sabine flushed with anger and mortification. "I didn't mean—"

"Didn't mean what?"

"I miss her, too."

"Don't," he snapped violently, his eyes blazing twin orbs of emerald fire. He felt his cerulean magic crackle about him, his hackles rising. Rage swept through him like an inferno, the conflagration of his grief the all-consuming fires of Hell. It was endless and constant and the whiplike reminder of her absence was an acute lash. All of it surged through his veins.

"Benedict," she said softly, pressing her hand to the barrier. "I know you didn't do it, even if no one else believes it. You would have never hurt Lucia."

His back had been ever so slightly turned towards Sabine, but with those five letters spoken in that order, he was whipping around to face her. As if branded. "Don't say her name," he managed in a ragged gasp. "Please, I cannot bear it."

"Not talking about Lucia does not remove her death. We should not let her name become forgotten."

"Forgotten like me? The convenient scapegoat? Who better to frame for her murder than the fiancé her family disapproved of? I did not do it, and yet she is still gone, and they feel vindicated with the knowledge they were right about me, even when her true murderer still roams free."

"I know," she acquiesced with regret. "Whoever did it had connections—with the constabulary and high ranking warlocks. It was all the odds against you, and when they found you with her bo—"

"I know how they found us."

The memory haunted him daily, nightly. Of finding Lucia's body. The disbelief. The horror. The fear. The agony. He remembered the sight, branded to his memory. Red light. Red blood. Red anger. Her cold corpse stiffening in his arms, her blood staining his clothes, his hands, his soul. Ebony hair, chalk white skin, flat blue eyes, crimson everywhere.

Sabine's full lips thinned and tears brimmed in her dark eyes. She opened her mouth once, twice, then inhaled sharply, brushing fallen tears from her cheeks with the back of her hand.

"I apologize for upsetting you, Lord Edwards." Sabine sniffed and let out a half sigh, shaking herself from the painful emotions. Her eyes were glassy as they met Benedict's through the magical wall, her chin tilted up despite the quiver there. "Merry Christmas."

And with that she flattened her hands together and the scarlet-edged doorway shrank away, the metal reappearing—eating up the invisibility—as Sabine turned, a whirl of deep red hair and emerald velvet. The last thing he saw was her retreating form, held proud. She did not turn back and the metal door reformed.

Benedict pressed his forehead into his knees and let silent tears course down his face.

As the clock began to toll out the midnight hour, the temperature in Benedict's cell plummeted. His small orb of fire was nearly doused as he was plunged into arctic degrees. Benedict startled and pulled his blankets up about him, drawing himself up into a sitting position.

He casted his gaze around his dreary, windowless cell, seeing endless, repeating gray stone with warding sigils carved into the brick and some of the mortar. He could practice magic within the cell, but that magic could not penetrate the charms and wards compressing him. Not warlock sigils. His furniture was all still ruined where he left it, but something was off. Something was different.

Something was present.

Benedict resisted the urge to call out a foolish "Hello?" or "Who's there?" and instead heightened his alertness. He scanned the darkness, awareness strung high and tight, looking for any differentiation in the shadows.

The scent of frost came as ice crusted in the corners of his cell, the smell of fresh-turned earth and smoke mingled in the air. Something prickled and charged, the energy shifted and anxiety rose in Benedict.

Momentarily melding from the wall was a figure. It stepped out, like breaking the surface of water, before it passed through the stone. He was an apparition of empty gray and ice blue, floating on an unseen current, feet dangling like someone from a hangman's noose. He was weighed with chains, heavy iron links that wrapped his form, twisting about his neck and trailing behind him. The chains themselves dangled or ended in large, dragging spheres.

Benedict scrambled back in horror, realizations splashing across his psyche like a violent kaleidoscope.

The Nightmare Curse.

It had come for him.

And the figure before him was the ghost of Nicholas Whitehill.

"Nicky…" Benedict whispered, his breath coiling like white cigarillo smoke in the frigid air.

Benedict's best friend and mentor had always been fair and tall, a few inches more than his six feet and two inches, but the Wasting had taken both those from him—turned his skin sallow and crippled his spine. But here, in death, he was restored. Despite the muted tones, his hair was still fair and carefully styled, gently waving on some unseen breeze. Then, his gray eyes that had always been soft, yet grave, now seemed only the latter.

The last time Benedict had seen Nicholas alive, he'd been a pale imitation of the warlock he'd been seven years ago, before the Wasting had tightened its fist on his health. He appeared a frail man, weaker than one in his ninth decade. Instead of the warlock who'd completed the Staying before thirty. That had been months ago, back in the height of summer where the heat in the cell was so oppressive Nicholas had to be whisked away by guards and helpers.

That was the memory that branded itself into his mind now. His best friend collapsed, carried out, looking like a corpse already. Sweat had beaded on his brow, his face flushed, then pale, his breathing thin and high. Benedict knew his friend was destined for death not long after, but the reality of it was a whole other thing.

"Ben," Nicholas began. "I'm here as your warning, I am the precursor to your curse. I have been sent from the fires of Hell, on the heels of demons, as a Harbinger of your doom." His voice was stuttering and garbled, like the afterlife was interfering with his ability to converse. His speech read like a script, like prophecy and formality.

Benedict had not truly thought Nicholas would end up in Hell, but perhaps there were some sins he did not know of. Or perhaps he resided in the first circle with the other restless spirits and minor demons.

"So, the Nightmare Curse has come for me after all," Benedict said with resignation.

He truly hadn't believed he was at risk of being pulled for the curse—there were many other people worse than him and more worthy of the trial. Someone clearly hated Benedict, enough to want an imprisoned man punished more.

The Nightmare Curse was like a lottery. A name was chosen and the demons tormented the selected warlock until dawn. Most people could not absolve themselves of the characteristics that brought down the curse—like greed, disdain, abuse—and so, the chains of those choices pulled them to Hell. But, if they repented from their sins, they survived the night, and the person who had cursed them would take their place.

In all the years only two people had ever survived the curse—Ebenezer Scrooge and Clarence Beaumont. And in those instances, the curser indeed took their place, dragged to Hell in chains by the visiting demons.

It took a terrible sort of person to cast the curse, usually fueled by hate or fury or jealousy. Most saw it as a quiet way to get rid of someone, as the curser was never revealed unless they spoke of it, or their cursed warlock survived.

Sometimes the curse was playfully coined the Scrooge Curse for its first survivor.

"It has," Nicholas confirmed solemnly. His mouth moved, but nothing came out. He could see him forming words, but Benedict heard nothing. He pulled out a pocket watch and glanced down at it angrily. "I come, begging you take heed and survive this. Get revenge—"

Nicholas's words cut off again, the demons surely pulling his puppet strings by the soul-binding chains. Countless infernal runes danced around him, twirling in the air, so dark a shade of red they were nearly black, a few of them so raven purple they were midnight.

"If you are my Enabler, who were my others? How did *I* fit the requirements?"

The Enabler was the equivalent of Scrooge's Jacob Marley. Marley enabled his miserly tendencies, urging him to follow in his footsteps. The Enabler was also the one character in the curse who must have died as a prerequisite.

All these players, all these characters. It was a game. Curses such as the Nightmare Curse were made up by demons—like ideas and toys flung into the abyss. Demons whispered these ploys in taverns, after sweet nothings to bedmates, hissed from forests. Once they were heard, those curses were thrown into the void and they landed in the laps of warlocks who began to recite them in their spell books. At any point a demon could make a new curse, but it wasn't given power until a warlock took it up.

Anger had started taking place of the acceptance. The word "revenge" unravelling something in his brain. He was an innocent man and so much had just been taken from him. Now, his life and soul were in jeopardy.

To be taken by the Nightmare Curse, one must have wronged several specific people. Surprisingly enough, there were always enough people done harm by many to qualify.

"Who is my Discarded? My Undervalued? My—"

He stopped himself from saying his Lost. His Belle. The one who was his great lost love. He knew Lucia was his Lost. He'd lost her, not due to his greed or avarice or disregard. He'd lost her to death's hand. But it was a loss nonetheless, and it fit the requisite role.

The "Scrooge" must be selfish in some form—miserly, knowledge hoarding, spurning family, scorning the poor. Their inaction must lead to a preventable death—the Discarded, and they had to have someone enabling that behavior, or similar behavior, even copying it from said person originally—"Jacob Marley". Someone must try to see the best in them, and not give up despite the odds—the Believer—while someone else was being undermined or under appreciated by them—the Undervalued. Then there was the Antithesis, the opposite of the cursed—Fezziwig in Scrooge's case. And finally, in some way they must lose their greatest love. Any wronged person could cast and trigger the curse without being a character in the curse, though just as often the caster *was* a character wronged.

"Lucia," Nicholas said answering Benedict's unsaid question, and his voice held so much pain. She was dear to him too. Lucia had often compared him to a brother, and no doubt that loss was still raw. His mouth moved in more missing words before sound returned. "Lucia is your Belle. You'll be seeing her a lot tonight, but you can't—" The words broke again.

"Can't what?"

More broken silence. "You're powerful enough. Save her."

"How? Does the curse not just operate within my mind? I can't change the past from my psyche."

The ghost flipped the pocket watch thrice, then put it away. "The demons take you back *in time*. You can break through the wards. You can change it all. Please, save m—"

Nicholas was suddenly yanked backward by an unseen force, his chains pulled taut. Forcibly, he was dragged through the wall, his eyes twin globes of surprise. Then the ghost of Nicholas Whitehill disappeared.

Some of the more unbearable chill vanished, sucked away with his best friend's ghost. It was cold but no longer coils of fog slipped from his lips. No longer did the chill bite into his exposed flesh.

The ensuing silence was poignant and sharp. It was so painfully blunt that it left him reeling. In the total absence of Nicholas's ghost, Benedict felt the palpable awareness from Christopher in the cell over.

The visitation wasn't in his head, and the curse did not play out within his mind. It was real. It was happening. He knew it. Christopher knew it. And there was nothing Benedict could do about it.

"My condolences, Lord Edwards…for everything," Christopher managed, tagging on a rough cough.

Benedict didn't know how to respond. He just sat there in his shock and horror, both emotions morphing into an amalgamation of fury and despair. There was so much woe and regret spiking through the coursing river of fear and doom.

The only hope—the light at the end of the tunnel—was Nicholas's declaration. That the demons actually took him back in time. What if he could change Lucia's fate? What if he could save her? Would that change *his* fate? Would there be a paradox? A new timeline? Benedict wasn't certain, but what he did know was that he wasn't giving up without a damn fight.

Benedict sat and mentally prepared. He waited, cross-legged and levitating. He slipped into his mental study and put it back together. He filed through the documents he owned and went over the events that preceded Lucia's death. Why she may have been killed—inspectors said a crime of passion, a couple's conflict; Benedict said fucking bullshit.

It was nearly an hour of researching and note taking when the clock tower struck one o'clock. Benedict extricated himself from the confines of his mind study and found himself, once again, in the dingy, frigid cell.

As he landed on his feet, patiently waiting and expectant, the temperature rose. It was like a hearth had been lit in his cell, lending ambiance and coziness.

It felt wrong.

Just then, through a flash of candlelight, a form began to unfurl from the flickering wick. The figure was shrouded in gauzy, ivory white, the thin material sticking to a feminine shape, features hugged by it. As if suffocating on it. Perfectly melded to its face—the hollows of its eye sockets, the gasping open mouth. High cheekbones and a straight nose were highlighted beneath. Circling its brow was a crown of holly, glossy red berries and waxy green leaves. Atop the laurel were twelve fat candles dripping down its countenance.

"I am Calanthe of Hell, Demon of Cronus and Christmas, the Ghost of Christmas Past."

The demon's voice was soft, breathy, and overall unsettling. It had the possibility of being either sinister or sweet, with no warning as to which facet you'd get.

"I am here as a guide through your past to discover and relive what you did to deserve to be delivered to this curse. You will experience untold guilt and regret, and I will gorge myself on your despair."

Benedict inclined his head. "I am ready."

Even below the shroud Benedict could see Calanthe's arched brow. "So eager to accept your fate? So eager to welcome death?"

"The curse is unavoidable. I'd prefer not entering it kicking and screaming like a petulant child. No amount of begging and pleading will release me."

"You could try."

"Why?"

"Because I enjoy denying prayers and bargains."

"Then I must deny you that pleasure."

Calanthe pouted. "Spoilsport."

Benedict merely shrugged.

Calanthe extended one hand; it was bone white and tipped in claws of cardinal red. She held it out, palm open, an infernal rune emblazoned on her palm, black like from a branding iron.

"Come with me to witness your doom or claim a fighting chance against your rival this night. The Demons of Cronus and Christmas will have their sacrifice by morn, and I am eager to see how desperate you become."

"I would not hold my breath."

Calanthe giggled, an eerie, chiming sound. "I do not need breath, young lordling." She bared her teeth through the shroud in a mockery of a smile. "Perhaps your Lucia could have learned that trick."

Fury, potent like sickness, like poison, like ink, rushed through him. The anger hit him as sharp as a blade, as hot as a flame, as explosive as a shot. He had been taken utterly unawares and that wrath had no bracers and this curse was the fuel.

Benedict prepared to attack the offending demon, but before he could, Calanthe grasped his wrist and pulled. Those claws yanked him off his feet and suddenly he was soaring through the air, through the night, and through time.

STAVE TWO

IN TIME

Time and space warped around him, icy wind and brimstone heat battering him. Lights like the Aurora Borealis undulated in gemstone hues of emerald and jade and sapphire. White pinpricks like dying stars flashed in and out as Benedict and Calanthe hurdled through a vortex of magic.

Benedict was too shocked to scream, but his mouth opened in a silent mockery. His eyes were large and round, limbs flailing despite Calanthe's monstrous hold. The demon glided on air, her shroud billowing about her, swept against her face and fanning out behind her.

The two of them twisted about until Calanthe arrowed her body and they dove for a portal of darkness. Benedict finally managed a yell as they breached the dark, freezing air nipping at him as they crossed the threshold. The darkness grasped them and wrapped around their forms as he began to plummet.

Benedict tumbled out of the magical transport, falling to his knees. He braced himself, breaths heaving his shoulders, dark hair wind-strewn. Calanthe landed gracefully beside him on bare white feet. Her nails were the same bold red as the ones on her fingers.

They had arrived in the past.

It was the past, but it was still his cell, just many years blending together. It flickered past his eyes like the flipped pages of a book. Snippets and moments of his downfall.

"We are invisible and intangible here," Calanthe informed him, brushing her hand over the stone wall and then through it. "You cannot change anything here as *you* are not truly here."

Benedict tried to put a hand to the wall, but like Calanthe's, it went through. His hand—his entire body—was wreathed in the darkness from the portal.

He wanted to rail against the injustice. It wasn't fair. Nicholas had lied, he could touch nothing, nothing could see him, he could not be heard. He was in another prison, one of space and time. He had to watch all of his worst moments. And see all the best ones with Lucia turn to ash.

The Ghost of Christmas Past prodded him, and he turned his attention to the past unfolding in a third-party perspective. Calanthe showed him the disdain, the scorn he dripped from every word spoken to Klaus, the kindly prison guard. The ignoring and complacency he showed Christopher, his cell-neighbor. He watched the most recent of his curse triggers grow, the guilt growing with it.

It was only hours or days before, but he was shown Christopher's cell, the cold and dingy state of it. Christopher had long brownish hair and a scraggly beard. He coughed wetly into his palm and Benedict was surprised to see blood there. Christopher looked down at it with resignation and wiped it on his stained pants—rusty spots covering the fabric already.

Benedict looked more deeply at Christopher and a realization struck him still.

Christopher was afflicted with the Wasting.

He put all the conversations together in his head. The questions and pleas that had gone ignored. Christopher had been asking for help that only he could give and Benedict was denying him it. He could have told the guards how to cure Christopher, he had the knowledge, and he wasn't sharing it. It was knowledge that could save the other man's life.

Christopher was his Discarded.

Christopher was going to die due to his inaction.

Benedict staggered back, but Calanthe gripped him and yanked him off his feet and back through the portal. It was a short whirlwind of travel next, but he landed in his own cell this time.

He saw himself in the past, facing the cell door, radiating fury and aggravation.

"What makes you think I give a single damn about your family, Klaus?" Past Benedict had sneered. "Congratulations on your infant daughter, is that what you wanted to hear? I'm in prison—your life is nothing to me."

"I had thought to bring you some joy this season. I know this time is hard for you." Klaus was cowed by Benedict's vitriol, but still tried at kindness.

He remembered this conversation last year. He remembered all the ones around Christmas and Yule in the prison. Every year he went into an episode of darkness and depression, anger and hate. The anniversary of Lucia's death ruined him every winter.

"You are a lowly prison guard and a weak warlock. Your mediocre life will not bring me joy."

Klaus had flinched, but did not return the insult. Benedict was hurting, and he wanted Klaus to hurt. Only the other man did not rise to the bait. He could've easily thrown at him that he was a convicted—though innocent—murderer and a prisoner serving a hundred-year sentence. But he did not, because he was a good man, and Benedict was no longer that.

He quickly put together that Klaus was his Undervalued.

The scene disappeared and the vortex swept them up again. Benedict's stomach turned, but he kept his nausea at bay. Calanthe's claws were pricking his wrists, but he did not yelp, he simply clenched his teeth and waited for the next showing of his sins.

Next, he was shown solitary research sessions, ignoring and dismissing of his colleagues. He was shown Nicholas, young, healthy, aiding and abetting this behaviour, also partaking in the same single-minded research. He was shown the sharing of notes and experimentation he and his best friend and mentor had undertaken. How many times he shirked his professor duties in pursuit of a medical breakthrough. Only to fail and be disciplined for lack of attendance in the studies he taught.

Then he was swept away again. The portal spat him out on snowy flagstones, crystalline specks of snow catching scraps of moonlight. Around them it was night, orbs of magic hovering over the street where people were bustling despite the late hour. Everyone was dressed in finery, most of them holding warming spells in their palms, or wrapped in fur or wool stoles.

Benedict caught sight of two familiar shapes and he jolted.

One was him, dressed in a fine obsidian suit, tailored to his tall frame. His vest was stitched with silver, snowflakes embroidered in a pattern of diamonds, filigree clasps running across his abdomen. His cuff links were Mother of Pearl, as were the buttons on his jacket. His cravat was snowy white, like the shirt beneath his ensemble.

Beside him was Sabine, her gown a confection of bronze beauty that brought out the coppery tones of her dark red hair and night-dark eyes. It had a low décolletage, a tight waist, and a dangerously high thigh slit that displayed dark gold flesh, and ivory stockings topped with black bows.

They were linked arm-in-arm, ascending the steps of the Snowden Estate for a holiday ball. Benedict immediately recognized the time, the place. This was three months into the physical relationship he shared with Sabine, and it was also the last night of said relationship because this was the very night he was introduced to Lucia.

DECEMBER 14, 1865

Benedict broke from Calanthe and raced for the grand staircase on bare feet. Past him and Sabine were ascending the last few steps, heads tilted together and laughing. The front doors of the Snowden home were wide open, warmth seeping out in the cold air. Thin barrier sigils lined the doorframe, symbols to keep the heat out, the cold in, and prevent demonic entrance.

Benedict was on the tails of his former self, close enough to touch, but when he reached out, his hand went through, and his Past Self did not react. Not a shiver or glance.

Calanthe was behind him, laughing. "I told you," she said as they passed the threshold—the very one meant to halt a demon's presence. "We are not truly here. Nothing touches us, and we touch nothing. We are on a separate plane."

Benedict's irritation rose with declining hope. How was he supposed to save Lucia like Nicholas had urged? Was he wrong? Or was Benedict not seeing something?

They entered the golden foyer, the parquet floor polished oak, the walls panelled with motifs of snowdrops. Crystal chandeliers shone with soft light, wreaths of evergreen, juniper and holly hanging from every window and door with big white bows. A centerpiece of evergreen boughs, ivory poinsettias, and pale berries rested on the receiving table.

Immediately, they were escorted to the ballroom on the right. Snowflakes fluttered atop the glass ceiling, painting the outside a scene worthy of a sonnet. Moonlight and starlight cast a silver glow, while below the ball enchanted with gilded wonder. All the hues of the warmer metal and verdant green complimented perfectly against the pure white. The parquet floor continued here, though sigils were painted on the floor with an artist's hand, symbols of warming, sure-footedness, balance, joy, and demon warding.

Servants milled about, clad in white and evergreen, gold halos atop their heads and gilded angel wings upon their backs—though they looked like no true angelic being. They carried wooden trays laden with delicacies, hors d'oeuvres, pastries, and drinks. Music from a similarly garbed orchestra on a newly erected, wooden dais, flowed through the air, gentle tinkling and plucking.

Benedict followed himself through the throng, eyes on the man who had no idea how much his life was about to change. Calanthe stayed on his heels, silent and watchful, gleefully taking in the emotional pain that was wrought from this night.

Past Benedict and Sabine were on the fringes of the crowd when Sabine straightened suddenly and a glowing smile overtook her face. She leaned toward the crowd and waved daintily. Past Benedict looked to where Sabine's attention was and froze. Benedict had already seen her, and he spared only a moment on his past self to watch his features soften, and a star-struck expression enter his eyes. He knew—though he couldn't see it—his Past's heart was melting. Because Current's was too.

Lucia Marie da Silva Turner.

She was an absolute vision. She was treacherous on his heart, having stolen it the moment he'd laid eyes on her. She was a promise on his soul because he knew she held the match, the other half.

Of course, Past Benedict did not know this. He just knew she was beautiful and was enchanted by the intelligence in her eyes.

Lucia was petite but full of lush curves. She had long raven black hair, the waves loose about her bare shoulders, save for a few pieces pinned on the sides by silver hair clips in the shape of antlers with opals clustered at the base. Her eyes were luminous jewels, like sapphires, and framed by thick, black lashes. Her skin, so exquisitely smooth, was slightly golden with the touch of her da Silva lineage. Her features were plush—full, pillowy lips, smoky doe eyes, high cheekbones, an elegantly sloping nose.

She was stunning. Ethereal. Perfection. She was an absolute masterpiece, more radiant than an angel.

Benedict watched his past self walk towards his true love. Lucia's feet were sure in their heels, adding height to her minute frame. Her Prussian blue gown swept the floor, falling in an A-line from her tiny waist and flaring around her generous hips. He could see the breaths she drew, heaving her breasts over the edge of her gown, the neckline baring her shoulders and drawing the eye to the center of her cleavage where a teardrop pearl hung between them.

Benedict of the Past blinked, attempting to avert his eyes from the captivating sight. He was a gentleman and he was meant to behave as such. Just because they did not keep the virginal and pure rules and expectations of Mortal London, did not mean that he was welcome to gawk at every bit of exposed flesh.

"My lord," Lucia had said to Past Benedict, dipping in an elegant curtsy. "It's a pleasure to meet you formally after so much correspondence."

"Correspondence?" Benedict had asked in confusion.

"Oh!" Lucia had said with realized surprise. She cupped a hand over her mouth. "My apologies, I'm getting ahead of myself. I'm Professor Turner."

Benedict remembered the shock vividly. For the past month he'd been corresponding with a Professor Turner who was planning to transfer to his university from a small college to teach and research exactly his study—immortal diseases. Professor Turner had made marked progress on the breakdown of Ember Fever, even creating an effective treatment plan. Benedict just hadn't realized that Professor Turner—who he'd been imagining was a stuffy, stodgy old man—was really an utterly beautiful and smart young woman of his own age. Internally, he'd kicked himself for the assumption.

"Professor Turner!" he'd finally responded, taking her hand and shaking it. "So lovely to meet you! I must say, I hadn't been expecting—"

"A woman?"

"Er. Yes, I apologize. I should have—"

"Do not worry. I made my sex unknown deliberately. So many men in academia and science have not come around to the modern ways. And please, we're past formalities after such a time. Call me Lucia."

"Lucia."

Benedict knew in that moment he was lost. And Sabine knew it too. She had given him a sly smirk and patted his arm, gently disentangling it. She was a clever woman and she held herself to a standard with so much self-respect. She was not going to hang onto a man whom desired another. Besides, they had not been committed.

Calanthe trailed clawed fingers up his arm as he watched the past play out, his heart completely on his sleeve. He shuddered from the demon's touch as she leaned in.

"How sickly sweet," she crooned. "Do you miss her? Of course, you do, I can sense your pain. It is exquisite."

Benedict ignored Calanthe and watched the interaction longer. He watched the warmth between Lucia and Sabine, witnessed the growing attraction between himself and the professor, saw the bonds that were forming between them. He was aware of the moment he and Sabine had locked eyes and a silent conversation had ensued, commencing the end of their private affair. It was quiet and without dramatics. Nostalgia struck him straight in the heart and turned into a dagger once a fourth member joined their party.

Nicholas.

His mentor waltzed up in a fine gray suit, crisp and clean, with a green-striped waistcoat and pewter buttons. Immediately, the energy of the trio shifted to greet him and instantly the dynamic changed. Current Benedict watched it unfold and saw Sabine gravitate, Benedict turn companionable, and Lucia welcome.

Tears brimmed in Benedict's eyes as he saw the life he'd lived—the life he'd loved—play out, knowing the doom of the friends was coming.

A song had begun playing and Lucia's eyes lit up. Past Benedict had noticed this and immediately asked her to the floor. She'd accepted and they swept elegantly out.

THE PAST

They whirled perfectly together, feet sure over the parquet and sigils, hands firm and graceful upon each other. They pressed together and apart as they danced, Benedict leading them through the motions, Lucia an excellent student.

"Your study on the Wasting could use some fine tuning," Lucia said.

"Oh really?" Benedict cocked a brow. "How so?"

"You are focusing too much on the why and not the how."

"Elaborate."

"You are determined to figure out why it attacks certain warlocks and not others. What you should be looking into is how it gets there in the first place."

"Is it not important to know who is at risk? What factors make an individual more susceptible?"

"It would be, if the disease were not random."

"Which is only what the current studies believe. I believe differently. I think that research is lacking and through it we are missing crucial information."

"Perhaps, but imagine applying that tactic to Ember Fever? We do not have the time to study who, it is a rapid disease and it takes quickly. The Wasting gives you years of time."

Benedict leaned into Lucia pressing his mouth to the shell of her ear. He was intoxicated by her scent of orange and clove, the scent infusing in his lungs like a drug. "Perhaps we should then put our heads together. Learn each other's mind. I believe we could be an incredible team, you and I."

He drew back and Lucia's cheeks were flushed. Her eyes glazed with desire.

"Is this the sort of welcome all your colleagues receive?"

"Only the incredibly clever ones. Nicholas refused my advances; I must say I was a fair bit disappointed."

"Did he really?"

"No, I did not even try. But you believed it."

"You likely were not smart enough for him."

"I think that's what dissuaded me from the attempt."

They laughed together, full of joy and mirth as they continued dancing.

Benedict felt himself falling, tumbling, crashing. Hard. The melding of the two people he knew—Professor Turner and

Lucia—was as close to magical as a non-magical moment could be. He saw beauty and intelligence before him, wit and pride, radiance and confidence. The young woman in his arms carried herself with such internal strength that he pitied the man who underestimated her.

Nearby, Sabine and Nicholas were dancing together. The spin of Sabine's bronze gown caught the light and drew attention to Nicholas's understated hues, the two of them oddly matching in a fashion. His heart warmed knowing that Sabine and him fell on the same terms, and it seemed clear that both were enamored with the other's confidante.

"Would you care to read over my notes tonight over the course of a nightcap?" Benedict asked, then realized how boldly the statement would come across. "I am not trying to get you into bed, Lucia. Truly, I apologize, I was just eager to engage in our mutual studies—"

"Should I be offended that you don't want to fuck me?"

Benedict drew a gasp, surprised by that word coming from that delicate mouth. The F that drew her teeth against that lush lower lip, the flick of her tongue against her teeth on the end sound. He was truly enraptured by everything this woman did.

"It's not that I don't—I didn't want to assume—I…"

Lucia laughed. "It is all right. I would love to see your research tonight. Nightcap or no."

Benedict smiled, pleased and though he didn't know it yet, Lucia Turner had his heart in her fist and his will wrapped around her littlest finger.

OBSERVANCE OF THE PAST SHOWN BY THE DEMON CALANTHE

Calanthe swept them up from the ball and back into the vortex of northern light magic. They spilled through moments of Lucia and Benedict's courtship. Shared research dates, garden strolls, visits to the café, another ball. It was during a night of research in January when Calanthe tossed them out of the spell.

JANUARY 17, 1866

"Ember Fever can be cured with an extract of blessed demon's blood, a cleansing spell, santonin, and morphine," Lucia announced breathlessly. "It's a demon blood borne disease and blessing the blood neutralizes its infernal qualities so the body can create a natural resistance! Santonin paralyzes the parasitic infection, the spell flushes it out, and morphine helps with the pain!" She spun to Benedict. "We did it!"

Lucia threw her arms around Benedict's neck after she sent off documents of the cure with a flick of her fingers to an awaiting messenger, describing her breakthrough to all the academic, medical, and scientific boards. He caught her, wrapping her up, completely caught up in her glee as the papers whisked out the window with the university's creed emblazoned on the sheets.

It was an incredible breakthrough. Revolutionary. This discovery of the cure would change lives—save lives. Lucia designed a full treatment plan for Ember Fever. Not just that, but a cure. Practically a vaccine. All of that accomplishment and she was only twenty-and-six, not even having yet performed the Staying.

"No, *you* did it," he corrected. "I was simply here."

"I could not have done it without your challenging mind!"

She drew back slightly and suddenly their eyes locked. Tension grew between them, pulling taut like a wire, the distance between them near painful. Lucia searched his gaze, her blue eyes taking in everything and missing nothing. Then, just as suddenly as she'd launched herself at him, she crushed her mouth to his.

Her lips were soft, but her kiss was all passion. It was full of the high she'd earned from her scientific progress. His mouth opened beneath hers and he captured her lower lip, sucking on it, pulling it in. Their tongues touched and with that, it unlocked something else. Lucia's hands went to his chestnut locks, fusing there, pulling. She moaned against his mouth and he couldn't help himself as he clutched her to him, his hands pressing at the small of her back. Her perfect form was flush against him, all her curves against his planes.

"Is this all right?" he managed on a breath.

"More than all right."

Their intensity grew and Benedict stumbled, his back hitting up against a table. It rocked once before settling, yet

Lucia continued her attack. He, in a rush of wicked desire, slid his hands down the black cotton of her dress and slipped his hands beneath her thighs. He picked her up, hitching her knees around his waist and spun them to the table. He cleared the contents with a swipe of his arm and set Lucia upon it, her bottom on the edge. He ground his pelvis into her core, hardness meeting her divine softness. She let out a soft sound of surprise, but did not stop him. Rather, her hands went to the buttons on his shirt.

She bit his lip and he groaned low in his throat. His hands roamed up and down her ribs, feeling her breath hitch beneath his touch. She got two of his buttons undone before a knock sounded at the door.

The two of them startled and broke apart, donning their disordered clothes and attempting to smooth their hair. There was no hiding their kiss-bruised mouths, though. They stood side by side, looking at whatever piece of research they could get their hands on.

Nicholas entered and it was clear from his smirk that he knew exactly what had gone on in that office. His gray eyes held an amused light, but he said nothing.

"How does it go?" Nicholas asked, pointedly not bringing up the elephant in the room, nor the fact that Benedict was holding a book upside down.

Lucia was practically bursting at the seams. "I found the cure for Ember Fever!"

Shock showed on Nicholas's entire body. "You did what?"

Lucia repeated herself and her previous explanation. Nicholas took it in with singular attention, the sort only a scholar can secure when blessed with groundbreaking information. When she was done, he blinked, and then congratulated her.

"Which board are you bringing this information to?"

"All of them, I suppose. I'm not patenting it. This treatment will be readily available for all."

Nicholas smiled. "You're such a kind soul, Lucia. I admire that in you. Have you sent word of this discovery yet?"

"I have."

Nicholas's smile got bigger. "This is truly wonderful. Would you like me to get in contact with my friends in the paper? We could have an article published about you and your discovery in the Oracle by Friday."

"That would be spectacular!"

"I'll see it done. Congratulations again, my dear."

Lucia beamed and Nicholas left. Once he was gone, she threw her arms around Benedict again.

"You will have to join me for the interview, please! I couldn't have done this without you."

Benedict mulled this over as Lucia's hands coasted over his chest. "On two conditions."

"Name them."

"One, I take no credit for the cure. I only offered moral support."

"Done. And the second?"

"You kiss me again."

Lucia grinned. "That's extortion."

"Take it or leave it."

"I'll take it," Lucia said, pulling on his lapels, and bringing his face down to hers.

MARCH 27, 1866

Lucia had been overwhelmed with the celebrity that came with being the individual responsible for discovering a cure for one of the three fatal immortal diseases. Interviews, studies, meetings, fawning, praise, and invites became a daily occurrence for Professor Turner. Most of the publicity was positive, but there were the negatives. The jealous, bitter rivals, the old misogynistic men in academia who felt inferior because a woman had been the one to discover a cure.

Then some of the attention was a bit of both.

Suitors came out of the woodwork of every class and sex, proposals of marriage and intercourse, courtship and dates. The amount of balls and galas Lucia had been eagerly welcomed to—on or off a certain person's arm—was egregious. Lucia, gently but firmly turned them all down, citing dedication to Benedict.

Benedict and Lucia had been courting for nearly three months, and Benedict knew he was in love. The two of them had not managed intimacy past kissing, the wildest one having been the day she'd discovered the cure. It was after that Lucia admitted she was not ready to engage in a physical aspect to their relationship.

Lucia had been born to a mortal mother, and a mortal-born, yet magic-blessed father. Lucia's parents had been married only one short year before they discovered his magic and that his wife—young Carlotta da Silva Turner—was pregnant. Everyone, all mortals and warlocks alike, knew of the existence of magic and it was virtually every human's dream to be blessed with the craft. Lucia's father's had just bloomed late. When it was clear he was a mortal-born warlock, the Turners made the leap from Blackfriars Bridge and into Vonor, the parallel London of magic.

Life in Vonor was easier; streamlined, freer, with looser societal pressures and room for increased fulfillment in studies, pastimes, and entertainment. Safety, to some degree, was traded. Due to the presence of so much prevalent magic, demons were drawn to the city, though there was a police force dedicated to their eradication.

Due to her parents' mortal upbringing, there were reservations and hesitations on their part regarding courtship and intimacy. They believed sex was designated to marriage only, and so they instilled that belief in Lucia. While she didn't judge others for partaking, she herself was drawn to the idea of waiting.

And Benedict was fine with that. He just had one question for her now.

"Will you marry me?"

Benedict was down on one knee with a sapphire and diamond ring in his hand, the two of them having been walking the poison gardens. They were surrounded by dark red blooms, black thorns, and green leafed plants. There were no bees or birds about, and at this time of year, warlocks typically ignored the gardens. It wasn't until Harvest or Samhain that that changed.

"What?" Lucia breathed in shock, her blue eyes wide, unshed tears glittering there.

"Marry me, Lucia. Become my wife, stay Professor Turner, just be mine. I love you beyond words. You captivate me, challenge me, and utterly possess me. You are everything I never knew I needed. I cannot breathe without you. You are the air in my lungs. Marry me, and I will endeavor every day to make you the happiest woman alive."

"Benedict…" she whispered; emotion thick in her voice. "Yes, yes of course, I'll marry you."

Benedict grinned and slipped the marquis-cut stone onto her slender finger, the silver band a perfect fit. He rose when she cupped his face, and he met her with the most ardent kiss. He wrapped his arms around her and melted into her mouth, parting it with his tongue. She made a soft sound of pleasure as his hands coasted up her back and into her thick fall of onyx hair.

She pulled away and smiled softly.

"Our children will be so lucky to have such a devoted father."

Benedict's heart swelled. "Children?"

Unlike mortals, having children was not a necessity of society, it was just as normal for a couple *not* to have them as it was for them *to* have them.

Benedict hadn't let himself consider them much, not sure if he was worth the supposed unconditional love they were rumored to possess. His father had sold his own soul to pay for gambling debts, and when he'd accrued more, he'd tried to sell Benedict. Benedict's mother—an alcoholic—killed his father for this in a fit of rage, not because she was horrified by the idea, but because she was planning on doing the very same to afford her vice. She was currently serving a prison sentence without visitation for two hundred years.

"I'd like them—one day."

He broke away from the dark thoughts. "I think our children will be very blessed indeed, to have such a caring and intelligent mother."

Emotion had Lucia biting her lip and then suddenly she was nipping his.

The date was set for January 17, 1867. Lucia wanted to wait till the vaccines were fully in production and distributed in case the research required some fine tuning. The laboratories producing it were confident all would be finished by the winter solstice.

Their engagement drew headlines, and with that, more celebrity—for the both of them. In response, Benedict grew more reclusive, hiding out at home or at the university more often, keeping notes and research to himself, no longer collaborating on projects or offering tutoring. He became a dragon with his hoarding of knowledge.

Which became his downfall by the Scrooge Curse.

IN TIME

Benedict was shown more and more moments of Lucia, their relationship, the moments that led to her becoming his Lost—his Belle. He was shown more and more of his Scrooge behaviors—keeping research and knowledge to himself, becoming reclusive, borderline selfishness.

Then he was shown the fight he'd had with Lucia, a little over a week before her untimely death.

Benedict and Calanthe exited the whirling magic and found themselves, mid-December, inside his townhouse.

A fire crackled merrily in the hearth, an enormous festive tree in the corner of the sitting room; bedecked in gold and crimson ribbon, covered in lighted candles, orbs of warlock magic, and glass balls. The velvet couches with throw pillows were arranged in a three-sided square, heavy wood bookcases lining the walls, diamond pane windows overlooking the snow fallen street. The scent of pine and allspice was heady, the slight citrus notes of furniture polish and smoke mingling with it.

Lucia was raging at him, and he was taking it in silence, jaw held firm.

"You completely snubbed that student, Benedict! He was just asking if you had an opinion on the rise of the Wasting and you very pointedly ignored him."

"He only wanted to get close to you. Besides, he said Midnight Malady first. He had no idea what he was talking about."

"Perhaps he was nervous! This isn't the first time you've shot down a student or a researcher." Lucia held up a halting hand. "And do not share your excuses, I do not wish to hear them."

"I fear for you," Benedict admitted. "I worry someone with terrible intentions will get to you."

"I can handle myself."

"I know you can. I know you're a very adept warlock, and a more than capable woman, but I cannot help but be cautious when it comes to you."

"Why? Because I am a woma—"

"Lucia," he snapped. "Do not make that accusation. You know your gender has nothing to do with it."

"Perhaps not, but you're one to talk of cautious! You shut yourself in your study for days and I never hear from you! How am I to know someone hasn't come for *you* and your research?"

"I can handle myself. You don't need to worry about that."

"Because you are a man?"

"*Lucia*," he groaned. "We've already established that's not the issue."

"Then what is it?" she demanded. "Because all I see is a double standard."

"It's…" he trailed off, losing words.

"Precisely," she hissed. She stepped forward, standing before him. Fury vibrated off her. "I am a powerful warlock and a smart woman. My magic is more than sufficient should an attacker be foolish enough to come upon me." She inclined her chin, nostrils flaring. "Is it jealousy? Do you worry that some other man wants to fuck me?"

"Of course, I do!" Benedict shouted, stepping into her space, forcing her to back up. "I don't want anyone thinking you could be theirs. You are mine."

Lucia hit the wall and startled. He towered over her, and something about his domineering presence lit something in her eyes. He watched the blue change—darken—as lust warred with her fury.

Feeling passion overtake him, he kissed her—hard. She met it just as hard. Her kiss was an attack and they used teeth and nails that turned to claws. They poured fury and desire into the other, moaning into each other's mouths. He fisted a hand in her hair and pulled her head back, seeking deeper entrance. She nipped his lip, but she did so a bit too roughly because he tasted blood. Lucia must've too, because she pulled back.

His fiancée stared at the bead of crimson that bloomed on his lip. Her cheeks were flushed, her eyes heated.

"We are not thinking clearly—I should leave."

"No, Lucia—wait."

"No, I think I need a moment alone."

"You're going to leave in the middle of an argument? Really? Lucia, be logical about this."

"Logical? When our fighting could turn to fucking?"

"Would that be so bad?"

He knew it was the wrong thing to say the moment it left his mouth. He saw it register and change in her eyes. Suddenly, ire replaced the fires of desire and her lip curled.

The fight had exacerbated from there and they were sniping back and forth. Eventually, Lucia had left, slamming the door behind her. She hadn't left her ring on the table, so he took it as a small victory. Eventually, they did make up, but it was a week later, and that wasted week was the last one he was to spend with her.

DECEMBER 21, 1866

He was sent an urgent letter on Lucia's behalf, stating dire circumstances. He was racing through the snow on foot, not able to secure a carriage this time of night during the infamous Winter Solstice Ball hosted by the Snowden family. Especially when his was down for repairs and he did not trust his skill as a rider on a horse.

Benedict's lungs filled with and expelled frigid air, wisps of snowflakes hurtling across his vision as he slipped and slid. His cheeks were flushed and tears formed crystal tracks down his cheeks.

Terror powered him on. He felt doom crawling all around him, descending upon him, crushing him already. Denial tried making its home in him, but he knew the situation was dire.

He raced up the stairs of the address he was given, the entire interior of the manor was lit up with crimson light, pouring out from every window. He broke through the doors, ignoring all the rose motifs as he hurtled through the corridors.

When he found the door he'd been directed to, he blasted through it, preparing a defensive spell on his fingertips. Cerulean magic danced over his hand as he entered the courtyard.

The magic immediately doused itself as his hand fell.

There, in the center of the courtyard was a fountain, full of icy water and burbling from a cherub's hand. Before the fountain, on the stone floor was Lucia, covered in blood, her ebony hair soaked around her like a violent spill of ink.

"Lucia!" he screamed. "No, no, no, no, no!"

He sprinted across the flagstones and practically fell before her. He took her in his arms. She lolled against him limply, skin chalk white, flesh frozen. Her once luminous blue eyes looked up blankly, a flat, muted blue.

"Lucia! Please, no, no, no!"

He clutched her, not caring about the blood that soaked his white shirt, not caring for the arctic water that streamed from her long locks and chilled him. He just needed her to respond, to be *okay.*

But he knew she wasn't.

He knew she was gone.

There were thirteen stab wounds in her chest and it was clear that at some point she'd been forced under the fountain's water. He didn't dare to imagine it, but the intrusive thoughts won.

Was she tortured? How long did it last? Why did it happen? Why *her*?

Benedict sobbed against Lucia's chest, so little of her orange and clove scent left on her skin. There was too much blood, the metallic notes taking over everything.

"Lucia…" he sobbed raggedly.

He howled to the night, his pain visceral, cracking through the stars and moonlight. Tears poured down his face, wracking pain splitting his chest wide open.

As Benedict sobbed, he was unaware of anything else around him. So absorbed in his agony was he, that he didn't know the constabulary had arrived until they were screaming at him to drop the body.

IN TIME

Benedict watched himself grieve and mourn Lucia. Despite knowing it was coming, he hadn't been able to adequately brace for it. When he caught sight of her corpse, he broke. He felt like his already ruined heart was wrenched out of his chest, through his soul.

Involuntarily, he'd lunged forward. To go to her. But Calanthe had gripped his shoulder and pulled him back.

"I do not think so, Lord Edwards," she chortled. "I told you before. You are not truly here. There is nothing you can do."

There was nothing he could do, so he just watched. He bore witness to the constabulary converging on him, two officers forcibly tearing him from Lucia's body, another screaming orders, countless others flooding the courtyard. One bent down to where he had been cradling Lucia's form and produced a knife from the ground. Benedict had been too involved to notice it, but notice it he did when the crimson moonlight caught it.

It was his.

A family heirloom. Wrought in roses and formed of true silver and steel. It bore his initials, it looked bad, but it should not have been the lynchpin it was. This was his family's estate after all, abandoned as it was. Of course, some of his belongings would be here. But that common sense was not taken into account.

They hauled him away while he kicked and screamed, casting messy spells to try to break away. An officer branded the sigil into him to lock away his magic. Anxiety melded with the grief and horror and he turned even more feral, his physical resistance increasing sevenfold.

Eventually, two more officers took him and the four hauled him away from Lucia—away from his fiancée, away from the love of his life, his purpose, his everything.

Officers began securing the crime scene as Benedict vanished through the doors.

With that, Calanthe sucked him back into the vortex of magic. She sighed with ecstasy, a low, near moan.

"That was utterly tragic. Your despair is so decadent…" she sighed again, sucking on her lower lip beneath the shroud.

"You are monstrous."

"I am a demon, little lord, of course I am." She tittered and pulled him along.

Calanthe drew him back into the waving light of the transport magic, letting them be swallowed by the greens and blues. The air felt charged differently this time; thinner, colder.

"My time with you is coming to an end," she informed him. "In moments I will be handing you off to the demon Azenor, Ghost of Christmas Present. She will be taking you through the trials of your current sins, and though it may be in the present, you are still intangible."

"Fuck you."

Calanthe chortled. "May I speak candidly?" She didn't wait for his response. "I think you are going to fail. You are too traumatized and depressed to change. I look forward to devouring your soul tonight."

Benedict resented the demon's role. She didn't want to help him, but the parameters of the curse dictated that she show him where he went wrong and allow him the grace to try to change his ways. But she didn't want him to succeed, she wanted him to struggle, then fail.

Suddenly, the colors began to shift, the greens and blues fading, transforming into reds and violets. In the distance, a form approached—feminine, curvaceous, winged, and horned. Her hair was a long fall of ebony silk, her eyes glowing red embers. Her fingers ended in deadly sharp claws of obsidian, the ruby flesh of her arms carved with infernal runes.

As the colors shifted, Benedict could see through the magic. He could see the past. Snippets of his life flashing beyond the whirl of false auroras.

Suddenly, Nicholas's words made sense.

They weren't truly in the past when Calanthe guided him, there was still a layer between them—the wreathing darkness keeping a plane there. This, whatever was beyond the vortex *was* the true past. Or at least a gateway to it, and Benedict knew he could break through it.

As Calanthe grinned beneath the ivory, Azenor approached, her wings flared wide, a smug smirk on her cruelly lovely face, and Benedict began to cast.

His fingers worked, cerulean sparking from his fingertips as he guided spells into one another, tangling them, tying them, melding them. During his imprisonment, he'd become supremely talented in magic—it had been one of the only things to do, allowed to practice to insanity if he wished, never able to breach the warded stone or daily muting sigils. Within the study of his mind, he'd perfected how to mesh multiple spells into one.

That's what he was doing.

He casted first for invisibility—confining it to his magic—and perception blocking, so the demons would not notice his spell work. Then he continued casting for ward breaking, demonic repulsion, incendiary power, balance, strength, resistance, and more. He became a flurry of magic, barely touching his reserves from all the years of rationing energy. Then, when he created this amalgamation, he met the eyes of his two demon captors.

"Are you prepared to experience the sins of your curse in the present?" Azenor asked, her voice smoky and coy.

Benedict twisted his lips in a mockery of a smile. "No."

And then he dropped the first two spells and revealed the monstrosity of a spell held in his hands. He released it and the demons shrieked. It shot out of him and blasted a hole through the vortex of magic. Benedict chased after it and leaped through the tear, casting for guidance and levitation.

Despite his casting, he tumbled through time and space. He added balance and his tumbling became somewhat more manageable. He tried to steer himself through the motley kaleidoscope of colors and found himself hurting through a vision of a frosty street. He quickly wound his fingers in a cast for reality and broke through just as he completed the spell.

75

THE PAST

Benedict fell to the ground, but did so with the oddest sensation. It was as if he had been walking on the street before suddenly becoming lightheaded and empty stomached. As if tripping over nothing as his world spun.

His breath coiled in the air as the freezing temperature penetrated his bones. Ice seeped through the knees of his viridian trousers, a patch in the elbow of his fine coat damp with snow.

Benedict froze.

Trousers? A coat?

He'd been wearing his prison garb, filthy rags made of pajama pants and an old sweater.

Benedict examined himself as he got to his feet. He brushed himself off, feeling the fabric of his favorite green suit, the wool of his gray coat, the supple leather of his black shoes. He brushed his hands down his abdomen to find healthy weight there. He'd been wraith-thin in prison, but now, while still lean, he'd filled out somewhat.

Standing in shock, Benedict realized he'd done it. He'd broken through the curse. Broken through time. He must be in the past—and in his past's body.

Abruptly, he heard a screech and looked up. Above him was an open portal, waves of green and blue and red and violet flashing. Two irate demons stared down on him.

Calanthe and Azenor leaped through the tear and Benedict did not hesitate as he took off running.

Benedict winded down the streets of Vonor, recognizing shops and architecture. He was only three blocks to the university and he knew the campus was completely warded against demons. Not even half demons could get on the grounds. He passed people he hadn't seen in more than seven years, ignoring the exclamations as he sprinted by.

He caught sight of the black iron university gates and picked up speed. But then a shadow swooped overhead and a figure landed on the flagstones before him. Two knives were brandished in Azenor's hands, a wicked grin set across her fanged mouth.

"Fuck," Benedict cursed.

He halted and then ran through his list of spells mentally, searching for banishment. Then he remembered, he was in the past, and he had his past's arsenal.

Dipping into his coat pocket he felt around and found a vial. Immediately, he uncorked it and spilled the contents over his hands. With that, he summoned a zephyr and had it carry the liquid on his hands to rain over Azenor.

The wind blasted her with droplets of holy water and Azenor screamed. It drew attention and then he heard someone screech.

"Demon! Call the constabulary! Demon!"

Azenor's hands were over her face, her skin sizzling, smoke rising from the burns that were burrowing through her flesh. Spots of black stood out against her snowy wings. Her skintight dress had protected most of her torso from the worst of the wounds but her face bore the brunt of it.

Warlocks began casting banishment, others screeching and summoning the constabulary. More than one person ran, children or babes clutched in arms or prams.

With the demon suffering her burns, Benedict skirted around her and crashed into the gates. He pushed them open with desperation and stumbled through. When he turned to look, Azenor was taking to the air and Calanthe stood off to the side in the shadows, candles on her brow flickering with fury.

Calanthe held up a single clawed finger and ticked it side to side before vanishing into the shadows behind her—her candle wicks the last to disappear.

Benedict heaved a sigh of relief and ran his hand through his dark hair, a mist of perspiration on his brow. Steeling himself, he turned and entered the university.

Benedict slammed the door of his faculty office, leaning desperately against his desk. It wasn't his research office—it was his teaching one. The one that he was stationed in when he had classes in session.

Luckily, he'd had his key on him, but why wouldn't he when this was his regular route at this time? Nothing was out of the ordinary, yet.

Tugging on his hair, he looked around, taking in the solid wood shelves, the leather-bound tomes, glass orbs and trinkets. On the floor was a blue Persian rug, enchanted to match the color of the owner's magic. A leather armchair faced his desk, a matching swivel chair behind it.

He was heaving breaths, running his hands through his hair, trying to get his bearings when a knock sounded at his door. Surprised, he drew his hands away from his head and crossed the threshold. As he swung open the door, he felt the air deflate from his lungs. Every thought fled his mind, all the strength left his body, all the blood drained from his face. He staggered, grasping the doorframe for dear life.

"Benedict, are you all right?"

No. No, he was not all right because standing in front of him was Lucia.

Alive and well.

STAVE THREE

DECEMBER 14, 1866

Lucia's fiancé stood before her, whiter than a ghost, before he collapsed in her arms. She went to him, just barely catching him before his knees buckled and he dropped.

"Benedict!" she cried out.

Concern had her searching his face, cupping his flushed cheeks, bitten by the bitter chill outside. His skin was damp, dewy with perspiration, his jade eyes glazed and lacking lucidity.

"What's wrong? And why did I hear you were running like Hell was on your heels?"

Benedict let out a sharp, barking laugh and Lucia startled. He began gripping her in earnest, clutching her to him, his hands all over her. Her previous anger faded with his clear desperation.

"How? How are you here?" he managed. His fingers coasted across her cheeks.

Lucia's dark brows narrowed in confusion. "We're having lunch today. You wanted to patch things up from last night's argument—don't think I've forgotten, even in light of…all this."

"What day is it?" he asked, near deliriously.

"What?"

"What day is it? Please, it's important."

"You're scaring me, Benedict."

"*Please*," he begged. "What is the date?"

"It's the fourteenth of December."

"In what year?" There was a frantic light in his eyes.

Lucia fearfully answered. "1866."

A broken sound slipped from him and Benedict grew boneless against her, burying his face in her chest, sobbing. He didn't let her go, even when she felt his tears stain the rose silk of her day gown. Worriedly, she trailed her fingers through his chestnut hair soothingly, a habit she'd made more than ten months ago. She couldn't stop herself from touching the soft waves.

She waited a time, waiting for his cries to abate, before she spoke. "Benedict, my love, what is going on?"

Benedict lifted his head and showed her red-rimmed eyes.

"I've traveled to the past. I was the victim of the Nightmare Curse and I broke out of it and found myself in my past's body. Now the demons chase me, waiting for my soul."

She froze. "That's impossible."

"I assure you; it is not."

Lucia blinked, staring off in the distance over his head. Fears rambled inside her mind, realizations clamoring for their moment. A branding hot iron questioned itself into her brain.

"Who is your Belle?"

She knew how the curse worked. A "Scrooge" must have a Belle, and a Belle must be lost to them.

Benedict looked at her squarely, pain scalding itself into those gem green depths.

"You. It could only ever be you."

A stab of hurt worked its way through her heart and she looked down, fiddling with the sapphire and diamond ring he'd given her this past spring. Tears burned behind her eyes.

She hadn't realized their fight had been so dire.

"So, we do not marry? We call it off?"

"No," Benedict said and then paused. "You die."

Lucia's head snapped up and her eyes grew wide.

"When?"

"A week from today."

Lucia broke from Benedict and stumbled back, falling into the cocoa leather chair, pressing a hand to her heart. Panic and anxiety weaved within her, thinning her breath, racing her blood.

"How?"

"Murder." Then he went on to tell her the details. The when and where and how. The night of the solstice at his abandoned family estate by stabbing and drowning—torture.

Lucia's throat thickened, her anxiety spiraling higher, urging her to hysterics. It wasn't normal to know the details of one's death, and despite the fact Benedict could be lying, she knew he wasn't. She was truly meant to die in one week. Meant to be *murdered.*

"Who did it?"

Benedict shook his head. "I do not know. It's unsolved, but I was framed for it."

Lucia's heart jumped. "But you would never."

Lucia trusted Benedict implicitly. She knew in her heart of hearts that he could never hurt her. He'd never touch her like that.

She reached for his hand and he took it eagerly. She looked up at him—she always had to look up due to her diminutive size—from the armchair. She poured faith and devotion into her gaze. Benedict visibly softened with her look.

"I know, but it didn't matter to them. No one believed me. Except Nicholas and Sabine."

Lucia nodded. Of course, their friends would believe him. They had all been so close, and despite knowing he and Sabine had once shared a physical relationship, it didn't matter to her. Sabine would never act out bitterly for the end of it, and she knew neither of them desired the other any longer. They had been their dearest friends—their unwavering faith was a guarantee.

Benedict sank to his knees before her, gazing deeply into her eyes. He took in every detail of her face and she took in his. His angular features, his narrow and sharp jawline…

His fingers were brushing every curve of her face. Her high cheekbones, her brow, the slope of her nose, chin, lips, jaw. She shuttered her eyes.

"I've missed you so much," he whispered ardently.

"I saw you just yesterday."

"It wasn't yesterday for me."

Still with her eyes closed, she asked, "How long has it been?"

"Seven years."

He choked on the words and Lucia let out a soft sound of pain. Seven years. He'd mourned her for seven years. In his life she'd been dead and gone and alone for *seven* years. She didn't wonder if it was the truth, and there were many questions, but she'd save them for later.

Lucia opened her eyes and placed her hand on Benedict's chest, the linen shirt beneath his suit warm to the touch and stuck to his flushed skin. She felt his heart pick up tempo when her hand met him. Her other hand went to one of his, twining their fingers together. Comfort and sparks danced beneath their skin.

Suddenly, she leaned in and kissed him.

Benedict made a sound of surprise, and groaned before melting into her touch and embracing her. He pulled her to him, her hands crushed to his chest as his mouth discovered hers. He was like a man starving as he pulled her lower lip between his teeth and nipped.

"Lucia. *Lucia.* My Lucia."

Lucia let slip a moan and dug her fingers into his chest. His heart was beating so fast. She let her fingers work beneath the buttons of his shirt, finding his smooth, hot skin.

Benedict gasped wildly, his hands tilting her jaw to allow him greater access, his tongue sweeping in to claim her. But his hands did not stop. They roved over her. One went to the nape of her neck, fusing in her long ebony locks. His other went to the small of her back, tugging her from the chair.

"My Lucia. My love."

She kneeled before him as he continued his devotions. He pressed them together, him arching over her, her long hair a free fall behind her, the ends touching the hardwood floor. He kept whispering her name over and over like a prayer. Like she was a goddess and he was worshiping at her altar.

Lucia pulled away slightly to catch her breath, and Benedict shifted his mouth downward. To her jaw, her throat, suckling lightly on the juncture of her shoulder. Her eyes rolled back in her head.

How could this feel so good?

She caught her breath and rallied herself to ask a question.

"Did we ever…?" Her eyes made deliberate contact. "You know? Fuck?"

Benedict shook his head, his lips brushing against her collarbone with the movement.

Disappointment rang through Lucia. She was still a virgin when she died. She wanted to experience sex, and learning she'd died without that activity come to pass made her reconsider her parents' ingrained values.

What did it matter if she found pleasures of the flesh? She wasn't damaged goods just because of intimacy. She wasn't going to be deprived of the ability to still find a husband. She wouldn't be a fallen woman. All these fears and facets were remnants of her parents' moral upbringing. Yes, she wanted it to be special, but it was Benedict. No matter where it would be special.

An idea struck her.

Why was she waiting at all? Truly? What was even the problem with right here, right now? The door had a lock. It was lunch hour. And that rug looked quite comfortable.

Feeling confident in her choices, Lucia gently pushed Benedict to the floor. His head settled softly against the deep blue rug as he gazed up with her with a look of lust and shock. She draped herself over him and carefully, she straddled his waist. His eyes were huge as they took her in.

"*Lucia…*"

"*Benedict.*"

She took his hands and very deliberately guided them to her waist, holding his green gaze all the while. Lucia settled them there and then she let her fingers slip to the buttons on his vest.

A knock sounded at the door.

They both froze.

"Ignore it," she whispered.

The knock sounded again.

"Lord Edwards, are you in there? I wanted to speak with you."

Lucia recognized the voice immediately.

"*Oh, fuck!*" She scrambled off her fiancé as she realized her father was on the opposite side of that wooden door.

Her father, like Benedict and Lucia, was a professor. Only he taught arithmetic while they taught runes, sigils, and epidemiology, respectively. In fact, his office was four doors down from Benedict's. Lucia's was two. They shared a research office in the Greenwood wing, though.

She straightened her skirts to her best ability and smoothed her hair—even if it was to no avail. She knew she could do nothing about her kiss-bruised lips, but she hoped he'd consider her flushed cheeks a result of the frosty weather.

As panic wove within her, Benedict was climbing up from the floor, straightening himself as well. Lucia went over to Benedict's desk and busied herself behind it, pretending to translate some infernal runes. They were blood runes, familiar to her, which was at least believable in her discoveries regarding Ember Fever.

Benedict checked with Lucia and nodded when he found her in a more appropriate state. He went to the door and opened it in one smooth motion.

There, Lucia's father stood. Large and imposing, dark salt and pepper hair, an immaculately trimmed beard, and the same blue eyes as Lucia's own. He adjusted his indigo coat as he stepped into Benedict's office.

Heat flushed down Lucia's neck. She was certain her father knew exactly what they'd been doing on the floor in the exact spot he was standing.

Lucia didn't know why her father was visiting Benedict. They seemed to get on fine, but they weren't particularly close. In fact, oftentimes there seemed to be a tension between them but Lucia could never seem to put her finger on it. She often wondered if her father had warned Benedict off from pursuing her, but she'd never voiced the thought aloud.

It had crossed her mind that perhaps Benedict struggled with a fatherly relationship, since his own was a right piece of work.

Benedict ruffled the back of his hair nervously.

"Good afternoon, Lord Turner. To what do I owe this pleasure?"

"I wished to warn you about some rumors circulating around the board." He paused and then looked over at Lucia. He delivered her a warm smile. "Hello, my darling."

"Oh?" Benedict asked, circling to her father's original line of conversation. "What rumors may these be?"

A dark look entered his blue eyes. "The word is you two are making marked progress with the Wasting."

"This is true," Benedict confirmed.

"Yes," Lucia said, piggybacking off her fiancé. "In fact, there are strong correlations between Ember Fever and the Wasting, linked to demon blood." Lucia held up the book she was falsely transcribing for emphasis. "It's become clear that they come from different circles of Hell, but there is a connection, nonetheless."

Concern etched itself in her father's brow. "I need you to be careful. There are people who'd rather see these diseases uncured. There is more money to make in treating a disease than curing it."

Lucia knew this, but it hadn't stopped her drive nor her passion in discovering the end of these immortal diseases.

"I mean no disrespect, sir," Benedict began. "But we know this. Why do you tell us now?"

Her father ground his jaw. "A warlock was apprehended recently. He was part of the Scarlet Brotherhood. They're a militia, hired by those with deep pockets in high places to carry out dirty acts. There is talk that someone on the board has hired some of these individuals to stop the cures—by any means necessary."

A lead weight sank in Lucia's gut and she watched Benedict turn to her slowly, all the blood draining from his face. He was white as he took her in. She swallowed.

By any means necessary.

It was clear that whomever was hired truly took those words seriously. Perhaps it was a coincidence, but it seemed unlikely. She was supposed to die in one week, and today she learned that someone had a vendetta against her life's work.

No. This was no coincidence. This was something akin to prophecy.

"We appreciate the warning," Benedict said after composing himself. "We'll be careful."

"Right. Well…" he cleared his throat, pulling out his pocket watch distractedly. "While I have you here, Ben, I'd like to invite you to dinner tonight."

Benedict blinked and shook his head a little. "Oh, of course. I'd be honored."

"Delightful. Dinner will be served at seven."

"I will be there."

Her father nodded. "Lucia, darling, good to see you. Keep up the good work and be careful."

"I will, father."

He nodded once to her, then nodded to Benedict. When he left the room, Benedict shut the door quickly and wheeled on Lucia.

"I need to figure out who killed you and who cursed me."

"Walk me through what you've experienced with the curse thus far."

Benedict did, recounting his prison stay and sentence, the demons Calanthe and Azenor, the traveling magic, who he'd figured his characters in the curse were, his first visit with a ghost. Suddenly, he gasped and looked at her with shock.

"Nicholas. He's alive."

"What?"

"He died. Three days ago—where I came from." He began looking around, grabbing vials of holy water from the shelves. "I have to go to him. Warn him, or I don't know, ask him about the curse and the rumors. Maybe he knows something. He's on one of the boards, too."

Lucia's hand was over her mouth.

Not only had Benedict lost her, he'd lost his best friend and mentor, too.

She dropped her hand and steeled her spine.

"I'm coming with you."

Benedict looked at her, holding a moment of silence. "Okay. But take some of these." He handed her three vials of holy water and a silver blade blessed by an angel, marked with seraphic runes.

She did not refuse them.

Tucking them into her skirt's pockets, she patted the small spell book that also resided there. It was the size of her palm and each page was inscribed with a sigil, both offense and defense, as well as convenience. They were for moments when she couldn't recall specific spells—though those moments were few and far between.

Benedict crossed the room and pulled her in by the nape of her neck, planting a damning and claiming kiss on her.

"I'm not letting anything happen to you this time," he swore against her lips.

"I believe you," she returned.

The two of them cancelled their afternoon classes and they set off across campus, armed to the teeth against the demons who sought to take her fiancé's soul.

DECEMBER 14, 1866

Nicholas's manor was five blocks from the campus. Rather than hailing a carriage, the two of them opted to travel on foot, erecting a shield of protection about them. Personal shields were typically more effective than those casted by the government to cover public carriage rides as they were not linked to a specific person. While individuals could cast over the government's wards, there was a chance of tangling them and making them null if attacked.

Benedict held Lucia's hand in his, walking together in disbelief. She was alive. She was truly alive. He could see her, touch her, smell her, feel her. It took everything in him not to break down and weep again. He couldn't get her out of his head. The silk of her hair, the satin of her skin, the sapphires of her eyes. Her scent was heady, intoxicating, all citrus and clove and *Lucia*.

Previously, he hadn't gone to his office and so he'd missed both Lucia's and Luther's visits. If he had, perhaps he and Lucia would have patched things up sooner. If he had, he may have gotten the warning about the Brotherhood in time. And she wouldn't have died.

She glanced over at him and smiled, squeezing his hand in her leather gloved palm. They were black, as were his own gloves, and her long wool coat was black and white, fashioned in a herringbone pattern with silver buttons.

"I meant to tell you about something," he began, "though, there didn't seem much time all things considered."

"What is it?"

"While I was imprisoned I—"

"Benedict, run!" Lucia shouted and tugged him hurriedly.

He didn't question Lucia, but he did look behind.

There, Azenor, burns healing, broken wings—likely injured from the previous crowd of warlocks—was chasing after them. The fury in her gaze rivalled that of all the fires and brimstone in Hell. Her teeth were bared in a feral growl and her clawed hands dripped blood from the raked wounds down her arms.

He watched the blood that poured from her hands morph in the air like a nebulous thing, warping into sigils.

No—infernal runes.

He cursed as he recognized the spiky shapes—wither, venom, ague, blight, and flame.

Shouts and screams went up around them, warlocks racing for the constabulary. Every warlock worth their salt knew how to banish a demon, but Azenor was no low-level demon, she was a demon from the seventh circle of Hell and could use the powers of that damned place through runes. Within moments the streets around them were clear of foot traffic entirely.

Azenor sent the manifested runes arrowing at them and Benedict quickly formed a second shield, melding it with an impervious sigil. The five crimson runes smashed against his cerulean magic, cracking and spiderwebbing across the expanse. It formed white cracks like broken ice on a frozen lake.

The shield held but wavered. A single impervious sigil was not designed to handle an onslaught from five infernal runes.

As the scent of sulfur and blood assaulted him, Benedict rounded a corner with Lucia and whirled on her, shoving her behind him. Lucia was twisting her fingers in a cast, a sigil of geometric patterns growing between her fingers with emerald light. She was working the banishment sigil. Benedict pulled a blade of silver, blessed by an angel and doused it with a vial of holy water. It was overkill, but it would be effective if he struck true.

Azenor was barreling towards them, her ruined wings adding to her demonic visage. She carved a rune down her arm again—illusion. Her dark red blood summoned the rune in the air and Benedict blasted it away with a destruction sigil. The demon hissed and Benedict charged her.

Behind him, Lucia had linked three banishment spells into one, creating a single large cast.

Benedict threw the silver blade and casted for precision and return. It spun through the air and though he aimed for Azenor's heart, she deflected with an infernal rune and it sank into her shoulder instead.

She squealed in agony as the heavenly mix of holy water and an angel's blessing burned her, the pure silver an undefiled carrier. Coils of smoke rose from the wound as Benedict's second charm pulled the knife free, flinging back into his hand.

It was then Lucia threw her banishment at her. Unfortunately, Azenor had a destruction rune wrought on her palm and she held up that hand as the blast collided with her. It blew her back, but the spell dissipated without sending her to Hell. Luckily though, the power sent her over a wrought iron fence, the spires of which were currently puncturing the demon's body.

Azenor roared as she flapped her pinned and injured wings, summoning enough to lift her from the sharp points. Once she was freed, she staggered, falling to her knees before carving a portal rune on the snowy ground in blood. A circle of Hell opened beneath her and she slipped through it to recover and lick her wounds.

Benedict stared at the spot Azenor disappeared through for a moment before he turned to Lucia. His fiancée was breathing rapidly, but she was uninjured. Even so…

"Are you all right?"

"I'm fine," she returned, a rasp to her voice.

"Are you certain?"

She crossed to him and took his hands in hers.

"I am well. Are you?"

He searched her bright eyes and then nodded.

"I am."

"All right. Let us get to Nicholas's manor before we are attacked once again."

They checked and restrengthened their protective shield before setting off once again. In the time it had taken for them to run Azenor off and rebuild their defenses, a light patter of snow had begun to fall. Delicate flakes landed against the shield and settled there. Other warlocks around them produced parasols or basic shields that covered them like an umbrella.

The rest of the travel passed without incident, but that didn't stop them from constantly looking over their shoulders, jumping at every unexpected sound, or readying their anti-demon weaponry. When they arrived at Nicholas's residence, Benedict pulled the bell and held his breath. Moments later, his butler answered the door and upon recognizing the two of them, immediately escorted them to Nicholas's receiving room—they had a completely open invitation.

Benedict and Lucia were seated only minutes on Nicholas's peridot couch cushions, having only had time to remove their gloves and overcoats, when the warlock himself graced through the door.

Some days the Wasting stole so much of his energy that Nicholas relied on a walking cane. Today was one such day. Three years into the Wasting and he was leaning heavily on the silver handled cane, the head of which was a perched owl.

Benedict clutched Lucia's hand for reassurance, tears burning in his eyes, a beaming grin on his face.

"Nicky," Benedict said softly, full of emotion.

"Benny!" Nicholas beamed. "Lucia! What are you two doing here?"

Benedict didn't say anything. Instead, he got up and crossed the room before capturing Nicholas in a tight embrace. Nicholas staggered but Benedict steadied him. His cane clattered to the ground.

"Benedict! What's going on?"

Benedict loosed a harsh breath and let slip a wavering laugh.

"I have a lot to tell you."

The three of them settled on the couches once Benedict helped Nicholas with his cane. Nicholas called for tea, which was delivered promptly. They had their cups in hand and prepared before Benedict launched into his ludicrous explanation of his life for the past seven years. He told him about the curse, his imprisonment, Lucia's death, his death, everything.

Nicholas took it all in stride until he heard of his own death. At that point he opted to add a splash of brandy to his tea.

"I think this was all because of our work on immortal diseases. Lucia's father told us just today about some rumors circulating around the board. I think whoever killed—kills—Lucia, is also the person who cursed me."

Nicholas exhaled and ran his hand through his light blond hair. "Well fuck me." He blinked rapidly. "All right. Well, we know the crux of the issue is your disease research, but what is the secondary motive? Jealousy? Money? Does someone want the claim to fame you two are building? Or do you think someone benefits more monetarily from the diseases not having a cure? Because I'll tell you this much, the cost to keep the Wasting at bay just at this point is astronomical."

"We think it's money."

Nicholas nodded. "That's my instinct, too."

"Is there anyone on the boards you can think of that could be behind this? I know you're on the one responsible for the Wasting."

It was true, Nicholas held a position on one of the three immortal diseases boards. Lucia's father held a spot invested in Midnight Malady. They had connections on the Ember Fever board, but no one they could trust. In fact, Benedict trusted the Ember Fever board less and less considering how emaciated their coffers were growing in light of Lucia's cure.

Midnight Malady was a vampiric illness. It was very likely what had spurned the legends of the vampire to begin with. During the daylight hours, the victim was normal, but come nightfall, an insatiable craving for blood struck and it could drive a person to insanity. If they did not get it, their cognition declined to madness, before they expired. They needed it every three days. However, the blood eventually made the victim sicker, and only prolonged the inevitable. Death. The longest living victim with Midnight Malady lasted ten years.

"I could make a list."

A realization struck Benedict right then.

"Nicky," he started passionately, inching to the edge of the sofa. "While I was imprisoned, I figured out the cure. Just the other day."

"You did what?" Both Lucia and Nicholas said in unison.

He turned to Lucia. "That's what I was about to tell you when Azenor attacked." He shifted to Nicholas. "Do you have laudanum, arsenic, and the bezoar of a goat?"

Nicholas arched a brow. "Naturally."

"And is your neighbor still of the cloth?"

"Yes...how does any of this help us?"

Benedict produced the silver knife he'd used to stick Azenor, her blood still coating it. "I have all the ingredients to cure you, right here, right now." He paused. "I also need some spirits."

Nicholas summoned for his neighbor, a middle-aged man who was hemming and hawing about his faith, but possessed the ability they needed nonetheless. The watery-eyed man blessed the blood on the blade with absolutions of the angels—purifying it. Of course, it couldn't be done out of the goodness of his heart and so the man demanded five pounds for the inconvenience. Nicholas slapped the payment into the man's greedy hand and had his butler usher him out.

Unlike humans, warlocks did not worship a deity. Any warlock who'd performed the Staying knew neither Heaven nor Hell possessed a ruler. It was just angels and demons, and angels kept their unearthliness apparent. Divine light, many eyed, winged, and gilded—they were complete celestial power. Demons, meanwhile, were mostly humanoid with non-human characteristics that lent them an "other" aspect. But their familiarity in form was enough to sow trickery in mortals and warlocks.

Lucia drew a vial of Nicholas's blood with her careful hands, perfectly tying a tourniquet and extracting another ingredient as painlessly as possible. She bandaged him up and handed it to Benedict.

Benedict stirred the silver blade with Azenor's blood in a tall vial of spirits, cleansing the blade and saving every drop of the blessed blood for the cure.

In a flask, Benedict combined Nicholas's and Azenor's liquor-soaked blood and with a gloved hand, and sprinkled arsenic into the mix. He corked the flask, shook it, and then reopened it. Then he took the brownish stone—the bezoar—and wrapped a sigil around it, followed by a confinement charm around that. The blue geometry formed the sigil for destruction. He added it to the blood and arsenic solution. A swirl later and he was adding more of the spirits. Next, he triggered the destruction sigil and the bezoar exploded into tiny granules. On the bottom of the flask, he casted for vitality—as an extra measure.

When everything was mixed, Lucia extracted the muted red solution and loaded it into a syringe. He could see she was holding her breath as she did so, anticipation glimmering in her eyes.

"Do you realize what this means if this works?" Lucia whispered.

Benedict nodded. "It means everything. It means we will be documented in history, we will have more celebrity than before, and the target on our heads will be tenfold larger."

"Exactly." Lucia exhaled. "It's time."

Benedict handed Nicholas a tincture of laudanum and his friend downed it like a shot. He knew this process was going to be painful and he hoped the laudanum would at least dull the edge.

Nicholas exposed his forearm and Lucia ventured over to him; syringe full in her hand. She prodded his inner arm with two fingers, searching for a vein.

"Are you prepared?" she asked.

Nicholas nodded frantically. "Please."

Without ceremony, Lucia administered the cure, injecting it straight into Nicholas's veins. They all watched the reddish liquid disappear from the syringe, waiting for some response. When it was emptied, Lucia set the needle aside and gently bandaged the wound.

"Keep pressure on it for a few minutes, the bleeding should stop soon," Lucia instructed.

Nicholas did as told, and looked up at them with anticipatory gray eyes. "So, what now?"

"We wait," Benedict said.

The waiting didn't take long. In the same amount of time it took for Nicholas to hold the pressure on the injection site, did he begin to squirm.

"I'm beginning to feel very hot."

"It's the demon blood," Lucia told him. "It's being burned out of you as the rest of the ingredients help fight off the progressing infection and create immunity. The cure for Ember Fever works similarly, I'm assuming that's why Benedict chose the laudanum. Do you require another dose?"

Nicholas squirmed and groaned. His hands flexed.

"I feel like I'm on fire."

His skin looked clear and flameless, in fact there was a healthy glow to it that wasn't there before.

"You're not," Benedict said. "I can add a slumber sigil for your comfort?"

"Please," Nicholas practically begged.

Benedict worked his hands and a blue glow emitted, moments later a fully formed shape took form. He pressed it to Nicholas's forehead and his best friend's eyes immediately shuttered. Lucia and Benedict both helped Nicholas to settle on the sofa. They arranged him as comfortable as possible and then draped a knitted blanket over him.

"We should celebrate," Nicholas mumbled. "Have a party for my good health."

"Another time," Benedict said softly. "You need to rest and we have a dinner to attend."

Nicholas sighed dramatically. "Lovesick fool." It was said with an air of endearment.

Benedict patted Nicholas on the head and then sought out the butler. He was a mild-looking fellow of middling age with short, sandy hair and a waxed moustache.

"Would you keep a look out on him?" Benedict asked. "He'll be quite weak a while, but if anything changes, please summon for me immediately."

The butler nodded. "Of course, Lord Edwards."

"Thank you, Dickens. Good afternoon."

"Good afternoon to you, sir."

Benedict and Lucia departed Nicholas's residence with soft waves and hope in their hearts.

Could they have really cured the Wasting this night?

Benedict prayed they did.

DECEMEBER 14, 1866

They'd casted cleansing spells to clear any evidence of their demonic encounter and cure from their person. Cleansing spells were effective, but lost their potency as they were recast over the same thing without a true clean. After that, they donned the same protections leaving Nicholas's residence as they did arriving. This time, they were even more vigilant than before and unlike before, they were lucky enough—and feeling brave enough—to hail a carriage.

Lucia's parents' townhouse was across the city, just on the outskirts of the baker's quarter. Lucia loved this area of the city; it always smelled like fresh bread or sugary pastries. There was, of course, the slight scent of horse, but Lucia was informed that the smell of Mortal London had been foul in many places. Due to the lack of ability to cast cleansing spells, the human city reeked of horse and shit and a motley assortment of other things. Magic afforded the warlocks many advantages—a balm on the olfactory system one of them.

Benedict extended a gloved hand and helped Lucia into their hired transportation. Despite the two layers of leather separating their hands, she felt a spark of magic between them. Attraction. Arousal.

It was a sleek black thing with silver accents and hunter green velvet. The horses were equally dark and smooth with bridles in the same metallic accoutrements.

They settled in and together they casted protection sigils, weaving their combined azure and emerald magic together. The two undulated with each other like northern lights.

Tucked away into the close heat of the carriage, Lucia's mind turned fuzzy. All she could smell was Benedict's rich scent of bergamot and sandalwood. All she could feel was the warmth of Benedict's left side pressed against her. The lean strength in his arm. The jittery movement of his knee, brushing his thigh against hers over and over. All she wanted to do was get her mouth on him. All over him. In tender ways and depraved ways.

The thoughts that were currently coursing through her mind were utterly indecent and licentious. It didn't help that the jostle of the carriage wheels had her bumping up against Benedict, only adding to the ache between her thighs. She kept her knees closed tight, but the movement was giving her friction. She shifted in discomfort.

Benedict put a hand to her knee and she ignited. "Are you all right?"

Her face heated. "Yes, just uncomfortable."

All Lucia wanted was that hand to slip higher, slide beneath her skirts and between her legs. To do all the things he'd once whispered he could do to her in the dark.

The carriage trundled along, negotiating the cobblestones like a graceless deer. The clatter of horse hooves blended with the clicking of the gears.

"Ah, yes. These seats could use a refurbishment, no? The padding has gone flat in places."

Truth be told Lucia hadn't noticed the subpar stuffing. Her mind was consumed with the singular distraction of the wetness blooming between her legs.

"It seems so."

"Mm," Benedict mused, trailing his fingers on the inner curve of Lucia's knee. Her eyes practically rolled back in her head as he leaned into her. "Lucia darling, you and I both know there is nothing wrong with these seats." His nose skimmed against her throat and she saw stars. She stopped breathing. He continued. "Perhaps it has something to do with that hollow feeling between your legs. Your desire burning through you. Love, I know you, and I know what you want."

"What?" she managed thickly.

He chuckled softly, his mouth against her ear.

"Me."

She shivered and her eyes closed. "Yes."

"I know." He sighed. "But not yet."

Lucia's eyes flew wide. "Benedict, I meant to talk to you about that. I've changed—" She broke off as she noticed their lack of movement and Benedict's hand on the door. "Oh. We're here."

Perhaps now wasn't the best time to converse about possible intimacy and how badly she wanted her fiancé to fill the void between her legs. In light of her possible impending death, waiting till marriage seemed foolhardy.

Benedict opened the door and a bracing breeze rushed in, taking with it the warmth and most of the sexually charged air. Benedict swept out and then waited for Lucia, hand upraised. She took it.

They were just outside of the Turner's brownstone, her parents having lived there her entire life. It was all familiar, the slate roof, the two poised gargoyles, the leaded windows. Flanking the staircase entrance were shrubs that stayed green year-round. In the summer there were yellow blooms that erupted quickly and died days later. In the winter, as it was now, they dressed the foliage in glass baubles and magic—just as they did for the tall, proud tree within their sitting room.

Benedict suddenly tugged Lucia against him. She stumbled over her own feet and crashed to him. Their breaths mingled in the cold air, melding like their magic. He ducked his head down to hers, his face just a breath away.

"Were you going to say you've changed your mind about waiting, my Lucia?" His mouth whispered across her cheek. She dug her fingers into his chest.

"I—I'm not sure," she said, even though she *was* sure.

"Do you require some convincing?"

"What sort of convincing?"

He practically purred in her ear. This was a side of Benedict she nearly never saw but she'd be lying if she said she didn't like it.

"I think perhaps on the carriage ride back I could show you." His hand skimmed down her front, slipping below her navel. His palm splayed there, hot and heavy. "Would you like that demonstration?"

"Very much."

"Then it's settled."

He pulled back and linked their hands as they started for the townhouse. She shook the fantasies from her head as they ascended the steps.

When they entered, the family's longtime butler, Charles, took their coats and gloves. Lucia was greeted warmly with childhood familiarity and Benedict was welcomed with respect and friendliness. A small smile was on his clean-shaven face, his blue eyes twinkling with mirth.

Fresh evergreen wreaths hung on the dark wood doors, large red ribbons tied in fat bows bedecking each. Golden bells were fastened to their centers, jewel-toned holly tucked in artfully. Garland wrapped the staircase banister in swooping arcs, more fat bows fashioned against them. The dark floors gleamed with fresh polish, the walls boasting a new spread of wallpaper in yellows and reds, designed in muted florals.

The scent of roasting chicken was thick in the air and Lucia followed it, detecting savory, rosemary, and thyme. In the dining room, the cook was just placing the silver dishes on the long mahogany table. Tureens of buttery mashed potatoes, gravy, honey glazed carrots, seasoned green beans, fresh dinner rolls, and a bowl of cranberry sauce. The sizzling chicken was set in the center and the cook set to carve it.

Lucia's mother and father were already seated in the paisley chairs at the head of the table and to the right. Lucia dipped to first her mother's cheek and then her father's, giving them a quick kiss in greeting. Benedict, behind her, nodded politely to both her parents before pulling Lucia's chair out for her to sit. She beamed and took it. Benedict took the seat beside her.

Lady Turner was a very mild woman. Petite, like Lucia, and quiet, with a gentle voice and soft-spoken manners, she was the antithesis of Lucia's father. It didn't help that she was one of the very few citizens of this city who did not possess magic. Her status was entirely dependent on her marriage to Lucia's father—spouses were the only people afforded this grace. It was just another juxtaposition between them, as Lord Turner was big, brash, intelligent, and outspoken. Though some of his ideals were archaic or mortal in source, he was clever and sharp-witted.

Pleasantries were made and they plated their meals. Lucia knew something was coming, her father didn't typically invite Benedict over unless he wanted to discuss something. She braced herself for that moment. It was after Lucia was halfway through her meal, and they'd just commenced with talk of the weather when her father cleared his throat purposefully.

"So, Lucia, Ben," Lord Turner began. "What are your intentions after marriage?"

Lucia dabbed her mouth with a napkin. "What do you mean?"

"Do you still intend to teach and research?"

Lucia hesitated, taken aback. "Yes, of course. Why wouldn't I?"

"Well…children."

He said it like children were such a done deal. As if that was explanation enough. Lucia had to remind herself that her parents came from a part of the world where people had children regardless of desire to. It was an expectation in Mortal London. Having babies was just something a person did. Society demanded it. Here, it wasn't the same. It was more deliberate—elective.

"*If* we choose to have children," Lucia began, not revealing that children had already been a discussion between her and her fiancé. "Benedict and I will both be continuing our research and teaching."

Lucia's mother was conspicuously quiet, olive hands folded in her lap, dark head tucked down. She stared at the flickering candle flames from the white candlesticks running the length of the table on a scarlet runner. Her brown eyes turned gold beneath the small flame. Her face was placid, but around the eyes some tightness betrayed her ire.

Lucia's father stammered, gaping. "But how will you provide—"

"I would stop with this mortal thinking," Benedict inserted. "Should one of us take a step back from their careers, I would be the first to do so. Lucia is the one who has discovered Ember Fever's cure."

Lucia noticed that Benedict did not bring up his part in the potential—though quite certain—cure for the Wasting. He was eager to show Lucia in a successful and ambitious light.

"No, that just isn't done. The man should be out working, the mother stays home with the babes."

"That's not how it's done here. That's an option, but it is certainly not the demand. Those backwards values are archaic, and quite frankly, fucked."

"I have worked tirelessly in academia, father," Lucia enunciated carefully, not letting her father comment on Benedict's use of 'fucked'. "I have constantly had to prove myself, again and again. Despite my awards! Despite finding the bloody cure to Ember Fever, mind you! Men have children and continue teaching and researching. Why must I stop?"

Lord Turner's face turned puce. "Lucia, your studies are far too dangerous. She should stop them now."

"So, that's what this is really about," Lucia snapped, slamming down her utensils. "Are you and your mighty board so threatened by my discoveries?"

Lord Turner flattened his hands on the table. "I am concerned about the threats on your *life*. You have no idea how dangerous this has become. People want you *dead*."

Lucia and Benedict were both stunned to silence.

"Luther, please," her mother admonished. "Do not crush her dreams."

"No, you don't understand. I've watched this sort of thing happen before. Any time the board senses its coffers might go dry, they react harshly. Retaliatory. They don't think before they act and oftentimes, they seek to eliminate that threat."

"Father…"

"This—this ambition of yours, it's going to get you killed, and I can't bear to lose you."

Lucia swallowed thickly, tears prickling her eyes. Her father had no idea how right he was. Her eyes fluttered to Benedict, and his knuckles were whitening on his fork.

"The board doesn't care about you. It cares about its way of living. They don't want to change their lifestyles even if blood must get on their hands. The money those of us on the board will lose could be tantamount to losing our house staff. Our homes."

Lucia's head snapped up. "Our?" Her eyes narrowed. "Do you benefit so greatly from there being no cure for Midnight Malady?"

Lord Turner blustered. "Well, to a certain degree, yes, I do, but—"

"So, really anyone—even a well-respected man like yourself—could be sending the Brotherhood or another organization to silence me."

It felt like a dagger was plunged into her heart with her father's callous words. Blood thrummed in her head; her heartbeat was a drum in her ears. Beside her, Benedict reached for her leg to steady her. Support her.

"I would never!" Luther Turner choked.

"Why?" Lucia challenged. "Because I'm your daughter? Or is the idea reprehensible enough that you'd never dream of condemning a stranger in my shoes?"

"I love you. I could never hurt you. But others might. Others *will*."

"That is an evasive answer." Lucia stood up, her heart breaking in her chest. She was sure she could hear the crack in the beats that hammered her head. "And I think this dinner is over."

She pushed her chair back from the table and the legs screeched across the hardwood. She smoothed her hands down her rose-colored dress. Benedict, in support, stood also.

"Mother. Father. I will send a letter when I am ready to speak to you again. Until such time, I think it's for the best if I find my stay elsewhere."

Luther hung his head in shame but said nothing.

"What about Christmas?" Lucia's mother asked, breaking her nearly complete silence.

Lucia took in her mother's cowed brown eyes, her hunched shoulders. She was a small woman, both in form and power and confidence. She had nothing here without her husband. Not even her child would be enough to allow her to stay should something happen to her husband. Lucia didn't even know if her parents still loved each other, or if it was just convenience or societal expectation at this point.

"I do not know, but I will be staying with Benedict for the foreseeable future, and I'll hear no remarks on it."

"Lucia..." Luther began.

"No. I have had enough. I am more than capable. My magic is powerful, you know that better than anyone else."

Lucia wheeled around and strut for the door with her back held straight. She heard Benedict address her parents succinctly and probably nod as he caught up to her anger-powered stride. Snatching her coat and gloves from the rack before Charles could assist her, Lucia was striding out the door—fuming.

She donned her coat in the cold evening air, snowflakes falling on her dress before she had a chance to button up. Angrily, she pulled her black hair from being trapped beneath the wool.

"I cannot believe him!" Lucia raged, casting protections as Benedict struggled to catch up. Sparks flew from her hands as she drew lines together. "He may as well have hired the Brotherhood himself to take me out! Truly, my own father, undermining my studies and intelligence under the guise of children and archaic values! It's sickening."

Benedict's approaching footsteps we're getting louder. Lucia tugged on her leather gloves after the first spell took form. She'd already made it two blocks when she felt a hand on her shoulder, she whirled.

Her fiancé stood there, concern written across his face. "Do you truly think your father sentenced you to death?"

He was talking about in his time. The coming future. A week.

She huffed a breath. "I don't know. Complicit, even just by allowing this sort of practice? I believe it. Actually carrying it out? I'm not sure."

Lucia tugged her hair, stressed and confused.

Blue and green magic writhed around them, her emerald waves staticky and intermittent—she didn't do a very good job. She casted a patch-up as Benedict took her in.

"Maybe Nicholas can help sort it out. We can run all the names by him and see if they have more motive than your father. But I still think your…death, and my curse are connected. I think it's the same person at hand."

"Well. You'll certainly be useful as we determine who is still alive during your time then."

"It won't be you."

Spinning toward the hissing voice, Lucia came face to face with a white-shrouded demon. The demon was standing just outside their webs of protection, face eerily clear beneath the shroud. As if water had painted the fabric to her skin, Lucia could see high cheekbones and the tip of her nose. The wreathed crown of candles flickered against the deepening night sky, carving shadows through the dark.

"Calanthe," Benedict said through gritted teeth.

Calanthe cocked her head at Lucia's fiancé. "You're not supposed to be here, soul-cursed."

"But indeed I am."

"This goes against the fabric of time. Of fate."

"And I certainly do not care. *She*—" he grabbed Lucia's hand— "is all that matters to me."

"Her soul is destined for the afterlife."

"Somehow, I believe she's been given a second chance. Tell me, where does her soul currently reside?"

Calanthe visibly pursed her lips, tightening them in a damning non-answer. Clearly, Lucia's soul was not in the afterlife.

"You may have plucked it from the fires for now, but in due time, destiny will claim her," Calanthe growled.

"No one will be claiming her."

Lucia saw Calanthe's sharp grin form beneath the whiteness. "Are you willing to stake your life on that?"

Just then, Calanthe reached out with a long-clawed fingertip and dragged it through their magic. It caught on Benedict's power, but slipped through hers. Lucia's breath caught and Benedict shoved her behind him. Then, before she could blink, Benedict threw a spell at Calanthe. She hadn't even seen him cast.

Calanthe flew back as the orb of blue hit her, the sigils for power and propulsion etched upon it. The demon slammed into the brick pillar of a staircase. The brick made an odd cracking noise as debris filtered down on her, mixing with the snow in stark contrast.

"Go!" Benedict commanded.

Lucia hiked up her skirts and bolted.

The icy night air was like knives in her lungs, the snowflakes like razor blades. Lucia, cursing her skirts, couldn't cast as she ran. Behind her, Benedict was forming and tossing spells, attacking Calanthe with vigor.

A bolt of red-hot flame swept past her and Lucia yelped, veering away.

"Holy fuck!" Benedict cursed. "She can use hellfire!"

Dread turned Lucia's blood cold.

Demons who could summon hellfire were from the sixth circle. Only certain demons could summon hellfire, just like only some could cast infernal runes. It was all dependent on the circle and ring of Hell the demon originated from.

Jets of flame followed Lucia as she sprinted, heading in the direction of Benedict's home. Her breaths huffed as her feet ate up the distance. They were so far away, they should have hailed a cab, they should have—

Benedict suddenly tackled Lucia into the snow, rolling them over and over as a stream of fire blazed ahead, burning without reprieve. Immediately her dress was soaked and her knee smarted from where she'd knocked it against the curb.

At this time in the evening there was no one on the streets. It was too late for the business workers, the banks and shops having closed over an hour ago, yet it was too early for the ladies of the night and the men who sought them. Too early was it also for any of the bars or gambling halls to open their doors, with wafts of hot boozy air and boisterous, drunken shouts. It was quiet and eerie, and the perfect timing for a demon attack.

Lucia cursed.

Suddenly, a very cold hand wrapped around her ankle and pulled. Lucia was dragged through the snow, her skirts bunching up around her hips, the cold penetrating her bones. She felt the first pricks of claws break through her flesh, the ensuing liquid turning icy against her bare leg. Lucia screamed and kicked the demon in the face with her opposite foot.

Messily, Lucia casted the first sigil she could think of. Calanthe shrieked and released her as the sunlight spell slammed into her face. Lucia hoped it blinded her.

The demon began clawing at her face and Lucia got to her feet, yanking Benedict with her. Her fiancé covered his hand in holy water and threw a spell behind them—pure water, dousing Calanthe's building flame.

The holy water mixture doused Calanthe's hellfire and the remaining liquid scorched her. She shrieked in agony. Blinded by sunlight and burned by holy water, the demon opened up crevasses on her flesh through the shroud. Blackish blood flooded out.

Together, Lucia and Benedict ran, turning a corner. It was pure luck when a taxi carriage rounded the opposite one. Immediately they hailed it and wasted no time jumping in. The carriage hadn't even stopped yet.

"Drive!" Benedict yelled. "North!"

The driver didn't hesitate. He whipped the reins and they took off at an alarming speed.

They collapsed against the benches, catching their breath. They were wet, dirty, and bloody. Her dress was torn, her shoes ruined—her coat might've been salvageable. Lucia's hair was a mess and dirt streaked Benedict's face. She was sure hers was probably just as filthy. Fruitlessly, she casted cleansing and mending spells but only a thin layer of grime disappeared—she hadn't washed after her last cleansing spell earlier—and the rips in the gown repaired themselves, but it was clear where it had been torn.

After a few minutes of composing themselves, Benedict gave his address to the driver.

"Well," Benedict said with a dry chuckle. "So much for our previous carriage plans. I was going to li—"

The carriage was airborne and then it was crashing to its side. The horses cried out, piercing whinnies, and the driver shouted, surprise in the sound. Lucia and Benedict flew across the bench and slammed into the western side of the cab. Lucia landed hard on her shoulder and hip while Benedict caught himself with both hands, his forehead knocking against the hard side. A gash opened on his head, blood streaking down his face.

"Fuck!" Benedict cried out, palming his wound.

"What in the nine hells was that?" Lucia groaned, getting to her feet in the upturned carriage. She stood, and due to her short stature, her head barely brushed the opposite side.

The carriage door was yanked off its hinges and a bearded man's face peered in. A malicious smile crossed his mouth as he produced a knife and held an orb of amber magic in his palm.

Lucia sucked in a breath and quickly summoned a defensive spell, blasting him free from the upturned carriage. He let out a grunt and she heard him hit the ground a few seconds later. She didn't even process which spell it was.

A new face was revealed over the broken door and a hand reached in—it had bitten nails and a scarred palm. The man had gingery mutton chops and rubbery lips which peeled back over yellowing teeth. He caught a handful of Lucia's hair and pulled.

Her scalp stung and she grabbed onto his wrist with both hands, trying to relieve the sharp pressure.

A cerulean flash of light snagged her peripheral vision and the man grabbing her screamed as Benedict's magic hit him. He released her and soared away. Lucia turned and found her fiancé, blood dripping from his forehead and down his nose, face a mask of fury.

Benedict hoisted himself out of the carriage, a spell already loaded, protections revolving around him. He cleared the broken door and immediately launched himself out, tackling one of their assailants.

Lucia scrambled out behind him, aided by the sigil of agility. When she climbed out, she discovered she'd knocked their first attacker out cold, his head resting against the sidewalk, having cracked the back of his head on the edge. One of the horses had broken free of the carriage, the other scrambling and panicking as it kicked its legs and thrashed its head, squealing in terror. The driver was speared through on the bench, a javelin in his chest, blood leaking from his mouth.

Benedict was casting spells, thwarting two attackers— Mutton chops and a third. The third man was clean shaven with hay-colored hair and a thin build. Benedict's hands were a blur, his cerulean light lashing against the gray of the hay-haired man and shattering the sickly green of Mutton chops.

It was clear to even a human that Benedict was far more powerful and held far more control.

Benedict held the rare talent of being able to blend unlike spells together, likely honed from all his years imprisoned. Many warlocks—like herself—could combine several like spells into a larger and more potent version, but to take destruction and combine it with flame? Nearly unheard of.

Lashes of blue lit up the night sky and Benedict whirled away from a dart of gray magic. His viridian coattails flew out behind him with the speed of his movement, his fancy shoes gliding over the snow. Benedict casted, geometric lines erupting from his hands.

Lucia took advantage of the distracted attackers and crept around wide. Skirting the sidewalk, creeping forward past storefronts and townhouses, Lucia began casting. Tangling her fingers, deep green bloomed, and she built the fire sigil. Over and over. She combined it five times.

When she was directly behind Mutton chops, she lined up the spell and let that green magic bloom into flame. It appeared with a whoosh, and she released it. It slammed into him, and then it consumed him.

Mutton chops went down screaming, his mildewy magic evaporating with his broken cast. He began rolling in the snow but Lucia had been thorough—he could not douse five spells without a significant body of water.

His companion whirled in shock, a gray orb warbling in his hand. Immediately, she watched him cast for water, but Benedict was quicker.

Her fiancé created a lash and whip and then wrapped the sizzling cerulean around hay-haired's throat. With one forceful tug, Benedict yanked his magic and a sickening snap echoed through the air.

The man's eyes went glassy as his neck canted to an odd angle and then he dropped.

Benedict had broken his neck.

Benedict had killed him.

Lucia sucked in a breath. She was no better. She was currently letting a man burn alive at her feet. His wails of agony doing nothing to implore her movement. He thrashed and then suddenly he stopped. The fire crackled.

Lucia and Benedict gazed at each other without a word before she quickly crossed over to him and threw herself into his arms.

"I am unharmed," he said before she could ask.

"As am I," she replied breathily.

They held each other for a moment, absorbing the love and affection, safety and concern that all rose between them. Eventually, they broke apart and stared at the carnage.

A ruined taxi carriage. A dead driver. A terrified horse. Another missing. Three bodies with various methods of murder.

Murder.

They'd killed three people.

Lucia, feeling a sudden flash of clarity, needed answers. She waved away the flames of her spell—they'd already done their job and this much was overkill. Crossing over to the first man she'd ejected from the carriage, she checked his pulse— or lack thereof—to confirm his death. Next, with extreme focus, she shoved aside any conscience or guilt and dug around in the dead man's pockets.

She found a bag of silver and a contract. She read it over and her blood ran cold.

"Benedict," she started, her tone high-pitched and shaky. "They were hired to kill me."

She held up the paper, stamped, with a broken seal. A contract between the Scarlet Brotherhood and an unnamed employer, stating half the payment upon acceptance of the job, and half after the completion of. The sum was a great amount. It was dated December 14, 1866. Today.

Benedict rushed to her and took the contract from her hands. He perused it, shock painting his face more and more with every word read. As he did, she bent to the body and tugged the collar of his shirt away from his neck. There the Brotherhood's symbol was branded into his skin—a wolf's head with a bloody drop on its brow.

She went over to the other two bodies and found the same thing. A brand, a bag of silver and a contract. The burned man's contract was all but ash, but she was able to make out scraps and the remains of wax that revealed the once formed seal.

"This didn't happen before." Benedict's voice was grave. "It didn't. Something changed." His head whipped up to hers. "Not unless you never told me of an attack before—" He swallowed. "We were not on speaking terms for nearly a week. It's not entirely implausible, but it is very uncharacteristic for you."

Lucia shook her head. "No matter how angry I was at you, there is no realm of possibility where I kept this from you."

Benedict looked as if he'd seen a ghost.
"We need to get off the streets. Now."

When they finally arrived at Benedict's townhouse their adrenaline was finally dissipating. All of a sudden Lucia could feel all of the cold, the exhaustion, and the fear from the past few hours. It wasn't until she'd made several steps into his foyer that she noticed he'd stopped. She turned and looked at him quizzically.

"I haven't seen my home in nearly seven years," he said forlornly.

Lucia watched his jade eyes take in the rich red wallpaper—the golden florals printed on it. The heavy wood wainscoting and rich parquet floors. The gold frames that held art and family portraits. The table holding a pot of poinsettias.

Concern and empathy rose in her and she made her way to her fiancé, taking his arm.

"I'm here," she whispered. "And this time I'm not going anywhere."

He tightened his grip on her arm and nodded. He swallowed once, twice, then together they stepped further into his home.

The sitting room was similar to the front entry. Reds and golds, dark woods, but here there were wreaths and a tall tree decorated for Christmas. The tree had red bows, flickering candles, hovering sigils of protection and peace in blue and green circling, glass ornaments, all topped with a bright, seven-pointed Elven Star. Leaded windows had drawn drapes of crimson, couches of similar shade were arranged artfully, a polished piano sat in a corner near a wall of bookshelves. At the center of the furthest wall a fire burned happily in the grate of the grand fireplace, a landscape painting of a battle between angels and demons hung above it.

Lucia glanced at Benedict and saw tears silvering his eyes. She could see the longing there. She squeezed him tightly.

From the kitchen bustled Benedict's butler, a soft-hearted man, dark of hair and eye with a rich ochre complexion. In his white-gloved hands was a tray with sandwiches and tea.

"Good evening, Lord Ed—" Huffam, the butler paused. "Good grief, my lord, my lady, you look a mess!"

Benedict smiled sheepishly and ruffled the back of his head. "Apologies, Huffam. We've had quite the evening."

Huffam nodded and set the tray down. "I'll leave this here and draw you two baths?"

"That would be appreciated, yes."

"Right then."

"Oh, and Huffam?" The butler turned and Benedict continued. "Please be careful coming and going from the house. To be frank, I'd be most comfortable if you either stayed here within the wards, or your personal residence for the foreseeable future."

"May I ask why?"

"Demons and the Brotherhood, Huffam."

"Sir," Huffam said sternly. "I am old—far older than you might think—I have been around since the dawn of Vonor, and before we discovered demonic warding. I have fought many a demon in my day, and I remember when the streets were never safe to walk—one was always on guard. If you are having demonic encounters, know it is not my first time facing them, and I am confident in my abilities. Any thought less of me, and I may consider it an insult."

"I worry that my business may end with your harm."

"Thank you, sir, but I can handle these risks."

Benedict sighed, defeated. "All right. But, feel free to take the rest of the night and tomorrow morning off. Or until after Christmas."

"I can't do that, sir."

Benedict glanced aside. "Then please just cast extra protections and take the morning."

"Are you certain, sir?"

"Quite. Thank you for all you've done."

"Of course."

Huffam left to run their water. They were left alone, but rather than speak or engage in intimacies, they went for the food. After wiping their hands on the warm cloths provided, they made their tea and picked at their sandwiches. Halfway through the platter, Huffam returned.

"Your baths are waiting. I've set out fresh linens and robes. Miss Lucia, your things are in the upstairs powder room."

"Thank you, Huffam," Lucia said around a bite of sandwich.

Huffam locked up behind him as he left, leaving the two of them completely alone. Lucia swallowed, suddenly feeling the intensity between them. Benedict seemed to feel it the same moment she did, staring hotly at her over the rim of his teacup.

Lucia cleared her throat. "I think I'll go bathe now." She stopped, horror striking her. "I never asked. Benedict, is it all right if I stay with you?"

Benedict chortled. "It's more than all right." He leaned forward and captured his hand. "Maybe we can even make this a permanent thing."

Her heart lodged in her throat. "You mean before the wedding?"

"I do."

She slipped a small smile on her face. "I think that's our line next month."

"It works right now too."

She bit her lip. "I think there's also something else I'd like to do before the wedding."

Benedict's eyes widened. "Like what?"

She smirked. "Use your imagination." And then she extricated herself from his grasp and sauntered away to her bath.

When she got to the claw-footed tub, she stripped off her nearly ruined dress, shredded stockings, and filthy shoes. As she slipped into the water, she nearly moaned. Coils of steam rose from the surface, seeping into her bones and flushing out the cold. Adding orange oil to the bath, she scrubbed her face and scalp, feeling grit gather beneath her nails. After she lathered and rinsed her hair, she used a bristle brush to clean her nails, and then she eyed the straight razor on the tray.

She thought about all the lustful things she wanted do to with Benedict. How she'd heard from her female companions about their preparations before intimacy. It varied between each woman, but Lucia knew she liked the feeling of smooth legs.

Quickly, she took the razor.

Thoughts of Benedict plagued her, memories of his touch, and fantasies of his seductions. She had gotten a taste of the things he might say to her in the carriage and suddenly she felt a stirring low in her belly. She set the razor down and curiously, she slipped her hand beneath the water and over her soft abdomen. Down, she ventured, feeling the fine black curls between her legs, and there—

She gasped as her touch made contact with a very sensitive spot. Lucia pulled her hand away as if shocked and stared blankly for a moment. She'd never touched herself before, having had her parents' values drilled into her, but that single touch was like a spark of magic.

Again, she reached down and touched herself, feeling a small nub that sent thrills through her entire being. She bit her lip to keep the sound at bay. And then she travelled lower. She found the slit between her legs and slipped a finger in. She was slick, and despite the fact she was in the water, she knew she was wet in a different way.

Lucia yanked her hand from between her legs and promptly finished her bath. Pulling the plug, she stepped out and hastily towelled off, wringing her hair. Huffam had left her a dressing robe and she donned it, tying the ruby sash haphazardly.

She padded out into the hall, the sound of water sucking down the drain behind her. Her black hair was still wet, she could feel it soaking the back of her robe as she went down the hallway. The sound of Benedict's puttering in the bedroom drew her attention and she boldly followed it.

When she pushed open the half-closed door, she found Benedict, a towel around his waist, dressing robe open. Candlelight caught specks of water like amber gems on his skin. That same light casted devastating shadows on his high cheekbones, the shape of his mouth, the line of his clavicle. He turned from his wardrobe in surprise, revealing his smooth chest, the finest scattering of hair there. She noticed the trail of hair that started at his navel and she most definitely noticed the V that dipped to the towel; something about it made her want to lick him. She was shocked by her own response.

"Lucia, I—"

"Don't put your clothes on," she said, striding into the room and closing the door behind her.

"What? I—"

She approached him and pushed his hands from the sleep shirt he was pulling from the drawer. In the space of his arms, she reached up and pulled his face down to hers.

Her kiss was devouring. There was nothing sweet in it. It was claiming and fierce and wild. She wanted him, and she wanted him to know she wanted him. Now. Fear from the day had turned to passion and she filled Benedict with it.

Lucia opened her mouth to allow him entrance and their tongues slipped together, tasting and dancing. She tugged on his hair as she swept the tip of her tongue over his lower lip before pulling it in.

As if his hands had been hesitating, they finally went to the small of her back, tugging her against him. She felt the hardness between his legs push against the towel, the thick ridge prodding her belly. She gasped into his mouth at the sensation.

"Lucia…" he half moaned.

"Benedict."

She tugged on his towel and it fell away between them. Skirting her fingers down, she grazed the length he pushed against her. Her fingertips just brushed his sensitive skin before he was groaning and suddenly picking her up.

Benedict carried her to the bed, her legs wrapped around his waist. His mouth never left her, even as she broke for breath, he just trailed open-mouthed kisses down her jaw, her throat. They crashed on the red coverlet, Benedict's weight a seductive promise atop her.

Thrusting her hips upward while her hands scrabbled for any purchase on her fiancé, Benedict bit lightly on her collarbone. A thrill shot through her and she shoved his robe from his shoulders, pushing it away until he was utterly naked above her.

"Lucia, are you sure?" he murmured, near pained against her throat. "I don't want you rushing things or making a hasty decision because—"

"I'm sure." And then she took him confidently in hand and stroked him.

His devastating moan sent liquid heat between her legs. He pumped into her hand, and a jolt of anxious excitement struck her.

"We don't have any protection," he whispered.

Lucia pondered while feeling him. "I'm okay with taking the chance. We both want children and we marry next month. We're established in our careers. I am six-and-twenty, you are little more than that."

"That is my dream. *You* are my dream," he said ardently. "I love you, Lucia."

"I love you, too."

They kissed and it was tender. Sweet. But then the sweetness melted away and Benedict's hands were on her waist, untying the sash that held her robe closed. He pushed it apart and then his hands roamed her soft abdomen. His hot mouth coasted down her neck and down, low, lower than he'd ever gone before.

Suddenly, his mouth was on her breast and he flicked her nipple with his tongue. She gasped and arched. He took that tight bud in his mouth and rapidly moved his tongue against it.

Her one hand was still stroking his length, the other dug nails into his back. But then, he began moving lower and she was forced to release him, his hand taking over, playing where his mouth once was. He rolled her nipple between his thumb and forefinger, and she didn't know how such an incredible sensation could exist.

Benedict's mouth was on her lower abdomen and he continued even lower. She held her breath as she watched him slip between her legs, his mouth so close to her core.

"I want to taste your honey, Lucia." The vibrations from his gravelly tone had her curling her toes. "I want to give you every pleasure tonight."

"I've never…" She blushed.

"Can I show you?"

"Yes. Please."

He set his mouth on her and curled his tongue around that tiny, sensitive spot. She nearly flew off the bed from the lash of pleasure.

"*Oh fuck,*" she moaned.

Benedict continued licking her and tasting her, and ecstasy started to build within her. His tongue moved cleverly and she began making sounds that had never escaped her before—mewling, begging. Something began building within her, expanding, pressing the limits. Pleasure coiled and a pang of fear struck her. A feeling—a sensation—needed to be released, but she didn't know how.

"Oh, Benedict, I can't, I—I—"

She suddenly shattered, pleasure racing through her. Bliss overwhelmed her and she let out a keening sound—a high-pitched moan—as her hips undulated with the waves of what she suddenly realized was a climax.

Lucia came down from the high, panting. A faint dewy layer of perspiration speckled her skin. Her breasts were heaving with her breaths. She stared down at Benedict, his sultry green eyes looking up at her as he tasted her again.

She jolted.

"How did you do that? I—" she moaned as he licked her again. "Fuck."

"Mm, you're delicious, my darling." He trailed his fingers down her belly and then down, parting her. He slid a fingertip through her sex, sweeping her wetness. "Can I try something else?"

She nodded very quickly.

Gently, he slipped a finger inside her tight channel and immediately and reflexively she clenched around him. Slowly, he plunged it deeper and then curved his finger in a come-hither motion. It struck something in her and she let out a sound of surprise.

"You're so wet, darling."

"That's a good thing?"

"Oh, it's a very good thing."

He continued fingering her, curving and playing as she felt herself loosen with his touch.

"Benedict," she whispered. "Stop a moment."

He immediately did and withdrew.

"Come up here," she told him.

He did as commanded and crawled up her body. His eyes were eager, and obedience was in his form. He looked as if he'd do anything for her. Anything she asked of him, he'd bend over backwards to do.

They were level and she reached up, tracing his lips with a fingertip.

"I want to try it now. I want you inside me."

"You do?"

"I do."

He cracked a coy smile. "I think that's the line for next month."

"It works now, as well," she replied, playing along.

Carefully, he maneuvered himself over her, spreading her thighs with his hands. He gazed down at her hungrily, eyes devouring her center that he'd just so recently pleasured.

"I'll be gentle."

"If you must."

He lined his proud length with her entrance, and reached for her hands. They intertwined their fingers and then slowly, holding her gaze, he pushed in.

The pressure was intense, the stretching of her core. He'd hardly entered her, but reading the slight discomfort in her eyes, he stopped and let her adjust. A moment later she let her thighs fall open more and then she released one of his hands and set it at the small of his back. Staring at him with intent, she gently prodded him inside her, urging him on. He continued, and then the pressure shifted. It was anticipation and the first inklings of a newfound pleasure. He paused again and a few seconds later she guided him in more. He then sank to the hilt and surprise lit both their eyes at the connection between them.

Lucia rolled her hips and there was a delicious friction of her clitoris against his pelvis.

"*Oh,*" she breathed.

Benedict ducked his head to the juncture of her shoulder. "'*Oh*' is right. Fuck, you feel divine, Lucia."

She wriggled again and Benedict responded with a thrust.

OH.

Pleasure zapped between her legs and suddenly they were moving together, a tandem dance only they knew. Benedict pumped in and out of her as she met his strokes with the rise and fall of her hips. She raked her fingers down his back, his free hand going to her hip, guiding their lovemaking. They kept one hand intertwined.

Everything was Benedict. Everything was the scent of bergamot and sandalwood and musk. Everything was jade eyes and chestnut hair. Everything was this moment.

Their rhythm became faster and suddenly Benedict was leveraging her hips up. Whatever he had done had put glorious friction exactly where she wanted and she felt another orgasm climbing through her, like an orchestra built to a crescendo. Benedict began losing the dance, his thrusts becoming disjointed.

"I'm so close, love."

She pressed them more firmly together, hooking her heels around the small of his back. "Benedict, you're going to make me—ah," she managed breathlessly before her very air was stolen by a moan.

Lucia came, the pleasure tearing through her. She saw stars behind her eyes as her delicate inner muscles squeezed around Benedict. Quickly, he followed her over the edge and she felt his cock pulse inside her, spilling his release.

They crashed down together as the waves of bliss slipped away on the ocean of their lovemaking. Benedict fell aside, a leg over hers, his hand on her waist, face in her citrus-scented hair.

"I've been waiting so long for this," Benedict rasped, his teeth scraping her shoulder as he pressed a kiss there.

"Have I met your expectations?"

"Surpassed them," he replied, his hot mouth moving higher.

"Indeed?" she asked, propping herself up on an elbow.

"Indeed."

Benedict helped her clean up while she used the facilities, noticing the tenderness between her legs. It was not pain, per se, but it gave her a surge of pride.

She'd finally had sexual relations.

She'd finally made love to her fiancé.

Lucia caught sight of her sex-mussed hair in the gilt-edged mirror in the bathing chamber. Her black locks were wild about her head, her lips bee-stung by kisses, her cheeks flushed. She smiled to herself.

When she returned to the bedroom, Benedict was lounging on the covers, an arm behind his head, knee bent at an alluring angle. Suddenly, her mind was taken over by the desire between her legs and she found herself sauntering across the room and to the bed.

Lucia climbed astride him, straddling his hips as she bent down to kiss him. Their tongues tangled and she felt hardness rise against her core. Once he was fully aroused, she shifted her hips and then took him inside her. She sank deep onto his length, revelling in the fullness he gave her, the stretch of her channel to take him all.

"Lucia," he groaned.

Benedict sat up as she rode him and he wrapped his arms around her, clutching her close, before dipping to her breasts and taking a nipple into his mouth. He sucked on one and then took the other. The pinkened peaks hard and tight from his touch and the wanting of him.

This new angle, of being atop him provided such intimate friction that she decided this was her favorite. To be the one doing the fucking rather than being the fucked.

Her orgasm built and she felt it coiling low in her belly. Lucia's rolling hips sped up and Benedict tensed, it was clear he wanted—needed—her to come first. A few moments later she did, slamming her hips into his and carried herself over the edge, crying out. Benedict followed her and their climaxes crashed together as they spilled into ecstasy in unison.

DECEMBER 15, 1866

Benedict couldn't have been in more bliss. When he awoke after their night of lovemaking, he took in his fiancée's beautiful form—her golden skin, ink-spill hair, kiss-bruised lips, lush curves, and peaceful features. He couldn't believe his luck, that such a majestic creature of a woman—a warlock, a professor, a brilliant genius—was asleep in his bed next to him. He'd wanted to stay there, luxuriate in the absolute joy of having her back. Having her *alive*.

Carefully, as it was early yet, Benedict slipped from the covers and dressed without disturbing her. He pulled on black trousers and a white shirt—billowy with long sleeves. With dress slippers on his feet, he made his way downstairs.

In his kitchen, Benedict lit the stove with a sigil and found a pan. Normally Huffam cooked for him, but Benedict had given him the morning off and truth be told he wanted this domestic task. He wanted to do something for Lucia.

Besides, he couldn't remember the last time he had control of his meal. For the past seven years he'd eaten virtual scraps and near inedible food, forcibly served. And he had to accept or starve. His stomach turned at the thought. It had been so difficult to turn from the supper at the Turner's last night, but for Lucia he'd do anything.

Twenty minutes later he was plating eggs, ham, potatoes, toast, and an orange for him and Lucia. Just as the coffee finished brewing, a creak on the staircase reached his ears, and he turned with a smile on his face.

Lucia entered the kitchen, dressed in the robe he'd divested her of last night. She shyly tucked a lock of hair behind her ear.

"Good morning," she murmured.

Benedict crossed to her and swept her into his arms. He kissed her ardently and cupped her cheek. "Good morning to you, too," he whispered against her lips. "Are you hungry?"

"Starving."

"Good. Go sit down and I'll bring breakfast over."

Lucia padded happily to the dining room and Benedict followed after preparing the carry tray. He found her seated, anticipation making her wiggly. Benedict smiled, charmed by her—as he always was, always had been, and always would be.

"I meant to tell you about this fascinating article I read, Benedict. It was about a synthetic blood replacement for

Midnight Malady. It was positively spectacular news. Of course, it's not a cure for the disease, but it is a step towards a better treatment than blood theft."

"That is truly groundbreaking."

"It is, isn't it?" she said, so cheerful.

Benedict then set the food down in front of her.

"I'd love to hear more, but you said you were hungry," he said, lifting the lid of the tray. "I forgot to mention that I am positively starved too."

She blushed. "I think we worked up quite the appetite."

"Indeed, we did. And I must admit, I have a very specific craving right now."

Benedict went down on his knees and Lucia's blue eyes widened. His palms went to her knees and he could feel her silky, hot skin through the parting of the robe. Locking eyes, he spread her legs and then kissed up the inside of her thigh. Then he found her center and his mouth took her.

He flicked his tongue against her clitoris. Lucia's hands immediately found his hair, fusing into the locks. She pressed herself firmly against his mouth, writhing and mewling. Benedict tasted and licked, winding her up tight. He applied suction to that sensitized bundle of nerves and her reaction was instantaneous.

She bucked against him, tugging his hair, making sounds of desperation. He continued alternating suction and flicks of his tongue until she was panting and begging.

"Please Benedict—oh fuck please, yes."

She threw her head back and cried out. He felt her orgasm tear through her, her legs trembling around his head, her thrusts against his face. Lucia panted as the pleasure sapped her energy and Benedict grinned with purely male pride.

"Will you take me right here, right now?" she asked.

"If my lady asks."

"She asks."

Benedict rose from his knees and began tugging on his pants. Just then, he heard the bell on his door chime and he froze. He checked the clock in confusion—it was only nine o'clock in the morning.

"Eat your breakfast. I'll see to the door," he told her, wiping his mouth with a napkin.

When he opened the door, he was surprised to see Huffam with an armload of groceries and Nicholas beside him.

"My apologies sir," Huffam started sheepishly. "I encountered Lord Whitehill at the market and he informed me he had pertinent information for you."

"I'm so sorry, Benny. It really shouldn't wait."

"No, of course, come in. Nicholas, I'll meet you in the study. Huffam, you can find your way?"

"Of course, sir. I apologize if I was interrupting anything."

Benedict flushed but shook his head. "No, all is well. Thank you for your concern."

Huffam nodded but Benedict saw a glimmer of mirth in his eyes. Benedict shut the door behind them and made his way back to the dining room. Lucia was just finishing up her plate and she looked up with his return.

"Nicholas is here. When you're done with breakfast feel free to join us in the study. There are some spare clothes for you in my room."

She smiled behind her coffee. "I will. Oh, and Benedict?" Benedict had started to walk away but her voice stopped him. "I also have a very particular craving today." Her blue eyes darkened as she looked very pointedly southward—towards his trousers.

"Oh."

"Mm," she replied, a coy tilt to her head. "Later though."

"Later," he echoed.

He left the dining room, his blood roaring with a raging ache in his cock.

Benedict was trying very hard not to be bitter with Nicholas for interrupting possibly the third round of fucking with Lucia. At the same time, he felt a flash of guilt. This was his best friend whom he hadn't seen in a very long time and who was, until very recently, quite dead.

It was clear though that any effects the Wasting once had on him had vanished or reversed entirely. He had a healthy glow about him, and while he still walked with his cane, he did not depend on it so heavily. He was also dressed in ivory white, a suit with silver chains crossing his chest in three swoops. A lacy collar ruffled about his throat, matching the same fabric that fanned at his wrists. A heavy coat perched on his shoulders, pinned by silver clasps of owl heads.

"You are well?" Benedict had ventured.

"I have not felt better in more than three years, Benny."

Benedict's heart swelled. "So, you are cured?"

Nicholas beamed. "It seems so."

Benedict pulled him into an embrace and Nicholas held him just as tightly. Into his shoulder, Nicholas released a sob.

"Thank you. Thank you so much."

Benedict just held him tighter, engulfed in his pine and mint scent. After a time, Nicholas released him and gave his shoulder a squeeze, his gray eyes fighting off a line of silver that threatened to spill.

In the study, Benedict had cleared off his desk and Nicholas had replaced it with documents pertaining to all of the immortal diseases board members and financials. Huffam helped carry in the files. Some of the papers showed investments and debts. It was with these papers that the two men intended to discover who had set out to murder Lucia and frame Benedict for it.

"These are copies, correct? They are not the originals?" Benedict asked.

"That is correct."

"Good."

Benedict took a quill and from the first page, struck three names from the paper.

"How are you eliminating these men already?" Nicholas asked.

"Easy," Benedict replied as he scratched out Nicholas Whitehill's name. "All these ones are dead."

Some curses the dead could cast, but the Nightmare Curse was not one of them.

Benedict went on to explain. "Seven years from now, several of the board members have succumbed to some of the immortal diseases—a near plague having swept through the city in 1870. I'd also kept up with all the obituaries during my imprisonment and memorized the names." He had an entire book with important deaths written down in his mind's study. "Others are gone due to more unfortunate accidents—an arson, a carriage accident—but it's enough to eliminate them. The same person who framed me is the same one who cursed me, I'm certain of it."

Nicholas ran his hand through his light blond waves. "Bloody hell, all right. Let's get down to business."

They settled into seats and then took up documents, vetting who benefitted greatest from treating rather than curing the diseases, and then moving on to whoever had a most vested interest in actually seeking a cure. They looked into those who had invested in and endorsed both Lucia's and Benedict's research, as well as other warlocks who studied the same epidemiology. They then looked into how many of them had lost loved ones to the diseases. Who have been most outspoken and hosted charities and banquets and balls. Then they determined if they'd performed the Staying. They compiled the list of suspects ranging from impossible, unlikely, possible, likely, and then suspicious.

After an hour, Lucia knocked on the study door and entered. She was dressed in snug fitting black pants that rose high on her waist, a tucked-in blousy white shirt, and emerald wool socks that reached her knees. Her hair was partly pulled back, a few black tendrils hanging around her face, a light dusting of cosmetics highlighting her features— a balm on her lips, something on her lashes.

"Well, aren't you a sight?" Benedict commented, taking in his fiancée and the way the new clothing clung to all her curves in the best way. Fuck, she was radiant.

Lucia preened and then skipped over to him. She leaned down to give him a peck on the lips but he quickly deepened it.

"Benedict!" she chastised, eyes flickering to Nicholas, who quite obviously was trying to hide his smirk behind a dossier.

"Fine, fine!"

Lucia smirked as she plopped down onto an ottoman and plucked up a document from an unfinished stack.

"Tell me what I'm looking for."

Benedict relayed all the criteria and information regarding anyone they'd be vetting, adding them to the list in a specific order and noting which part of their life required deeper investigation. Upon receiving the information, Lucia set to work with single-minded focus.

The three of them were ensconced in the study for hours, Huffam periodically checking on them and bringing them trays of food and coffee or tea. As soon as he'd clear one empty one, he'd return with new refreshments. It was late evening when they'd compiled their list and all three of them stared at the top name with varying degrees of horror and disappointment.

All three had drawn the same conclusion.

Luther Turner.

Lucia's hand shook, even as she wrote her own father's name at the top of her list. It was clear she couldn't deny the facts. Far too much was lining up with her father's interests; the greed he'd retained from his mortal upbringing, the argument at dinner just last night, the financials he had invested in the treatment of Midnight Malady, the lack of any support amongst researchers. It didn't bode well.

Lucia stood. "I think I need a moment alone. And I think I need a drink."

Vacant-eyed, Lucia left the room, walking stiffly. Benedict heard the clink of glass bottles and a pour. He sighed and rubbed his face.

This was not the answer he had been hoping for. He didn't want it to be Lucia's father, but every arrow pointed to him. Their recent fight just cemented it all. But he would not say that. He would reserve his words and wait for Lucia to broach the topic first.

Nicholas scrubbed at his jaw. "This is unprecedented."

"It is. I just don't see how it was anyone else."

Benedict scanned the top three names, but neither Edith Smith-Williams nor Gilbert Davis held as much promise as

Luther. Still, he made a mental note to investigate them as deeply as possible.

Nicholas left shortly after, sensing Lucia's solemnity. The rest of the evening Lucia withdrew herself, sitting in the window seat of the sitting room, staring at the window and the falling snowflakes. She clutched a hot whiskey in her palms, a book on infernal runes beside her, and every so often she sipped and sighed.

When he asked what she wanted from him she gave him a sad shrug.

"I don't want to be touched right now, but I'd like you near."

So, there they sat; Lucia in the window with her vice, Benedict on one of the sofas with a book. Eventually, she gently discarded her drink and made her way to Benedict. She slowly curled herself on his lap and he just held her, being whatever she needed.

"Did you know there is a seraphic equivalent of the Elven Star banishing spell?" Lucia asked softly.

"I did not."

"Supposedly it can kill any demons in a certain radius."

"Unfortunate that we do not have a rune caster among our acquaintances, then."

Lucia was tired, sleepy, as she finally responded, "Quite."

Time passed and Lucia fell to slumber.

Benedict carried Lucia to bed and he watched her, his heart hurting for her pain. Though despite it all, she never cried once.

DECEMBER 16, 1866

Lucia was awoken the next day just after seven in the morning by harsh banging on Benedict's front door. She jolted out of bed, her heart hammering in its cage while Benedict shot from the room in his bed clothes. Lucia chased after him.

Lucia was still wearing the same outfit from yesterday, having fallen asleep in them, and Benedict being a gentleman, had not undressed her.

The banging continued and it matched the pounding in her skull from two stiff drinks, and a lack of water. Her mouth was dry and cottony, her stomach sour.

They flew down the staircase and suddenly a familiar yelling voice reached her ears. Lucia cursed and then put a hand to her forehead in exasperation.

"It's Sabine," Lucia told him. "Why in the nine Hells is she here? And at this hour?"

"I haven't the faintest clue."

Benedict opened the door and it practically flew off its hinges as Sabine pushed inside.

"Lucia had better be here, otherwise you have some serious explaining to do!"

Sabine was frazzled, her dark eyes full of frantic light, her dark auburn hair tousled in a very unfashionable way. She was fuming as she stood in the entryway, dressed in pewter blue and white wool.

"What have you gotten yourselves into?" Sabine finally caught sight of her best friend, still bearing marks from sleep. "Oh, hello my dear, care to tell me why I was *attacked* outside of your office?"

"You were what?" Lucia asked, making her way down the last few steps.

"Attacked!" Sabine repeated, yanking off her gloves and tossing them on the entry table. "After you missed our afternoon tea yesterday, I went to seek you out at your parent's home and your father informed me you'd had a falling out. Then this morning I try to catch you at the university before your classes and right outside your office someone threw me to the floor and tried to stab me! I fought him off, of course, but it begs the question: Why was someone from the Brotherhood after you?"

A lead weight dropped in Lucia's sour stomach. "Are you all right?"

"I'm fine," Sabine said dismissively, face furious and concerned. She popped her hands on her hips. "I nearly killed him, but that's besides the point. He could have gotten *you*! He was lying in wait, Lucia. The only reason I got the chance in is because he hesitated when he saw my face. My assumption is that he was expecting you and wasn't sure what to do with me."

Lucia's eyes widened. Her and Sabine looked hardly alike, however they had similar builds. They were both below average height—Lucia being 5'2" and Sabine only two inches taller—and both with curvaceous bodies—busty, round-hipped, and tapered waists. That's where the similarities ended. Lucia had long raven hair, and while Sabine's was long too, it was deep auburn. Lucia was light of eye, Sabine dark. She had a golden complexion from her mother's Latin heritage, while her best friend had a bronze complexion.

But, if Sabine was wearing her hood, it was an easy mistake to make.

"I—" Lucia glanced over at Benedict but his face was stoic. She couldn't get a proper read on him. She swallowed and looked back to Sabine.

Sabine had an eyebrow cocked and was quite literally tapping her foot. "Well?"

"I don't want to involve you. It's dangerous."

"Oh, fuck that," Sabine nearly shouted. "I'm your closest friend and I've already gotten involved—or have you already forgotten my near murder and my near killing of a man?"

"You shouldn't be associated with us right now, it's far too risky. You should just go home and—and stay indoors. Stay behind wards."

Sabine stared. "How serious is this?"

Lucia shifted from foot to foot. "Very."

"I want to help."

"And I want to keep you safe."

Sabine was silent. "This is not fair."

"I know."

"For how long?"

Lucia glanced at Benedict. He cleared his throat and answered. "Christmas Day."

Sabine raised her brows dubiously. "You cannot be serious."

Lucia and Benedict were both horribly silent.

"Mother fuck, what have you done?" Sabine's voice rose on the last word.

"Please, just trust us," Lucia implored.

Sabine visibly deliberated and then sighed. "Fine! But if I'm attacked again, I'm demanding answers and I will not be leaving until I get them. Is that understood?"

Lucia nodded like a scolded schoolgirl. "Understood."

"Good. I love you. Please keep yourself safe."

"I love you, too," Lucia whispered.

Sabine shook her head, took up her gloves and strut for the still open door, twisting a protective sigil between her fingers.

Lucia watched her make her way down the stairs, Benedict beside her. Sabine's footsteps made perfect impressions on the untouched snow as she started down the street.

Suddenly, that untouched snow was trampled as Calanthe materialized from the shadows.

She shot a line of hellfire at Sabine and it smashed into her personal shield. Sabine gasped and whirled, already forming an attack sigil with her ruby magic. Sabine was unusually fast at casting, a talent that held her far and above others.

An incendiary symbol took form faster than Lucia could blink, and then Sabine was launching it at Calanthe. It crashed against her face in a hail of bloody sparks and she screeched, tones of demonic nature like a reptilian call echoing down the street.

Calanthe blindly rushed Sabine, and it was then that Benedict and Lucia finally got their bearings.

Benedict raced out in his house slippers, donning a protective shield, and casting an amalgamation of spells that Lucia couldn't decipher. Lucia herself shoved her feet into a pair of her boots she'd left here—she'd slowly been moving items over the last couple of weeks in anticipation for the upcoming move in after their wedding. Shoes on, Lucia dashed outside.

Together the three of them took on Calanthe with Benedict's cerulean, Sabine's ruby, and Lucia's emerald. The three different magics lashed the demon, sigils slamming and branding into her. Calanthe shrieked. Sabine was the fastest, but Benedict could tie multiple complex spells together, while Lucia created bigger casts by combining several of the same over and over.

Lucia scythed a line of magic at Calanthe and spun around her to avoid a physical blow. Benedict hurled a monstrous medley of spells at Calanthe and it launched her off her feet. She flew across the street and slammed into Lucia, the two of them tumbling together until they came to an abrupt stop at a brick fence.

"Lucia!" Benedict shouted.

A hot line of pain opened on Lucia's arm and she looked down to see crimson blooming on her white shirtsleeves. She hissed as the sting grew larger.

Sabine threw an incendiary spell at Calanthe but the demon dodged it, throwing a jet of fire at the female warlock. Sabine yelled as it caught the hem of her dress afire, shock and curses flowing from her lips.

Calanthe then knocked Lucia to her back and straddled her, her demonic face warped and twisted beneath the shroud and shadows from her candle's flame. Lucia slammed a fist into her chin, a strength sigil clutched in her palm. Calanthe's head shot back, but she just wrapped her hands around Lucia's throat and squeezed.

Lucia's eyes widened, her chest tightening. She kicked her legs as her hands scrabbled for purchase on Calanthe's claws.

"You little bitch," Calanthe sneered. "Your destiny is to die and I will savor your torment down in Hell." She leaned over her, hot hellfire breath at Lucia's ear. Lucia was running out of air. "Do you care to know how they ate your soul from the true timeline? How you squealed—"

"Get the fuck off of her!" Benedict forcibly yanked the demon up and then blasted her in the chest with a sigil.

Calanthe's claws raked furrows in Lucia's throat and she gasped for breath once her unrestricted airway returned. She turned and coughed into the dirty snow—her clothes soaked.

Lucia got up, clutching her throat and wheezing. She turned in time to watch Benedict add a destruction spell to his amassed artillery that spanned his cupped hands. Before her very eyes she watched it careen into Calanthe's face, but rather than land, it encompassed the entirety of her head. The blue magic wrapped Calanthe's visage and candle crown before it suddenly exploded, raining brackish blood and bone.

Calanthe's headless corpse fell into the snow, spilling blood from the stump her head once occupied. Lucia stared in disbelief. Then, the remains erupted into a pillar of scarlet fire, leaving nothing but ash and scorch marks.

Benedict immediately gathered Lucia into his arms.

"I thought I was too late," he rasped.

Lucia shook her head into his shirtsleeves. "You got to me in time."

"I don't mean to be a bother and break up this beautiful moment, but that was quite literally a demon," Sabine started, fury in her voice. "And I am no fool, we all know what the Ghost of Christmas Past looks like, so why is she after you?" Sabine marched right up to them; the skirts of her dress burnt to her thighs. "What fucking disaster warrants the Scarlet Brotherhood and the Nightmare Curse to come down on your heads? I want answers, and I want them now."

Benedict nodded. "Okay, but not out here. We need to get inside before the others show up."

DECEMBER 16, 1866

Inside, Benedict urged Sabine to change into some of the spare clothes he kept for Lucia and to wash up while he bandaged his fiancée. Sabine acquiesced after promises of an explanation.

In the bathing room, Benedict laid out supplies, bandages and bottles spilling across the vanity. Lucia was perched on the sink's edge while Benedict assembled what he needed. First, he examined her throat, seeing the ragged grooves from Calanthe's claws and the bruises blooming from her fingers. He then checked the gash in her arm. Already, the blood was clotting and the shirt was sticking to it.

"We need to take this off," Benedict informed her.

Lucia quirked a smile. "Excuses to get me naked, hmm?"

He stepped into the cradle of her open thighs, heat burning between them.

"I don't need excuses," Benedict said, sultry, as he grasped her shirt and untucked it from her pants. "If I want you undressed, I'll just do it."

He worked the ruined fabric over her head and discarded it. He had to forcibly bite back a groan. She had nothing on underneath. Her breasts were perfect—full and plump with peaked nipples that he wanted in his mouth.

Ignoring his lust, he set to work.

Gently, he took her arm in hand and cleaned it, removing the grit from the wound. Then he flushed it out—to which Lucia hissed during. After it was cleaned to his satisfaction, he applied a salve and then he drew on her skin with magic. He added a healing spell to aid the process. With her arm still in his grasp, he took up the roll of bandages. With care he wrapped her upper arm, winding the gauze over and over. When he tucked the end of the bandage in, he trailed his fingers down her arm, along the crease of her elbow. They continued skirting up. Across her shoulders, over her collarbones.

She placed her hands on his hips to steady herself.

At her neck Benedict made a sound of displeasure. It looked painful, and he wanted to kill Calanthe all over again for it. Taking wet cloths, he swiped it through the blood and dirt the demon had lodged there. Lucia tightened her grip on his hips in response.

After applying a healing salve and numbing cream, Benedict repeated the healing sigil.

Lucia tilted her head back and winced. Benedict was quick to cradle the back of her neck, feeling the spill of her silky locks over his fingers. He tipped her head to the side and pressed a chaste kiss to the corner of her jaw.

"I will kill anyone who tries to hurt you," he vowed.

Lucia shifted. "That shouldn't elicit the reaction in me that it does."

"And what reaction is that?"

"A lascivious one."

"Good." He grinned, kissing her again.

Carefully, he wrapped her throat similarly as he'd done to her arm, aware of the tightness—he didn't want too much pressure to remind her of Calanthe's touch. Just as he finished, Sabine knocked at the door.

"I'm still waiting for an explanation, but I swear to fuck, if you two have finally decided to consummate your relationship under demonic duress in there, I will debate a voluntary commitment to a sanatorium."

Benedict chuckled and leaned his forehead against Lucia's. Lucia cupped his cheek with a wry smile, pecking him quickly.

"Not to worry, that was already completed the night before last," Lucia called back.

There was a palpable silence from the other side of the door.

"*Finally!*" Sabine yelled. "Hell, it took you long enough. Okay, you have much to tell me."

Benedict cracked a smile. "We'll meet you in the drawing room shortly," he informed her.

"Yes, yes. Fine, all right. I'll be waiting!"

Sabine's retreating footsteps sounded outside the room and Lucia laid a hand on her forehead. "Fuck," she swore, before sliding off the countertop and tugging on a spare shirt and knitted sweater.

She headed for the door and Benedict followed.

When they arrived in the drawing room Sabine was sitting on one of the red couches, dressed in a plain brown dress with a high collar—a relic from Lucia's mother's mortal world days. A tray of tea and coffee was set before her and she was adding several heaps of brown sugar to her cup. She leaned back and crossed her legs with their arrival.

"I did say if I was attacked again, I wanted answers. I cannot believe how short-lived that was. Sit, explain. Now."

Benedict sighed and the two of them sat across from her. Sabine took them in with perceptive dark eyes, the natural smokiness adding an intensity that made Benedict want to squirm.

"I was cursed in 1873 and broke free."

And so, Benedict told the tale for the third time. His curse, his imprisonment, his being framed, Lucia's death, the immortal diseases and their subsequent cures, the Brotherhood, their suspicions about Luther, the attacks, Nicholas's death and un-death, everything. Sabine took it all in, never interrupting, but the reactions that spanned her facial features betrayed much she wanted to say. It took a while, but finally Benedict concluded the history.

Sabine's mouth hung open, her coffee cooled and untouched in her hands. She snapped it shut and then turned to Lucia.

"So, you're with a much older man now," she quipped finally.

Lucia blinked. "Pardon?"

Sabine twisted a smile behind her cup, sipping her coffee. "Is he not thirty-and-four now?"

Benedict was affronted. "I returned to my previous body. Besides, I've completed the Staying—I no longer age."

"As have I, but it's all about up here—" she tapped her temple. "You're old now."

"I take offense to that."

"You can have it."

Benedict sighed, but there was endearment in it. There was a reason why Sabine was Lucia's closest friend and a dear one to him.

"May I remind you then, that you hold affection for a significantly older man. Nicholas performed the Staying nearly seventy years ago."

Sabine dismissed it with a wave of a hand. "That's irrelevant."

"I think it's quite relevant—"

"Anyway, if we're so sure Lord Turner is behind it all, why haven't you confronted him?"

"Well for starters, anytime we leave an anti-demon dwelling we are almost instantly attacked," Benedict answered, folding his hands together. "But also, because we haven't confirmed he's the one who cursed me." He deliberately didn't bring up the killing of Lucia. Who wants to hear their parent had the hand who dealt their death?

Sabine sighed. "We can't stay inside forever."

"No," Benedict agreed. "We can't. But also, in the meantime I'd encourage you to stay here until this is all resolved. I can have Huffam prepare the guest room for you."

Sabine shrugged. "As long as I'm not intruding."

"You're not," Lucia answered for him.

Benedict turned to Lucia hesitantly. "I did want to speak to you about something, though."

"Oh?" Lucia asked, sitting up straighter.

"Would you consider completing the Staying soon? It would be an added protection."

The Staying was a ritual that turned warlocks immortal. Upon commencement, aging stopped, though the ability to retain children and eventually die was still possible. But the rite provided some invulnerability. Aside from the immortal diseases, warlocks who performed the Staying did not get sick, and in addition to that, wounds healed more quickly. It also took much more to harm them. The only thing was that the Staying was dangerous itself.

To perform the Staying, as protections, a warlock would drink a vial of angel ichor and bathe in demon blood before descending to the circle of Hell where their most prominent sin resided. There, they would swallow the piece of their soul that Hell had claimed by their birth. Because as warlocks, a piece of one's soul resided in Hell—just as a piece of it resided in Heaven.

After consuming the soul piece, the warlock would then ascend to the celestial plane and split the remaining shard of soul and send it down to appease Hell.

It could be a dangerous journey. At any point the warlock could fail—be killed by a demon, be torn apart by unhappy souls, fall during the ascent to divinity, forget to split the soul shard. But hearing of failures was uncommon. Warlocks were taught this ordeal since infancy.

The hold of the afterlives was the defining difference—aside from the ability to cast—between humans and warlocks.

Cosmically, warlocks were chosen to straddle the lines of magic, therefore to access such power, both afterlives held a definitive claim on them. It was why some warlocks could utilize infernal or seraphic runes.

Meanwhile, human souls were tethered to earth, and beings so earthly could be influenced by either domain or neither—depending on faith and the individual.

Lucia visibly swallowed. "Which sins held your shards?" Lucia asked Benedict and Sabine nervously.

"Greed," Benedict answered.

"Lust," Sabine replied, finishing her coffee.

"I'll think about it."

Benedict placed his hand on Lucia's knee. "That's all I ask, darling."

"All right. As happy as I am for you—and do not misunderstand me, I am, especially after learning you've technically been apart for seven years—we should come up with a plan." Sabine poured herself another cup of coffee. "I think we should go over all those names again, see if something was missed." She added more brown sugar again. "And we should consider attending the Whittaker Ball. Lord Whittaker is on the board for Midnight Malady so your murderous rival will most likely be there."

"That's in two days," Lucia chimed.

Sabine shrugged. "I know an excellent modiste, but if it cannot be done, we have magic. We'll figure out something." She sipped her coffee. "Lucia, I already know your measurements, Benedict, could you write yours down?"

Benedict did as bid and then handed Sabine the paper and quill. Sabine quickly sketched out two sets of measurements and design directions, waited for the ink to dry, then folded the paper, and gave it back to him.

"Would you give this to Huffam? And tell him to relay to the modiste that it's on my account."

"I can pay," Benedict protested.

"No," Sabine held up a hand. "I insist."

Benedict sighed but rang for Huffam with Sabine's directions. Huffam nodded and departed.

"Now, where are those names?" Sabine asked, already prepping her third cup of coffee.

A while later they had two more leads.

"A Christopher Taylor and Lady Beryl Snowden," Sabine announced. "The lady was overlooked as Lord Snowden had hosted a charity gala for the Wasting last summer and had several researchers give presentations—Benedict had been one of them—as well as lost his sister to Ember Fever. But Lady Snowden had no such charitable events and has several investments in the treatment of Ember Fever, in addition to a cousin in the Scarlet Brotherhood. Then Mister Taylor is currently renegotiating the budget for the Wasting research, and we're unsure if he's trying to decrease or increase it."

Benedict scrubbed a hand over his face. "All right, so we have five people to more deeply investigate. Should we decide who targets whom?"

The conversation continued similarly, deciding which person the three of them would interrogate, safe words, safety nets in case something went awry, excuses and cover stories—

they ensured all their bases were covered. They had also decided it best that Lucia not be the only one to look into her father—as he was their top suspect all three of them would attempt speaking to and looking into him.

Lucia suddenly set down her papers with a slam. She stared down at them and splayed her hands. She didn't look at either Benedict or Sabine when she spoke.

"I want to perform the Staying. Tonight."

Benedict inhaled sharply. Despite this being exactly what he'd hope she'd want to do, he couldn't help the flare of panic that darted through him. Her previous death date was only days off, and now she wanted to perform a ritual that had potentially lethal consequences. Anxiety wove within him, a tapestry of twisted emotions. But she was strong. She would prevail. He knew she would.

He wouldn't consider the alternative.

STAVE FOUR

LUCIA TURNER

DECEMBER 16, 1866

Lucia was terrified.

Ultimately, she knew her life had always been heading in this direction. All her life she'd prepared for this. But having it come so soon was sending her into a spiral.

Lucia counted her lucky stars that Benedict had both angel ichor and demon's blood on hand—a significant quantity of the latter as well. It seemed he'd be prepared for her to change her mind about the Staying for a while. She'd always been stalwart in saying she wanted to wait till her twenty-seventh birthday, but now seemed as good a time as ever. It was only a handful of months sooner.

And if it gave her the advantage to thwart her untimely death? Well, it seemed ludicrous not to.

Night had fallen with diamond dust stars, the moon swollen above. They stood in the back garden of an unconsecrated church ground a block from Benedict's town house. The church itself had been demolished in a demon attack a hundred years ago when it was revealed the priest was corrupt and unholy. It became a common place to complete the Staying, as the grounds for the ritual couldn't be protected by anti-demon wards, all that remained was rubble. In the garden, red, enchanted roses bloomed upon thorny bushes, frosted by another powdery layer of snow—an unusual amount had fallen in the last few days. They were on the stone patio portion of the church yard, Sabine bundled on a bench with two blankets and an orb of scarlet flame hovering near her chest.

Benedict was drawing sigils on the pavers, both in chalk and in his cerulean magic. They glowed as he casted. Around a circle he carved an infernal rune for Hell at the southernmost edge and a celestial rune at true north for Heaven. Between them he spelled symbols of protection, strength, healing, reality, vitality, agility, true-sight, and power. In the center of the circle, he wrote her full name, which when the ritual would commence, she would cast a sigil on top of while she stood over it.

Lucia stood on the edge, wringing her hands and drawing deep night air into her lungs. It was scented with the chill and threat of snow, gathering just the barest notes of Benedict's bergamot and sandalwood cologne. She breathed in again and the slightest floral aroma from the roses penetrated through the overwhelming smell of winter.

She was grateful they'd arrived unscathed, largely due to the minuscule distance between locations, but Lucia couldn't help but search over her shoulders. She was constantly ready for one of the demons to arrive, to rip her from this earth. She felt cursed. Destined to death.

Benedict finished the circle and then crossed to Lucia. His eyes were grave, but she knew it was due to worry regarding the death they were trying to escape her from, and not because he doubted her abilities this night.

"The angel ichor," Benedict said, handing her an iridescent vial.

The liquid in it danced silver and gold, like molten starlight or the sun's essence. It was pure, divine, and unearthly. Too much was a curse for madness, insanity having touched one too many warlocks who thought they could handle great quantities of angel ichor. Lucia knew no one should indulge in more than one dose.

Lucia took it and drained it. It tasted like nothing she'd ever experienced. Pure light and sweet, warmth like the sun on her skin, cool like stardust gracing her flesh. It was incredible. Euphoric. Bliss. Lucia suddenly understood how one sought this and traded it for insanity.

"Oh," she whispered, touching her lips.

"I know. Don't focus on the feeling, it will fade. Best to try to forget about it," Benedict advised her.

She nodded as the high began to dim.

Benedict leaned in and kissed her desperately, tangling their tongues, and tilting her head for better access. She cupped his face and tried to fill him with every adoration she held for him.

They broke apart and he pressed his cheek to hers. His stubble tickled her face, but she liked it.

"I have every faith in you."

"I'm still scared."

"As am I," he admitted.

She sighed and nuzzled against him. After a moment Benedict pulled away.

"Here is the demon's blood."

Benedict produced a jug filled with blackish red fluid and Lucia's stomach turned. She knew that apothecaries carried the blood, but to see that amount in one place was unsettling.

"You must pour it over yourself. The blood will be your best protection in Hell."

Lucia sighed and removed her sweater before she took up the jug. Standing in the borrowed shirtsleeves, she uncorked it and then lofted it overhead, upturning it and spilling the contents over her crown.

The blood struck her, warm and thick as it rained down her face. It flooded over her, soaking her to the bone, saturating and matting her hair. Her once white shirtsleeves were forever stained and ruined, drenched crimson. When she set the empty jar down all the blood ran down her arms, winding around her fingers. Her skin was streaked, her hands turned to gloves of red. She blinked blood from her lashes and she didn't dare imagine what she looked like.

A horror. A nightmare.

Lucia glanced at Sabine and she gave her a reassuring smile. "You will succeed, my dearest. I have every faith in you."

Lucia nodded and then turned to Benedict.

"I'll be right here the entire time," he told her softly.

She nodded. "I love you."

"I love you, too."

Bracing herself, Lucia stepped into the circle and felt the air prickle and charge. She stood in the center, directly over her name, and built a cast. A viridian sigil took form, floating before her eyes as her fingers twisted.

Transference.

Once she finished the spell all the cerulean sigils Benedict casted flared in brightness, morphing from blue to emerald before their very eyes. Taking on her signature magic. And then fire erupted along the lines of the circle, rising up beyond her height between Lucia and Benedict in an impenetrable shield.

Suddenly, heat flooded her veins and she felt light, like her bones had hollowed out. She felt weightless, bodiless, limitless. Her vision blurred—her reality blurred—and then, through the flames, she saw a feast.

The flames parted and Lucia narrowed her brow in concentration. She stepped through and saw the spread more clearly.

She was in a grand dining room, a large table set out with a crimson tablecloth laden with an excessive meal. A whole roasted turkey, baskets of dinner rolls, tureens of gravy, fig jams, various styled potatoes, a glazed honey ham, green beans and carrots, corn on cobs, bowls of fat purple grapes, mince pies, cakes, and pastries. Candelabras on the table provided an amber glow that illuminated the dim space. Upon the walls were gilt-edge frames holding masterpieces with garish extravagance. They were all landscapes and royal portraits, or depictions of angels and demons falling from Heaven, and others were of still life—like florals and fruits.

The more Lucia looked, the more she noticed the excess and the waste that this room held. Among all the decadence there was rot and ruin. Hidden beneath a veneer of finery, she saw the decay.

Layers of wallpaper curled from each other, dust coated marble busts and golden statues, countless vases held bouquets of dried flowers. Towers of fine glassware were in haphazard stacks in front of an overfilled cabinet, the mahogany shelves sagging and bowing beneath the weight.

This was gluttony.

It was excess in food and finery and decadence.

Lucia realized her voracious appetite in discovering the cures for the immortal diseases highlighted her cardinal sin. It was the same way Benedict was greedy for knowledge, and had later hoarded it. That was his sin. This was hers.

Lucia ventured deeper into Hell, cautious of any demonic presence. The blood on her skin was getting tacky and the bits on her lashes were turning gummy. Even so, she was grateful for it. It hid her earthliness. Through a doorway glowing gold with candlelight, she heard the sound of an overlapping orchestra. Several songs were playing at once, over each other and clashing in an anxiety-inducing discord. Feeling a pull in that direction, she went.

The next room was a ballroom filled with souls dancing, each of them bearing masks of misery and agony. They were twirling and spinning on bleeding feet, wearing several gowns each, showing off hats and crowns, drowning in jewels. It was a disgusting over-indulgence. The musicians' fingers were worn to the bone, tears tracking down their cheeks. Lucia detected at least three different songs overlapping each other.

Still, she knew she had to go deeper into the gluttonous circle.

Another doorway had a softer light and Lucia made strides towards it, over the chessboard floor, aware of all the souls she passed. She was halfway through the room when she stumbled, drawing attention. The orchestra came to a screeching halt and all the faces turned to her in unison.

Lucia froze as the ruinous faces turned starved—feral. Suddenly, there was life in Hell and they wanted it.

Turning on her heel Lucia sprinted for the next door. They gave chase. Hundreds of footsteps hammered on the ballroom floor as Lucia raced. Her breaths—though she wasn't in her natural body—heaved from her. She panted as she pumped her legs faster, crossing the threshold of the next room.

She was an award-winning researcher, a brilliant fucking professor, and the only person to discover a cure for one of the immortal diseases. She would not die in Hell. She would not fail the Staying.

Slamming the door behind her, she snapped the lock into place and quickly took in her surroundings.

She was in a study overflowing with books and papers. Towers of books reached to the ceiling, taller than her diminutive frame. Documents littered the desk, the floor, the walls, trinkets and alchemical objects scattered about the room.

There, in the center of the desk, sitting in a pewter box, was her soul shard. It glowed an ethereal white, hovering just above the base of the box.

Lucia approached slowly. At the desk, she dipped her hand in and plucked up the shard. Immediately upon touching it she was overwhelmed by the very essence of *her.* The scent of citrus and clove, the flash of her viridian magic, the feel of paper beneath her fingers, the thrill of Ember Fever's cure discovery, the press of bergamot kisses, the silk of her raven hair over long fingers that then cupped her jaw, the love she held for Benedict. It was everything that made her, *her*. Her experiences, her memories, her wants.

The souls began their barrage on the door, the banging and wailing on the wood sending fear through her. She didn't know if the door could hold an onslaught like this.

Not hesitating, Lucia popped the shard into her mouth and swallowed.

The light emitted from her and all the sensations that made up Lucia Turner heightened. She felt utterly herself, so settled in her place as a person—in the world.

A missing piece had been reunited with the whole.

After swallowing the shard, Lucia drew a circle with her magic and then added a seraphic rune at the northernmost curve, affixing protections along the remaining spaces.

The door groaned and Lucia increased her speed. She stood in the center, writing out her name, before casting another transference sigil.

The light feeling returned as fire erupted around her again. Her sight warbled and she saw flickers of green and blue as she hurtled towards the stars.

Suddenly, she stopped and she couldn't get a clear picture. Everything before her was a haze, silver and gold threading through her vision. Directly before her was a small orb light.

Another one of Lucia's soul shards.

She was only on the fringes of Heaven. The divine realm didn't want to encourage one to linger beyond what was necessary for the Staying.

She gently brushed her fingers over the light and immediately was overpowered by the sense of herself. Confirming it was truly hers, Lucia took it in hand and casted a splitting spell. Briefly, it flashed green before halving.

The rule was always take from Hell. Rather than having the demons taste Heaven in the air, and tempt an attack. It was also easier to send the soul-shard down, rather than try to work against gravity and send it up.

She returned one half to the divine realm she was currently in, and then she hurled the other half down, sending it to the depths of Hell where it could continue to live in gluttony. She watched it twinkle and then wink out from existence as she braced herself. When it was out of sight, she began casting transference again to return home.

By letting the afterlives keep only a half of a soul shard, they were locked in an eternal battle of push and pull where neither won and aging of a warlock stopped. It was only the bearer of the soul piece that could manipulate it. For anyone else to touch a soul shard that didn't belong to them, and try to shape it, was like trying to touch the moon—impossible.

For a final time, the light sensation overwhelmed her before she was brought to a snowy courtyard, filled with flame and magic. She looked around and there, standing with hope in his eyes, was Benedict.

"I did it," she breathed, taking a step towards the man she loved.

And then she collapsed.

DECEMBER 16, 1866

Benedict caught Lucia before she fell to the ground. He slid in the snow and through the chalk circle, scooping her up, disregarding the sticky blood that coated her. Her breaths were even, her congealed lashes fluttering, full lips parted.

It wasn't uncommon for warlocks to lose consciousness after the rite. The ordeal took much out of them, and if Lucia had experienced anything that threatened her during her descent, the return to her body would have drastic consequences. All Benedict knew at this point was that she had succeeded and she was alive.

He brushed her bloody hair back from her face, taking her in, noticing her brow narrowed in concentration—even in unconsciousness. He wondered what she saw, if anything at all. Was she dreaming? Or was it all just darkness?

Sabine made her way over, an air of nervousness about her as she scanned the perimeter and critically stared past the gates. "Is she okay?"

"I think so."

Sabine rubbed her upper arms, eyes flickering. "I don't like this. We need to go."

Benedict looked up, searching the night around them. He saw nothing, but he felt uneasy. He glanced at Sabine. He could see her rising worry and he elected to trust her.

"I agree. Something doesn't feel right."

Benedict picked Lucia up, cradling her like a babe. Her head lolled against his shoulder, blood smearing his white shirt. She weighed so little, even with the dead weight of her dangling arms and legs.

As he adjusted his fiancée, he noticed her temperature. But of course, he knew she'd run hot after the ordeal—especially considering hellfire barriers.

No less than a moment after they voiced their concerns came bone-chilling baying.

Benedict's gaze shot to the horizon and then snagged on Sabine. She wore a similar mask of horror, her dark eyes showing whites all around as they both came to the same conclusion.

Hellhounds.

The baying came again. Though Benedict had never heard a hellhound howl before, it was a sound one knew intrinsically. It was a soul-deep terror, promising rending of flesh and bone.

Terror raced through Benedict. He couldn't cast and carry Lucia at the same time. Running through options in his mind he weighed the possibilities. He could place Lucia in a circle of protections with him and Sabine defending her till she woke—the problem was, they didn't know when that could be and it could be a day before she rose. Or, they could make a run for it.

Fire suddenly illuminated the far end of the ruin's grounds, scrabbling nails, and large pounding footfalls accompanying it. Over the grounds came three massive dogs, the size of ponies, sleek and black with flames skimming off their body. Sparks danced from their immense paws, and leaped from their pointed ears. Their eyes were burning embers, their jaws black and salivating.

"Oh, *fuck!*" Benedict uttered.

He tried casting, but he was clumsy trying to hold Lucia at the same time. He managed a protection sigil over his fiancée, but the beasts were coming alarmingly fast and he didn't want to risk failure with another.

"Go!" Sabine shouted at him, pushing him away. "Go! I'll hold them off! Get her to safety."

Benedict stared at her in shock, absolute determination carving her face into firm lines. In her eyes he saw resignation. She knew the odds were against her, and though there was fear mingled, there was also acceptance.

"Sabine…"

"Fucking go!" she commanded him again, shoving.

Immediately she began casting faster than he could process. In seconds she had three protection sigils, ruby red glowing above her, before she moved onto offensive spells.

Benedict ran with Lucia as he saw her beginnings of a destruction sigil.

Benedict raced out of the unconsecrated grounds, casting for sure-footedness so that Sabine's sacrifice would not be in vain. He prayed he didn't fall with Lucia—they could not afford a grievous injury.

Behind, he heard the first yips of pain as Sabine's spells made contact with the hellhounds. Benedict's heart clenched at her devotion to Lucia, her willingness to put her life at risk for her.

On the street, he made for his townhouse, the night illuminated by golden lamps powered by magic and oil. The townhouse was less than a block away and he determined to get Lucia there to safety before doubling back and praying he was in time to save Sabine.

Suddenly, a force struck him and he and Lucia went tumbling to the snowy street. He managed to protect Lucia's head, his elbow cracking against the curb, his knees smarting as they took most of the impact. His shoulder bumped against a lamppost, halting their momentum. Luckily, neither of their heads were knocked.

Benedict looked up and dread poisoned through him as he came face to face with a third demon. He knew without introduction that this was the final demon in his curse. The Ghost of Christmas Yet-to-Come.

The figure was tall and draped in smoky black shadows, and garbed in white, almost like the depictions of a grim reaper—only this one had no scythe. Beneath the hooded cloak, the demon had no face. It was a cosmic swirl of night and stars. It evoked a feeling of existential fear and immense despair.

"Benedict Edwards," the demon intoned, his voice filled with the abyss. "I am Hollis, Ghost of Christmas Yet-to-Come. You have been claimed by the Demons of Cronus and

Christmas, and thus your soul is damned. Cease running and accept your fate."

"No," Benedict said, emphasizing his answer with a spell blast.

Hollis managed to thwart it. His movements were shimmery, as if he were not truly there or here. That he wavered, like rippling water from a rock thrown in a pond.

He hissed through no mouth and snapped fingers. Immediately, new howling started up.

Shit, shit, shit.

Hollis could command hellhounds, Azenor possessed the ability to cast infernal runes, and Calanthe had been able to summon hellfire. The demons were from the third, seventh, and sixth circles of Hell.

Fuck.

The sounds of Sabine's battle carried on in the distance, crashes of magic and the keens of pained hounds. He heard a yell and then an answering bark.

Benedict got to his knees, bracing in front of Lucia's prone form. He threw protections into the air and offensive spells. He began tying and twisting an amalgamation of spells, the lines warping and becoming anew. When it became something to truly fear, he threw it at Hollis, not waiting for the strike while he casted for sunlight—hoping to blind or take him off guard.

Gathering Lucia up, Benedict sprinted for their lives. He managed her into a position where he could clumsily cast and he awkwardly threw the spells behind him. His house was in sight and Hollis kept pursuit. He counted down the seconds until he was at his door.

Five…

Four…

Three…

Two…

One…

He crashed through his door heedlessly, busting it off its hinges. Benedict's shoulder ached from the fall and this most recent impact, but he ignored it, focusing on the adrenaline surge.

Placing Lucia on the settee in the foyer, he turned to find Hollis lingering like a horrifying apparition on his front step.

He was framed in the doorway, the shadows obscuring any fine details, but adding to the hellish visage. Hollis did not move. He didn't do anything but stand and stare, eyeless.

"You cannot remain behind those wards forever, little warlock."

"Can't I?" Benedict challenged, plucking up a vial of holy water from a side table. "Do you want to test that theory?"

Benedict uncorked the vial and Hollis reared back, hissing like a scalded cat.

"You dare threaten me?"

"I dare."

Hollis let out a sharp sound of indignation. "This night, I leave you. But I make no promises for the woman who opposes my hounds. Her life will be forfeit." He retreated backwards. "One way or another we shall take you come Christmas Eve."

Before Benedict could answer, Hollis vanished and a chill raced through him.

Sabine.

Benedict bolted out the door and flew down his steps just as he heard a furious scream and an explosion rocked the streets. He looked up in shock to see a flaming ball of crimson magic from the ruins. It rose into the sky, vibrant against the black and gem-speckled sky.

There was silence in its wake.

No hellhounds.

No Sabine.

Grief gripped his heart. Although he did not love Sabine romantically, he cared for her deeply. She was one of his closest friends. She was Lucia's closest friend. And now…

He stood foolishly at the base of his stairs on the street, staring in the distance at where everything had gone so wrong. Benedict hung his head and thanked Sabine for saving Lucia. He did not let himself cry, though he felt the prickle.

"What the fuck are you doing out in the open? Get inside!"

Benedict's head flew up to see Sabine running full tilt from the ruins, shouting at him. Her hair was a mess, streaming tangled behind her, her dress was scorched and torn. A black streak crossed the bridge of her nose and the same darkness stained her fingertips. He was almost certain she was missing a shoe, as well.

Benedict felt relief rush him as Sabine dashed on with the energy of a zephyr, carried by a speed sigil hovering blood red over her. He managed to hurry up the stairs just as Sabine made it to the base of them.

They stumbled through the doorway together, Sabine crashing to the floor in exhaustion, Benedict falling against the closest wall—both physically and mentally drained. The emotions wreaked havoc on his mind, and though he wasn't one to take to vice, he could use a drink.

The scent of smoke and sulfur clung to Sabine, burning his nostrils and permeating his entryway. He could also smell the slight musk from his own perspiration, and the coppery scent of demon blood and brimstone that covered Lucia. It was a blend of odors that Benedict did not care to repeat smelling.

"They won't stop," Benedict rasped. "Not until I thwart who cursed me."

"Or until the demons are dead," Sabine returned, tilting her head against the wall. She fluffed her ruined skirts. "Why is it always *my* dress catching on fire?"

DECEMBER 17, 1866

Benedict had washed Lucia as best as he could, waiting until the pink water turned clear, and with the most care and respect possible, he and Sabine got her dressed in a clean nightgown. They tucked her into Benedict's bed and then went their separate ways for the night. He'd cleaned the filth off himself then quickly changed, slipping into bed beside his newly immortal fiancée.

The following morning Lucia was still sleeping. He ensured she was comfortable and then slipped from the bed.

Huffam was in the kitchen at the stove. He turned with Benedict's approach.

"Good morning, sir. Miss Sabine is in the drawing room. I believe she is sketching."

Sabine was a highly talented artist, though many proclaimed her approach was too modern. She focused mainly on portraits, but in those portraits, she was more keen to capture the emotion and atmosphere, rather than the likeness.

"Right, thank you, Huffam. Also, when you have a spare moment, could you call for the doctor? Lucia completed the Staying last night and I just want to ensure she's still in good health."

Huffam turned with a smile. "Of course, sir. And I suppose congratulations to the lady are in order? Perhaps I should prepare a cake to celebrate."

Benedict grinned. "I'm sure she'd appreciate that."

He wrapped up his conversation with Huffam and took the butler's proffered plate as he made his way to the drawing room. There, on the red sofa was Sabine, legs curled up beneath her, dressed in green. On her lap was a sketchbook, and upon it she was drawing Lucia.

It was her at the moment she casted for the Staying, moments before her soul slipped to Hell. Her eyes were fierce and determined with a slight tinge of fear that Sabine had somehow conveyed through charcoal, and through that fear she looked powerful. Blood drenched her, slicking her hair down, strands sticking to the curve of her cheeks. In her hands was the last sigil.

"That's good," Benedict commented as he approached.

Sabine jumped and turned. "*Angels*, don't sneak up on me like that!"

"It's my house," he said wryly.

"I don't give a damn if it's the Queen's palace."

Benedict laughed and sat across from her. He noticed that on the table in front of her, in addition to the pastels and graphite were documents pertaining to Lucia's studies.

The papers documented collaborators and admirers as well as the opposite, competitors and detractors. Some issued flat out threats on her person, others insulting her character—especially as a warlock born to a human mother, and a mortal born father.

"Were you trying to figure out who might've paid for those assassins?"

"I was," she admitted, setting down the book and charcoal. "But I just got frustrated. There's so much anonymity, I don't know where to start."

That was a significant issue they'd come across also.

"I was thinking we needed to access banking records. Find out who withdrew the sum the Brotherhood was promised."

"And if they've been holding the money in a personal safe?"

She sighed. "Which is where I stopped."

A knocking at the door halted any more progress in discussion. They both paused and watched as Huffam went to answer. Immediately, he recognized Nicholas's voice.

Both Benedict and Sabine rushed to the door.

Nicholas was standing on the stoop in a burgundy suit, bronze chains holding his fur cloak on his shoulders. His near white hair swooped over his brow, a brow which instantly drew together at the sight of them.

"What the fuck is this?" Nicholas demanded pushing past Huffam. "Are you two messing around behind Lucia's back? How could you do this to her?"

He didn't even wait for Benedict's defense before shoving him. Benedict stumbled against the wall, hastily casting a mild defensive charm. It knocked Nicholas back a couple steps.

"No! Of course not!"

"Then where is she? It's eight in the morning, Benny, why is Sabine here?" He turned his steely gray eyes to the woman in question. "I thought you were better than this. I thought that you liked—" Nicholas cut himself off. "What is wrong with you?"

Benedict had to admit, it looked bad. It was early in the morning and Benedict was still dressed in his bed clothes; a robe tied over them. He and Sabine both bore the marks of a lack of sleep—and the sleep they had gotten was surely restless. He could understand Nicholas's assumption.

"Nicky!" Benedict shouted. "Lucia is asleep. In my bed. She completed the Staying last night and is recovering."

Nicholas froze, his rage sobering.

"Oh. Oh, I'm so sorry, Benny. I…I just didn't want to see Lucia wronged. I jumped to conclusions."

Benedict ruffled the back of his head. "I'm just grateful you didn't demand a duel here and now."

"You know I'm a shit shot."

"I know."

The two men took each other in and then laughed. Sabine rolled her eyes but smiled as she leaned against the wall.

"I'm assuming your company is welcome, sir?" Huffam asked.

"Yes, yes he is."

"Right then," he replied, shutting the door. Huffam returned to his duties.

"Not that I'm not delighted to see you, but why are you here?"

Nicholas produced a leather folder Benedict had missed previously. "I have recorded transcripts of the most recent board meetings with details and every word uttered there is documented within. I thought it might help."

"*How* did you get this?" Benedict could only imagine how classified such musings were.

"It helps to know people."

"Well, I appreciate the people you know." He clapped Nicholas on the shoulder. "Should we take to the drawing room? I'll be there shortly."

"Of course," Nicholas said and then turned his attentions to Sabine. He visibly softened. "Good morning, Sabine."

"Good morning, Nicholas," she practically purred. "Would you be a gentleman and escort me to the drawing room?"

He held out an arm. "It would be my pleasure."

Sabine took it and she positively glowed. Benedict could see the adoration in her eyes. She looked at Nicholas with her whole heart on her sleeve. Nicholas leaned into her, warmth and desire on his face.

Finally, with the Wasting cured, Nicholas and Sabine could pursue each other. He need not worry about leaving her a widow should they chose to marry—at least in regards to the disease.

"Say, I think our Benny is going to be the third survivor of the Scrooge Curse," Nicholas was saying to Sabine. "Do you reckon this one counts? He did break down the barriers of space and time."

They disappeared down the hallway and Benedict turned to his study with an epiphany. In the room, he pulled out ink and paper. Quickly, he jotted down a letter, imploring the receiver for their assistance. Benedict read the letter over twice before folding and sealing it with the Edwards rose crest stamp. Once dried, he hurried to the kitchen.

"Huffam, would you see to it that this gets delivered?"

"Certainly. Ah, just so you are aware the physician will be here at noon to assess Miss Lucia."

Benedict thanked him and took over the tray of coffee and tea the butler was preparing, bringing it to the drawing room where Sabine and Nicholas were sitting closely together—looking *very* cozy. Benedict held his tongue on a comment as he set the tray down.

The rest of the morning passed by reading the transcripts, drinking tea and coffee, and growing frustrated with dead ends. The physician arrived at noon and luckily gave Benedict a reprieve from the monotony of papers. He stood by as the doctor clinically assessed his fiancée, checking vitals and her magic status. He didn't seem concerned, which Benedict took as a good sign.

"She should wake by tomorrow morning I think," the doctor told him. "She has expended quite a bit of power recently and the Staying drained her further. She's not in any danger, but her body needs rest."

"But she will wake up?" Benedict couldn't help the thread of anxiety that worked into his voice.

"Of that I am certain. Should she not wake by this time tomorrow—which I deem highly unlikely—summon for me and I will come immediately."

Benedict thanked the doctor and saw him out. At the door, he breathed a sigh of relief, not realizing how much fear and worry he was internalizing. Without him allowing it to happen, tears eked out of his eyes. He hastily wiped them away and then returned to Nicholas and Sabine, anxious for Lucia's awakening.

LUCIA TURNER

DECEMBER 18, 1866

It was dark and she was warm when she awoke. Her body was buzzing with energy, her blood positively humming. The Staying had invigorated Lucia beyond comprehension. She felt entirely rejuvenated. She felt brand new.

Why had she waited so long?

Stretching, she felt the fabric of a white nightgown slip over her. She knew this is not what she had worn to sleep.

Suddenly, it all hit her with startling clarity.

The Staying.

Her unconsciousness following the ritual.

Darkness.

And then this.

She began breathing quickly.

Was Benedict okay? Was Sabine?

Lucia threw off the covers and dashed from Benedict's bed, out of his chambers, and down the stairs. She heard voices so she raced for them. She careened around the corner and found Benedict, Sabine, and Nicholas in the drawing room. The men had discarded their coats and remained in shirtsleeves, while Sabine had loosened the stays in her corset and kicked off her stockings. Papers and ink surrounded them, with empty cups and half-drunk tea.

"You're both okay." Lucia sagged in relief, gripping the doorway.

Benedict sprung up and froze.

"Lucia."

He looked at her like…like she was everything. The sun, the moon, the stars. Like she was magic. Like she was his whole world. His jade eyes filled with so much longing, so much desire, that Lucia had to draw breath. The tension was palpable, and though her attention was all on Benedict, she couldn't help but note the look passed between Sabine and Nicholas.

Nicholas made a face of discomfort, his lips twisting. "Well, I think this is my cue to leave," Nicholas announced.

"Mm, agreed," Sabine demurred. "I think I shall walk you out and then go to my bed where I will read my book and charm the room soundless. Yes, that sounds nice. Goodnight lovebirds." Sabine sent a finger wave over her shoulder as she went with Nicholas to the door.

Nicholas gave them a curious look, but ultimately pulled on his cloak at the door. Sabine shut it behind him.

"The door is locked, and I will be in my room till morning. Don't bother me unless the house is on fire or someone is dying." Sabine's footsteps hurried away and the sound of her shutting door echoed through the hall.

Lucia and Benedict were still locked together, their gazes heated—growing hotter with every taut second. Lucia felt heat pool between her legs, liquid rushing, aching for friction. The intensity in his eyes was doing all sorts of naughty things to her body.

"I'm immortal now," she whispered, spreading her arms. "This is what I'll look like—forever."

Benedict stepped forward. "You look absolutely breathtaking and I will be lucky to wake up to your beautiful face every morning." He took another step. "To challenge your clever mind every day." Another step. "To touch your lush body every night." A step. "To taste the sweetness between your legs every chance I get."

He was directly before her, her heart in her throat. She bit her lip and Benedict tracked the movement. His gaze darkened with lust and she couldn't help but look down, to catch sight of the hardness that pressed against his trousers.

"I was so afraid of losing you—I still am," he admitted, changing course. "My life without you in it was worse than dark. It was colorless, joyless, despairing. You, with your intelligence and ceaseless drive. With your beauty and kindness. Your wit and fire." He cupped her face. "If I shall be sliced by your razor-quipped tongue—then cut me. If I shall be burned by your passion—then scorch me. Just let me keep you. Let me love you."

Lucia's heart swelled. It was such a juxtaposition to the emptiness between her legs. The channel begged to be filled, while her chest overfilled.

"You have me—forever. I would be lost without you. Directionless without you. It would be as if you dropped me in the forest and took away my map. I love you. I need you."

"I need you, too," he whispered, wicked heat in his gaze.

"Do you think we should go to the bedroom?" she asked.

"I can't wait that long."

And with that Benedict swept her up desperately.

His hands were everywhere, clutching her, caressing her. His mouth fell upon hers, hot and devouring. He kissed like it was the last time he would ever touch her. Their tongues tangled, lips slanting over each other. Suckling and nipping. His fingers dug into her hip as he hitched her nightgown up her legs.

"I love you. I love you," he whispered over her lips. It was like their first time, when he dropped worship on her body, pressing her name into her skin.

Lucia's hands roved over his chest, feeling the lean muscles beneath, fingers tugging the buttons free. She managed to undo every one of them, baring his midriff. Her hands went to his hot skin, exploring. She skimmed her fingers over his chest before shoving his shirt from his shoulders. He helped her out of it before he began gathering up the hem of her gown, bringing it over her thighs.

"I love you."

He began pulling her into the drawing room, urging her with kisses and touches. She worked the buttons on his trousers as they walked, never breaking their kiss.

"I love you too, Benedict."

The back of Benedict's knees hit the sofa and Lucia pushed him down to it. He dropped onto it, and she dropped to her knees. Working his cock free of his pants, she gazed up at him devilishly before taking him in her mouth.

"*Fuck. Lucia.*"

She'd never done this before, but she'd heard her friends talk about the act, and she imagined that whatever she did down there he would enjoy regardless—surely?

Her tongue swirled over the head of him and she licked at the pearl of arousal that built. She started bobbing up and down, slowly taking more, letting her tongue lave the underside of his length.

Benedict's hands went to her hair, cupping her head. She could feel him holding himself back.

"You're doing so good, my love."

Something about that praise sent desire roaring through her blood. Suddenly, she felt so hollow between her legs that all she wanted to do was let her fingers travel down and assuage the emptiness. Her nipples were painfully hard brushing against the fabric.

She took him so deep he hit the back of her throat and tears prickled at her eyes. Benedict groaned. She continued a while longer before Benedict gently pushed her away.

Lucia looked up, her lips wet from her own saliva, the same that coated his thick length. "Was I not doing a good job?"

"You were doing a spectacular job," Benedict practically growled. "But when I come inside you, I want it to be between those pretty thighs."

A thrill shot through her.

Benedict sank from the couch and crawled over her. Lucia slowly fell backwards, leaning on her elbows as Benedict hovered over her. All she could smell was him—bergamot and sandalwood.

"And when I fuck you, I want nothing on."

With that, Benedict tore her nightgown from neckline to hem.

Cool air brushed her hard nipples, tightening them to aching points with her lust. Benedict's mouth immediately dropped to them, taking them into his mouth. Lucia's back arched and her thighs dropped open. Benedict notched between them, pressing his hard length against her dripping core. She thrust up, begging for friction—for release.

"Please. Now. I need you," Lucia moaned.

Benedict lined up his cock with her core and then in one smooth motion he pushed in. As he began thrusting and filling her, his hand went between her legs and played with her clit, rubbing small rapid circles into her. She felt herself clench around him, wetness soaking her as pleasure began to ratchet up inside her.

"You are everything I ever dreamed of, Lucia," he moaned into her throat. "You're mine."

"I'm yours."

The sound of their flesh against each other filled the drawing room, their panting breaths and moans accompanying it. The only other noise was the crackle of the fireplace.

Benedict rolled his hips hard against hers and she let her pelvis undulate with the rhythm he set, but suddenly an urge struck her. Hooking her ankles around him, she rolled them over, tumbling on the rich red carpet. She was astride him, his member still buried deep in her, and suddenly she began to ride him.

"Fucking Hells," Benedict groaned, clutching her hips, bearing down on his cock. He ground her core against him as she chased her pleasure, sending sparks of bliss through her being.

"Oh! Oh fuck, Benedict. Yes!" She tossed her head back as she bounced and ground down on him.

Her hands went to his back, her nails raking his skin as she drew close to a climax. She rode him harder, feeling on the brink of a precipice, stars beginning to dance behind her eyes.

"Benedict, I'm so close."

"Yes love, take it."

She shattered on him, legs trembling as she moaned into his hair. Her hips rolled through the waves of her climax and suddenly she felt Benedict pulse inside her.

Benedict groaned as he released, his own pleasure consuming him while hers began to fade. He drove upwards into her hard with the last few strokes.

She collapsed on top of him, their sweat-slicked skin sticking together, both their chests heaving. Benedict's hands were on her hips, his thumbs moving in small circles.

Climbing off him, Lucia searched for the scraps of her night gown. Benedict helped her into her ruined gown with a purely self-satisfied male smirk, and then the two of them slipped up to his bathing chamber where he assisted her with cleaning his release from her thighs.

After, they laid in his bed, once again naked, wrapped in each other's arms. Lucia's head was on his chest and he was rubbing soothing strokes on her shoulder.

"Have you considered the possibility that my death and your curse are separate?"

Benedict shook his head. "I thought about it, but after consideration it doesn't make sense any other way. I was jailed for your murder; I was going to be put away for a hundred years. There was no need to kill me and curse me aside from eliminating the chance I release a cure upon the end of my sentence."

"Unless it was for revenge. Would no one avenge me?"

Benedict considered. "Anyone who would either could not or believed I was innocent. Sabine and Nicholas knew I did not do it, and your father…"

"My father might be behind it."

"Exactly."

She propped herself on an elbow. "But say he's innocent, say he's not the one. There's a chance he would curse you—unrelated to the cures—to avenge me."

"I suppose yes, there is a sliver of a chance under those circumstances." Benedict let his palm rest on the curve of her shoulder. "But I won't let your death come. Not this time. I won't be too late."

She kissed him.

"I know."

She didn't hold his perceived failure against him.

"This time will be different."

DECEMBER 19, 1866

The letter arrived first thing in the morning. The meeting was scheduled for that very afternoon and Benedict prepared for it as best he could. He was jittery with anticipation and hopeful for answers, both of which showed in the tremble in his hands.

It was one o'clock when the four of them piled into a carriage—Benedict, Lucia, Sabine, and Nicholas, the latter having been summoned via post for his assistance. The four of them were armed to the teeth in protection sigils, symbols of cerulean, viridian, crimson, and violet burning in the air.

The carriage negotiated over the cobbles, rocking them gently. Lucia jostled into Benedict, as Sabine did the same to Nicholas. For the most part, it smelled of lemon polish and brisk winter air, but within the compartment the various colognes of his companions—Benedict's bergamot and sandalwood, Lucia's clove and citrus, Sabine's cinnamon and vanilla, and Nicholas's peppermint and pine—made the space feel like *home*. That these people around him were his dearest and truest, and just being around them and in their presence gave him so much happiness.

"I trust you had a pleasant night?" Nicholas said with an edge of teasing, smirking.

Lucia flushed cranberry red—Benedict thought it a compliment to her deep blue gown. "It was perfectly pleasant, thank you for asking."

"Well, I'm sure you'll be glad to hear of it, but I heard no *pleasantness* last night," Sabine interjected. "Those soundless spells are quite effective. Truthfully, I would have kept you both up with my indignation! When I tell you the foolish cad in the book I'm reading! Well, she's the best thing he ever had and then he…"

Benedict appreciated how Sabine had saved Lucia from the discomfort of answering questions about their sexual proclivities. Even though Nicholas's comment was like a brotherly jibe, Lucia was not accustomed to them. Despite the fact that Vonor was more progressive than Mortal London, there were still shortfalls every so often, usually pertaining to sex and the fairer sex. It was made worse, of course, by Lucia's more mortal-influenced upbringing.

Sabine chattered on about her book, regaling them with the idiocy of the male love interest in her book—he had to agree with her points, the man was making grievous errors. It continued like that until conversation shifted to the upcoming ball.

A large weight thumped onto the top of the carriage and the horses cried out. Benedict's eyes swung to Lucia's immediately. As if suddenly possessing precognition, Benedict shouted.

"Get down!"

All four of them covered and ducked their heads as they dove for the floor just as a clawed fist smashed through the roof of the carriage. The red velvet ceiling hung in tatters around the demon's wrist like bloody viscera. The hand took the edge of the hole and ripped it backward, tearing it larger.

"Every fucking time we leave the house!" Sabine complained.

Screams rent the afternoon, fear and anger yelling warnings. Warlocks gearing up to cast spells, to banish the demon back to Hell.

Benedict began tying spells together, blue blooming between his fingers.

Sabine, the fastest of them, shot an incendiary spell at Azenor. She howled as her white feathered wings caught aflame. Sabine blasted her with a second one that she thwarted with an infernal rune.

Lucia assembled a cast of three power spells—pure magic—and aimed it through the hole at Azenor's demonic visage. The Ghost of Christmas Present reeled back, the spell just catching her shoulder, sending her sprawling. Azenor keened in pain and fury, ripping the rest of the carriage roof to shreds. She dragged her hand through her own blood and formed an infernal rune.

Nicholas immediately thwarted it, destroying it with a protection sigil.

A pink burst of magic struck her back from the street and suddenly Azenor carved the infernal rune for invisibility. Because Benedict and the others watched her cast it, it would not work on them. And so, they were privy to her attacks.

The horses carried on, fearing the demonic assault reigning above. Their panicked hooves beat and clopped against the stone, their chuffing breaths betraying their anxiety.

Benedict caught flashes of the sky through the hole; steely blue, grayish clouds, limp sunshine. Smoke from distant chimneys coiled into the atmosphere. Tall buildings obstructed much of the view—all stone and gray and gothic lines.

He didn't hear anything from the driver and began assuming the worst. The carriage wobbled as the horses took a corner sharply, the two of them picking up speed.

"You killed my companion," Azenor hissed between her sharp teeth as she peered down from the larger hole. "I will take a life for the one which was stolen."

"No," Benedict said, a snarl in his voice. "We will take yours."

Benedict launched a large entangled spell at Azenor, her eyes flying wide, her brows shooting her to her horns. It collided and she tumbled from the carriage top.

Lucia opened the curtains on the back window and watched as Azenor rolled through the snow, her wings flapping uselessly as they smoked from Sabine's spell. She stayed down, dazed and pained.

"Someone needs to drive!" Nicholas said frantically.

Benedict climbed onto the seats and then pulled himself up through the hole, balancing on the top of the racing carriage. They hit a dip and Benedict slipped, knocking his chin on the hard wood. He tasted blood.

"Bloody fucking hell," he cursed, climbing to the driver's bench.

The suspicious silence from their driver was answered by the gaping maw of his throat, as he slumped on the seat. Benedict cringed but climbed down and took the reins.

He didn't know the first thing about driving a carriage but he knew his subpar skills were better than a corpse.

Looking at the reins in his hands, he tried pulling on them. The horses started to respond but Benedict heard the sound of wing beats, and then Azenor was above him, wrapping her claws around his arms and hoisting him into the air. He thrashed and managed to cast a slicing spell, cutting her Achilles tendon. She screeched and then dropped him on the top of the carriage, landing hard, his knees smarting.

"I need some help up here!" Benedict shouted down to his friends as Azenor dove for him. He caught her with an offensive spell as Lucia began climbing from the ruined carriage.

His fiancée managed to get onto the roof, tearing the skirt of her sapphire gown.

"Fuck," she muttered. "I'm beginning to detest dresses."

Azenor tackled Benedict, claws going for his face. He caught her wrists and held them aloft, straining with the force of fighting her off. Rolling his body, he attempted to throw her. At the same time, Lucia hit her with a spell and knocked her aside, giving Benedict the leverage he needed to keep her claws from his throat.

Lucia managed to crawl past them and take over the reins, calming the horses, and steering them back on course. At some point the driver's body had fallen from the carriage, as Lucia was alone on the bench.

Once the driving was more settled, Benedict was able to maneuver more steadily, attacking Azenor. Coating his hands in holy water, he made a single cast and blasted her with it. Just as he did, Sabine popped through the top of the carriage, and in quick succession, delivered three holy water doused sigils into the demon.

Azenor screeched from their tandem attack, Nicholas reaching up through the hole to fight in the casting. Eventually, the demon decided three against her was not the odds she wanted to bargain for.

"I'll return for you, little warlock," she growled. "Your soul belongs to the Demons of Cronus and Christmas, and we will have what we are promised."

Azenor fled, soaring through the air on angelic wings that were wholly decided to be very un-angelic. Her invisible infernal rune was exhausted and she was completely visible to all in her flight. The streets called out with warnings of "demon" and "call the constabulary" as well as wordless screams.

"Lucia, are you okay?"

"I am well, and we're almost there."

"You're bleeding."

A thin trail of blood leaked from her hairline. She wiped it hastily. "It's nothing."

Lucia remained steadfast in her driving, focused ahead. Benedict climbed onto the bench beside her.

He was sure that they made a curious sight. A ruined carriage, a lady and a lord driving it, another balancing atop the roof, another leaning out the back, casting protection sigils in violet magic.

Benedict scanned the changing scenery, transforming from the gothic gray stone buildings of the city, to the more sprawling lands of the outskirts. The space between houses began to grow slightly larger, the roads more rural, a higher density of trees. Farmlands and cottages began to appear. They kept trundling on until Lucia made a turn.

They arrived in front of a well-kept cottage with artfully climbing ivy, the first breath of morning's frost still clinging to it. Smoke coiled from the chimney, the light from a decorated festive tree dancing in the window. The front door was painted a cheery Christmas red, a wreath with a gold bell and white bow hanging from it. It was modest, but beautiful.

Unloading from the carriage, they walked up the path, past the anti-demon wards, then knocked on the door. It swung open to reveal a dark-skinned man with gold eyes. He gave them a soft smile, a hint of solemnity in the look of him.

"So, you're being hunted by the Demons of Cronus and Christmas? And from the looks of you, there was a recent altercation. I'm curious to know how this came about. Though, I cannot say I'm excited to hear tell of them again." He opened the door wider. "Please come in."

"Thank you, Mister Beaumont," Benedict said.

He hoped the only living survivor of the Nightmare Curse had answers for him.

STAVE FIVE

DECEMBER 19, 1866

Clarence Beaumont sat on his well-worn couch across from the four of them on the opposite one. He had his legs crossed over a knee, his fingers steepled. Between them was a simple tray of sandwiches and tea. As he took them in, pondering their bedraggled appearances, Benedict cleared his throat.

"Thank you for meeting with us."

"I must admit, curiosity truly got the best of me. How are the demons hunting you? They only come out during the

Scrooge Curse." Clarence's voice was skeptical, but he was meeting with them so that had to count for something.

"I am the victim of the 1873 Nightmare Curse."

Clarence quirked a brow. "How is that possible?"

Benedict told him.

When he finished, Clarence was running his hand over his close-cropped hair, blinking rapidly. He exhaled slowly.

"I didn't know anyone could use the curse to effectively time travel," Clarence said, awed.

"I don't think the demons did either."

"If I had known…" Clarence trailed off, looking away. "I wouldn't have had to spend so long making amends."

"Ah, but I did quite enjoy your groveling," a new voice inserted, carrying a new pot of tea. "Our daughter is also finally down for her nap."

"Wonderful, thank you darling. Our other daughter is also out, she went to get new ribbons for her next project."

"Perfect," Clarence's husband, Antoine, dipped down to give him a quick kiss.

In Mortal London Clarence's and Antoine's marriage would have been illegal and sinful. In Vonor, it was just as valid and normal as a man and woman marriage. Many mortal humans decreed it grounds for an afterlife in Hell, but that truly wasn't the case—as any warlock who had performed the Staying could attest to. Seductresses and suicides were also improperly assumed to reside in Hell. Those things did not condemn a soul—cold-blooded murder, rape, and abuse, did.

"So, Antoine was your Belle, and you won him back after surviving?"

"I did," Clarence confirmed. "I imagine it was hard to resist, knowing the ordeal I'd suffered and must have truly repented from to survive…well, as he said groveling was involved, but I wore him down."

"Mmhmm," Antoine murmured, standing beside his husband as Clarence wound his forearm up Antoine's. He turned to Lucia. "I'm assuming *you* are his Belle?"

"You would assume correctly." Lucia then indicated Sabine, then Nicholas. "And his Believer and Enabler."

Clarence lifted a brow. "So many of your characters present."

Benedict shrugged humbly, eyes trained on the light floral rug. "If not for them I would not have been able to kill Calanthe."

Clarence and Antoine both froze.

"You killed the Ghost of Christmas Past? Calanthe is dead?" Clarence said, eyes wide. Benedict could practically see his racing heart showing on his face. "That's not possible."

"I assure you it is."

"When?"

"Three days ago."

"You've been in the past for three days?"

"I've been here since the fourteenth and I am determined to stay."

Clarence shook his head to clear his mind. "You just might be able to. Whatever curse this one is, it'll be the last time it is carried out."

"So, I'm free?"

"No, you said you broke out during the transition of past and present?" Benedict nodded, so Clarence continued. "You never carried out the present portion of your curse. If you happen to kill Azenor, then maybe, but I would not hedge all my bets on it."

"What should I do?"

"Well as I see it you have three options. One, you finish the Nightmare and truly repent."

"I can't do that. Lucia is dead in my time and we don't know if we can prevent it from happening this time." He clutched Lucia's hand in her lap. He needed her stability.

Clarence nodded soberly. "I understand. Then you have two options, kill all the demons, or kill the caster in this timeline. I'm sure either will end the curse."

Benedict leaned back and rubbed his forehead.

"May I ask who your caster was?" Benedict inquired.

The caster of the Nightmare Curse took the risk of being killed in exchange should the intended target truly repent. Whomever had cursed Clarence would be dead now. The aftermath of the curse was never quiet, some even took bets on who the demons would take that year and if they'd survive.

Clarence looked down sadly. "My brother. He was in love with Antoine and he figured my untimely death would bring them something to bond over, in addition to hammering in how depraved of a man I must be if I qualified for the Scrooge Curse. Clearly, it did not work. Oftentimes our casters are one of our characters. He was my Bob Cratchit—my Undervalued."

Benedict looked down at his hands. "Are we such bad people if we fit the prerequisites?"

"I think those who cast it are the evil ones. We are just people who make mistakes, and sometimes those mistakes fit the demon's game. A person who takes a failure or ignorance and manipulates it to play this curse truly must have hate in their heart."

They arrived back home without incident which raised all of their anxiety. Even as they passed the threshold unscathed, they didn't trust they were safe. Benedict was sure that Azenor or Hollis was going to be lurking just outside the door or standing on the edge of the street like some ominous apparition.

Inside, Huffam was setting three, long, white boxes on the entry table. They all had a tag indicating the modiste that Sabine had suggested.

"These were just delivered, sir."

"Thank you, Huffam. Any news?"

"Nothing sir."

"*This* is delightful news," Sabine cooed. "Much needed after that whole ordeal."

Huffam nodded and departed to the kitchen to fix tea.

Despite Huffam's conviction in staying, Benedict still had his anxieties.

Searching the tags, Sabine found the one with her name scrawled on it and untied the black bow holding it closed. When she lifted the lid, all one could see was satiny olive green. She lifted it up and a look of awe came over her.

"Oh, it's perfect," Sabine said, eyes tracing the deep neckline. "Lucia, darling, do you want to see yours?"

"Perhaps when I am not still bleeding and covered in filth."

Sabine whirled, dropping her gown. "Oh darling, fuck's sake, let's get you cleaned up."

Lucia was hustled away by Sabine, leaving Benedict and Nicholas alone.

"She really is something, isn't she?" Nicholas said yearningly, gazing after the retreating women.

Benedict elbowed him good-naturedly. "There's nothing stopping you now—you're cured."

Nicholas gave him an odd look, like a double take, as if he'd not realized the freedom the lack of the Wasting offered him. "She won't have me," he said dolefully.

"Why do you think not? She's infatuated with you." Benedict leaned in conspiratorially. "Even seven years from now she burns for you."

Nicholas raised a brow. "She does?"

"Indeed."

"Hmm." A self-satisfied smirk graced Nicholas's lips. "It's a nice thought."

Benedict clapped him on the shoulder. "Consider it."

The four of them had settled in the drawing room with notes and drinks. As the research grew more frustrating, the drinks became stronger. Eventually, they were all drinking scotch from fine crystal tumblers.

"Lord Kane has a wife who recently pulled investments from Midnight Malady research and exchanged it for some sort of serum," Nicholas started. "Should we investigate why?"

"No, that's a dead end. Adelaide Kane is this year's Scrooge Curse victim—and no, she does not make it."

"Oh," Lucia said sadly, brows drawn together. "That's too bad. She was kind to me. She taught me how to French braid at a party many years ago—it was a dreadfully boring affair and she seemed to take pity on me."

"Right," Nicholas said with finality. "Strike that one from the list. So, as it sits for suspects we have: Christopher Taylor, Edith Smith-Williams, Gilbert Davis, Beryl Snowden, and…"

Lucia sighed. "It's okay, you can say it. Luther Turner."

"I am sorry."

Lucia shrugged and sipped her scotch. "It is what it is. You cannot choose your family, can you?"

It was clear she didn't want to think about it.

Benedict set down the file he was poring over. Wrapping his arm around his fiancée, he offered her whatever strength and comfort he could.

"I think we've established all we can from here," Benedict informed like an announcement. He set several files aside and grabbed his drink. "I say we take tonight to relax before tomorrow's ball. Tomorrow is when the real work begins. When we must interrogate and investigate while being on our best behaviors."

Sabine lifted her glass. "I can drink to that."

Beside Sabine, Nicholas tossed aside his papers and undid the top button of his shirt. "Why not? These papers will still be here in the morning anyhow."

"'*Strike the harp, and join in chorus:*
Fa, la, la, la, la, la, la, la, la!
Follow me in merry measure—'" Sabine suddenly broke off her singing of *Deck the Halls* as she stumbled on the hem of her skirt and fell onto the rug, blindfolded on a drunken dare.

"Bloody hell!" Sabine cursed, tearing off the blindfold. She blinked away her dazedness. "I nearly broke my ankle in that fall."

"You only made it to the second part of the song! You must finish your drink!" Nicholas crowed. His shirt was several buttons undone—his cheeks flushed.

"Unfair!" Sabine retorted. "You try completing such a ridiculous task in a blasted gown!"

"I don't make the rules."

"You quite literally did in this instance."

"In that case—drink."

"Fine!" Sabine strode over to her drink and downed it. She made a face of distaste but kept it down. "Is it my turn now?"

"I believe it's Benny's," Nicholas answered, patting Benedict's shoulder.

Benedict grinned devilishly and Nicholas began regretting many decisions. Decisions which led to him donning a crinoline and skirt, attempting the very task he'd made Sabine attempt. He did not make it through the first stanza.

They all descended into raucous laughter. The drink flowed freely, loosening all the stressors of Benedict's life of late. It also occurred to him that he had not yet processed that he was practically *free*. There were not four walls trapping him. All of the good hit him at once.

Lucia was alive, wrapped in his arms, perched on his lap. She tilted her head against his neck, cradling two fingers of scotch. He tightened his hold on her. He loved her, she was alive, and she was his.

Nicholas was cured, dancing in a bloody *dress* over his trousers. He had a drink sloshing in his glass, a top hat tipped on his head. He was grinning, beatific, happy.

Sabine was not alone and muted, there was jubilance glowing on her face. She had her dress hiked up, freeing her legs as she got up and joined Nicholas. The two of them spun together, Sabine tilting her head and giggling. They had a chance at a happy ending this time.

The moment around them crystallized in Benedict's mind. The warmth of the fireplace, the music playing in the corner, light from the Christmas tree, happiness emanating from his friends. It struck him with a surge like nostalgia and he knew that despite it all, he was going to look back on this moment with fondness.

Regardless of how it all turned out.

DECEMBER 20, 1866

Benedict awoke to the crack of a gunshot.

He startled awake from the couch he and Lucia had passed out on together, Sabine and Nicholas sprawled on a blanket in front of the fire. All four of them were suddenly wide awake—and suddenly very sober.

They jerked from their sleeping positions and immediately casted protections and readied offensive spells.

"Front or back?" Nicholas asked.

"I think the front," Benedict answered.

They proceeded slowly, Benedict taking the lead. He held up a hand to halt Lucia who was sidling up next to him.

Lucia slowed as Benedict reached the door. Slowly, he unlocked it and pulled it open, the hinges creaking ominously.

It was dark out—three or four in the morning—so what little light there was, was provided by the lampposts on the street and what spilled from the open door.

There, on the front step was Huffam with a bullet hole in his forehead.

Benedict let out a sound of grief and dropped down next to his loyal butler. Blood pooled on the front step, staining it. Huffam's eyes were open in a shocked stare, flat and muted. His dark hair sported so much blood.

On his chest a note was pinned.

She's next. Report this and we take the red-haired bitch, too.

And a contract for Lucia's assassination, courtesy of the brotherhood.

Benedict grabbed the papers and crumpled them in his fist, rage coursing through him. He felt it boiling his blood, burning in his chest. Furious and white-knuckled he ignited the words with the barest thought. It was rare for a trained warlock's magic to lose control and manifest with their emotions, but every so often, a leash would fail. The cerulean flames ate along his fingers until the threat was nothing but ash.

Anger and regret coursed through him. He had just destroyed evidence relating to Huffam's murder. Due to his carelessness, his justice might've been jeopardized. Staring down at Huffam's corpse, he took a moment to grieve, then straightened. Resigned, he bowed his head.

"We need to call the constabulary, explain everything," Benedict said, sighing. He turned to Lucia. "Would you make the call?"

"Wait, stop!" Nicholas said as Lucia began to turn, casting an obscurity sigil. "What if we didn't call?"

"What?" Benedict asked, aghast. "Why wouldn't we?"

"That note said if we say anything they'll take Sabine out. But, the police are going to ask many questions, questions we don't have time for. Also, this is going to make news, people will gossip and no one will want to talk about anything with us but the tragic murder of your butler. It will bury any ability for us to interrogate our suspects."

Benedict balked. "And what do you suppose we do? Hide the body? Not report the crime?"

"Yes, that is what I am suggesting."

"No. No way. I already went to prison for a crime I did not commit, I'd prefer not to be framed for another."

"Benny, think about it. They might take the girls out for this."

"No." He shook his head. "No, I can't. They're bluffing."

"Maybe we *should* consider it…" Sabine inserted, fear in her face.

"Are you still drunk?" Benedict asked.

"Yes. But that's not the point. The Brotherhood has made a direct threat on me now. I deserve to have a say in what goes." She crossed her arms over her chest. "What if they think you did it? What if they arrest you? Maybe you're in a holding cell for a day or two. What then?"

Anxiety wove within Benedict. He couldn't afford to be falsely accused either. He couldn't afford to be taken away for questioning. He hadn't done this, and he was damned if he was going to spend a single second being questioned for it.

"Fuck." Benedict ran a hand through his hair. "Lucia, what do you think?"

His fiancée froze, blue eyes flickering side to side. "I don't know." She looked to the side guiltily. "I don't want to risk Sabine's life or you going to prison, but it feels so selfish to speak about this." She tugged on her hair. "Oh, bloody hell, yes, we should wait to report it."

The four of them with an air of depression casted spells of strength and stasis. Carefully, the four of them used their combined magics and carried Huffam's body through the house and out to the back. They maneuvered his body, floating on a cloud of cerulean, viridian, crimson, and violet. Benedict felt regret and remorse course through him as they guided him to the root cellar located below the greenhouse in the back garden.

They settled Huffam on the packed dirt floor, wrapped in a sheet. Together the four of them casted various stasis spells so that Huffam's body would not turn—for a least a week he would not rot. He would stay as he was.

Benedict stared down at his butler with sadness while the rest of them filed back to the house. Lucia hung next to the doorway.

"What were you doing outside in the middle of the night?" he whispered.

He stayed a while longer until Lucia gathered him in her arms and the two of them returned to the house.

They slept fitfully, Benedict plagued by nightmares of Huffam's dead face. Of being hauled to prison again for another crime he never committed. It brought back all the worst memories, morphing into Lucia's death. Her broken body, her battered corpse. Blood and fountain water. His devastated weeping. The constabulary dragging him off. Calanthe laughing at him before her head exploded. Azenor taking off with Lucia and dropping her from thousands of feet in the air. Hellhounds running her down in the street. Hollis wrapping her in chains and dragging her to Hell.

Benedict woke in a cold sweat, drenched, his shirtsleeves sticking to his chest. He was breathing heavy and quick. Beside him he patted the blankets, finding Lucia's gently stirring form. In the early dawn light, she was ethereal—celestial.

The pearly glow caught the slope of her nose, the high arch of her cheekbones, the smooth shape of her brow and the smokiness of her eyes. Her long black lashes cast shadows on her cheeks, her plush lips parted lightly in slumber.

Reaching for her, Lucia let out a soft sound of disturbance. In sleep, she went to him, cuddling into his arms, tucking her head beneath his chin. He held her, heart racing, but her presence slowly relaxed him, banishing the worst of the nightmares.

"Are you okay, love?" Lucia mumbled, lips ghosting across his collarbone.

He clutched her tighter. "I am now."

She awoke a little more and reached up to his face bringing him down to her. They kissed. Slowly. Decadently. They lingered on each other's lips, mouths a slow seduction, a devoted reassurance.

DECEMBER 20, 1866

Lucia descended Benedict's staircase dressed for the Whittaker ball. Sabine, dressed in her sumptuous green gown, was already standing with the two men at the foot, Nicholas having slipped away home—without incident, despite their concerns—for his ivory and jade formalwear. Benedict was in a dark suit with coattails and a white cravat, paired with a deep crimson waistcoat—the very same shade as her crushed velvet gown.

With her first footfall, Benedict's eyes locked on her and she watched them darken with arousal. Leave it to Sabine to make their winter formals risqué. In addition to the plunging neckline that accentuated and cupped her breasts, the gown had a high slit in the thigh, exposing her golden skin whenever she stepped with her left. A sweet bow tied the corset at the small of her back, snowy lace tracing the edges of the drop-shouldered neckline.

Benedict stepped forward as she landed on the last stair, awe painted across his face. He looked at her ruby lips. "You are absolutely breathtaking."

Lucia blushed and ducked her chin, feeling the heavy swing of the silver-encrusted garnet earrings Sabine had secured for her. Benedict tucked a finger beneath her chin, tipping it back up.

"It makes me ravenous," he whispered. "And it makes me want to do very ungentlemanly things to you." He trailed his fingers down her throat, watching their descent.

Lucia swallowed, suddenly hot all over. "Then perhaps I will not be a proper lady, and you can show me such things."

Heat flared in his eyes. "Later."

Lucia bit her lip and decided she couldn't wait for later.

"You look ravishing," Sabine cooed, coming up to Lucia and fixing a stray lock of hair by her ear. "Simply beautiful. Isn't she?" She threw over her shoulder.

"She is," Nicholas replied, but his heated eyes were on Sabine.

Sabine smirked. She was also stunning beyond compare. The olive-green satin slid over her every curve, the A-line silhouette emphasizing her tiny waist, the slit on her dress parting the fabric in the center, stopping just above her knees.

It was clearly made for an ease of access, whether that be fighting or fucking.

A bell rang outside.

"That'll be our carriage," Benedict said, wrapping an arm around Lucia's waist. Heat flooded her cheeks and between her legs.

The four of them loaded into the carriage and went over the plans. It was Nicholas's coach they were in, light gray, pewter blue interiors and the exterior a steely gray with white spoked wheels. The horses drawing it were equally white.

"So, we'll all take turns interrogating Lord Turner," Benedict began, tapping his hand on his knee. "Nicholas, you'll focus on Gilbert Davis, Sabine, you have Edith Smith-Williams, Lucia, you'll question Lady Snowden, and I will speak with Christopher Taylor."

"Didn't we decide I take on Mister Taylor since Lady Snowden takes a fancy to you?" Lucia interjected, recalling Sabine's recollection of Beryl Snowden's mild infatuation with her fiancé.

Benedict visibly thought back to their previous planning and conversations before nodding. "You're correct. With that clarified, does anyone have any questions?"

They did not.

When they arrived outside the Whittaker estate, it seemed it was the popular time to make an entrance as they waited behind four carriages offloading finely dressed guests in the curved drive before being able to disembark.

The estate was huge and imposing with lush lawns that were covered in snow, cypress trees glowing with golden lights, wreaths hanging from doors and windows, flames burning in braziers along the drive. The Whittaker Christmas Ball was an annual staple of the season, rivaling the Snowden Solstice Ball that always occurred on the very next day. It was a testament to their popularity and influence that virtually everyone attended both, despite the consecutive dates. And always people wore new and separate formal wear to the occasions.

On Benedict's arm she made her entrance to the ball, cutting across the frosty ground while her breath drew coils in the air. Behind her, Sabine was on Nicholas's arm, her dearest friend grinning from ear to ear.

The drastic change in temperature from the winter chill of outside to the warm glow of inside nearly stole Lucia's breath. She tightened her hold on Benedict as he guided her into the party.

"Do you remember what Mister Taylor looks like?" Benedict asked, leaning down to her.

"I've studied his portrait enough and seen him in passing, I'm sure I can determine his identity."

"Don't stare at his portrait too long, I might get the wrong idea."

"Are you jealous?"

"Perhaps," he whispered, then nipped her ear. She let out a gasp that threaded with a moan. He chuckled next to her ear. "But you know I'm the only one who can do that to you."

Bloody hell, he was right. That didn't mean she wasn't going to make him work for it though.

With a coy smile she disentangled from her fiancé. "In that case, maybe I should speak with Mister Taylor. See what secrets he has up his sleeve."

She began walking away but Benedict grasped her hand and tugged her to him. She was pulled, stumbling into his arms as he pressed an ardent kiss to her mouth. He cupped her jaw, tilting her up to him. As he bestowed her with this hot, passionate kiss, she felt eyes burn all around her. Even so, she opened her mouth to allow him further access.

When he broke from her, he was grinning. "I think I just gave him and everyone else something to talk about."

"Cad."

"Yes, but you love me."

She brushed her thumb over his lips, her heart swelling. "That I do."

She slipped away and wove through the fray, making her way over to the refreshments. Rather than indulge like she had last night, she opted for a non-alcoholic apple cider. As she sipped, she perused, watching the guests, waiting for a familiar face to strike her. Just then, she spotted exactly who she was looking for.

Confidently, she strode over to Mister Taylor with a pleasant smile on her face. She extended a hand upon reaching him.

"Mister Taylor, hello!" She shook his ungloved hand firmly. "I'm—"

"You're Professor Lucia Turner, yes, I've heard of you. How do you do this fine evening?"

Surprise lit through Lucia but she hid it. "I'm well thank you. I'm glad to see my reputation precedes me."

Christopher Taylor was an average and unimpressive looking man—mid-thirties, middling height, medium build, plain brown hair, and equally unmemorable brown eyes. He was clean shaven with an unoffensive haircut. Overall, he was a very milquetoast warlock.

Though to her surprise, he seemed exceedingly nice.

"Well certainly! The brilliant mind behind the cure for Ember Fever? And the paper on the leading theory as to why the immortal diseases afflict only warlocks who complete the Staying? You're a celebrity Professor Turner."

A surge of pride struck Lucia and she sipped her drink to hide her over-eager smile. "Such kind compliments."

"It's nothing but the truth. Speaking of your brilliance, is there any chance you're putting that head to researching the Wasting?"

Lucia was taken aback. This conversation was going perfectly in the direction she wanted it to. "Actually yes, I've been working with my fiancé in ascertaining a cure for the Wasting, as well. It's my understanding you've been petitioning for a budget change?"

"That is correct. I—"

"Lucia, I need to speak to you."

Lucia whirled at the interrupting voice, surprised and angered to see her father standing behind her.

"No, thank you. I have nothing to say to you."

"Lucia, please."

Lucia chanced a look at Christopher Taylor to which the man met and shrugged.

Weighing her frustrations and need to discover who killed her and framed the man she loved, she sighed. "Fine. You get five minutes." She turned to Mister Taylor. "I'm eager to continue our conversation later."

"I will be here."

She began walking away with her father until he stopped her.

"Dance with me. We'll talk as we do."

Lucia rolled her eyes but crossed the marble floor with him.

For the night, the Whittakers had painted a gorgeous pattern of snowflakes in gold across the dance floor, matching all the gold adornments in the room—bells, ribbons, garland. Hanging above were a multitude of glass blown snowflakes, the craftsmanship incomparable, spinning in the air.

The music slowed and Lucia took her father's hand and entered into a dance with him.

"Still planning to have me killed?" she quipped bitterly.

"Lucia," he chastised, then composed himself. "I told you—I would never do that to you."

"And if I were a faceless target?"

"No," he said with concrete certainty. "You didn't give me time to answer."

"It seems a pretty clear cut yes or no to me."

"There are politics to it that you must consider."

"These are lives," she hissed. "Are you telling me they come second to money?"

They danced around the floor, her long red skirt sweeping out with the bigger turns. Her heels clicked, his shoes tapped.

"Not like you might think. Have you stopped to consider that I may be in a precarious situation here? You are my daughter—heralding a cure—and I am in a place where many people would choose to see that cure and you vanish."

"So, you admit the board is corrupted?"

"Of course, there's no question about it. All three of them are vile and in the business of lining their pockets. It's the few who genuinely want to see these diseases eradicated that make the difference. They are what stand in the way of cutting your funding."

"Are you one of them?" she challenged as they spun around the floor. "Do you halt the corruption? Or do you enable it?"

"I stand with my daughter and her fiancé. I want these cures, Lucia."

Lucia bit back tears. She didn't know what to believe anymore. On one hand, this was her father who was supposed to love and protect her. On the other, in some alternate world, she was supposed to die tomorrow and Benedict was to be framed for it. How could she reconcile the two?

"Do you have any idea who specifically might want the cures to disappear?"

"Not off the top of my head, but I'd presume anyone on the boards could feasibly want that."

"Make a guess."

Luther paused, considering. "Lady Snowden perhaps. She's been speaking to your mother, filling her mind with ridiculous ideas. She regales her with these tales of riches if we invest in an upcoming researcher that has a long-term treatment plan for Midnight Malady, but…it seems, I don't know, calculated."

Lucia nodded. Beryl Snowden was already on their list. "Anyone else?"

"The Whitehill family is divided. There was recently an altercation after a board meeting between Charles Whitehill and Nicholas Whitehill. Charles was trying to destroy Nicholas's reputation by claiming he was fabricating his research."

"He what?" Lucia was shocked. Why hadn't Nicholas said anything about this?

"Charles accused Nicholas of inflating his successes in determining a genetic factor for the immortal diseases so he could manipulate the stocks in favor of his investments."

"Why would he do that? Nicholas is very publicly affected by the Wasting." Lucia decided not to reveal Benedict had cured him. "Why would he want money going towards something that's not a cure?"

"I'm not sure. Perhaps to afford the most experimental treatments to find a secret cure?"

Lucia pondered this. "And Mister Charles? What is he invested in?"

"He has investments in all three diseases, though his profits have considerably plummeted due to your finding Ember Fever's cure."

Lucia's stomach twisted uneasily.

"Lucia," Luther began, an edge of concern in his voice. The fatherly love had her heart aching. "Is there something you're not telling me? Are you in more danger?"

Lucia steeled herself and pulled from the dance. "I believe your five minutes are over, father. Thank you for your concern, but I can handle myself."

With that, she let go and walked briskly for the courtyard.

The glass doors were open to let in the cool night air. Frost was lining the balustrade and a soft fall of snow was just beginning. She crossed her arms over herself and stared down at the garden, enchanted roses frosted, magicked carnations iced, sigils of various colors hovering above the flowerbeds.

She sighed and closed her eyes, how was she supposed to trust the word of her father when all the evidence pointed to him? But he had raised her. Loved her. He taught her, her first sigil, he gave her books, he was the person who held her after a nightmare. Could he really be this person? Able to end the life of the person he gave it to?

Tilting her head back, perhaps even searching for answers in the starlit sky, Lucia was alerted to a new presence.

Benedict sidled up to her, his scent of bergamot and sandalwood a salve to her worries. It was her favorite smell in the world. It was comfort. It was home. It was him.

Without looking at him, she told him what she'd learned about the Whitehills and everything else her father told her. He was equally unsettled by the revelation. They were quiet, but then he spoke.

"I have a question for you."

She turned to him in surprise. "What is it?"

"Will you dance with me?"

A small smile spread across her face. "Of course." She started walking inside before he tugged her back.

"No. Out here. Just us."

Lucia's heart swelled. They could still hear the music on the courtyard balcony, crisp as the air. And while it was freezing outside, the lit braziers offered heat and her stress levels had required some cooling down.

"That sounds lovely."

He took her by the hand and guided her to the center, then he placed a hand on her waist and began. They stepped together, feet moving, hands holding, hips in line, their movements flowing in unison. Benedict was a superb dancer, Lucia a formidable one. They twirled and spun to the tune, falling apart and coming together.

"I've missed you so much," he murmured, tears a silver line in his eyes. "And reliving this week, when we had been arguing before…" He inhaled deeply. "I am so grateful I get to do everything differently."

"I'm here."

"Marry me then."

She smiled. "You know I already am. The countdown is on."

"No, marry me sooner. Marry me Christmas Day. When all of this is over."

Lucia stutter-stepped. "What?"

Benedict dipped her back, her long black hair a cascade. He trailed his lips down her throat. Kissing once. Twice.

"Marry me."

"But what about our guests—?"

"I don't care," he said, punctuating with another kiss. "Marry me."

She bit her lip and looked up at the stars and the falling snowflakes. Her heart thundered and she could feel Benedict kissing along her pulse point making it race faster.

"Okay," she agreed. "Let's get married. Christmas Day."

Benedict swept her up and kissed her deeply. She opened her mouth to him, tangling their tongues together. Their lips moved, giving and taking. He sucked on her lower lip. She flicked her tongue against his kiss.

She pulled back. "Should we leave early? Go back to your house?"

"We still have work to do. But…what if it was *our* house?"

"Our house. It has a nice ring to it."

"Oh! My apologies for interrupting."

Lucia turned and found Christopher Taylor standing just outside the threshold of the doors, face flushed, a faint hint of perspiration on his skin.

Benedict seemed to have his hackles up, ready to bite out a retort. Surely, the reaction a lingering wound from his imprisonment.

"I just came out for some fresh air—it's sweltering in there."

"No, no, it's okay. Mister Taylor, have you met my fiancé?"

Christopher strode out. "I haven't had the honor yet, but I've heard of you. Good evening, Professor Edwards."

He shook Benedict's hand and Benedict blinked in shock. "I know you."

"You do?" Christopher looked taken aback. "I assure you we have not met."

Lucia watched Benedict stare him down in concentration until suddenly his eyes lit up.

"I apologize, I had you mixed up with someone else. How do you do?"

"Well! Actually, earlier I was speaking to your lovely fiancée, but I realize now you maybe be able to help also. You are researching the Wasting, correct?"

"I am," Benedict said with reservation. Lucia narrowed her brows. Why was he acting so stiff?

"I was wondering if you could present some of your findings to the board. It's regarding funding—"

"Constabulary!" someone shouted inside.

The three of them whirled and dashed inside.

Why would the constabulary turn up to the Whittaker Christmas ball? Was there a demon near the grounds?

Inside they were greeted to the sight of a dozen black clad officers, canes in hand. The music had halted and all dancing ceased, everyone moved to the fringes of the dance floor. The lead officer—the captain—stepped forward.

"We're looking for Lord Benedict Edwards."

Ice shot through Lucia's spine, her blood running cold. She inhaled sharply and immediately cast her gaze at Benedict.

He was stock still beside her, whiter than a sheet. He visibly swallowed before stepping forward.

"I am Benedict Edwards."

The captain stepped up to him. "You're under arrest."

No.

No.

No, no, no, no, no.

"What for?" he asked.

Lucia thought she went into shock. Her ears began to ring. Her breathing came fast and short. Her vision tilted and spun. She watched, frozen in horror as Benedict was arrested, hands behind his back, cuffs locked around his wrists. She watched as they read him his rights. She watched as the gossip spread, voices tittering, hands over mouths, eyes looking on her with pity.

"For the murder of John Huffam."

DECEMBER 21, 1866

Benedict felt hollow.

This was exactly what he'd been terrified of. This was exactly why they hadn't reported Huffam's murder. This and the risk to Sabine. Now, it had happened regardless.

He had been hauled through the ball, judgmental eyes taking in his every expression. He refused to say anything aside from, "I didn't kill him," knowing it was best to wait for his solicitor. It was why he was now waiting in a derelict cell awaiting interrogation.

The cell was causing him significant anxiety. It was not so alike to his previous cell that he felt trapped, but it was a cell nonetheless. This one—albeit possessing bars—had a window. There were also bars separating him from the rest of the jail, and not a steel door. Although the bars did contain the same anti-magic warding his former cell walls did.

His question was, how did they find out about Huffam's death? His body was well hidden and protected. No one should have found it. Not yet at least.

Another thought haunted him. Christopher Taylor was his cell-neighbor dying of the Wasting. He was searching for a budget increase because he'd become recently diagnosed and he wanted the cure before he was too far afflicted.

Benedict wondered how much more the future was going to change with the cure to the Wasting in the world.

The jingling of keys alerted him to an approaching guard. Benedict stood from the bench—that doubled as a bed—he'd been seated on.

"It's your lucky day," the guard said, unlocking his cell. "Someone else confessed, you're free to go."

The door swung open and Benedict stepped out, staring down the guard. He was irked, his hackles raised due to a mix of anxiety and anger.

"Did any of you even start the semblance of an investigation before deciding to jail me?"

The guard ducked his head. "That's above my pay grade."

"Evidently."

Benedict strode past him and walked down the hallway to the lobby. To his surprise, it wasn't any of his friends there to greet him, it was his soon to be father-in-law.

Luther Turner stood with his arms crossed, twirling a silver pocket watch, shoulder against the wall. Despite him being Lucia's father, due to having completed the Staying he looked to be in his mid-thirties. He had some premature grays, but that made him look more distinguished rather than old.

As Benedict entered, Luther caught sight of him and flipped the watch three times before pocketing it. Benedict flinched, something about the action unsettling him.

"Hello Benedict," Luther started. "Glad to see this little misunderstanding cleared up."

"Where is Lucia?"

"With your friends. I handled this alone."

"What did you do?"

"I pulled some strings." He shrugged. "Went through some contacts—my less illustrious ones—and applied some…pressure. They tracked down who in the Brotherhood was responsible for your butler's murder and the additional blackmail. Why didn't you speak to me about these threats?"

Benedict gave him a dubious look. "Because there was a high probability you were behind it."

Anger clouded Luther's eyes. "I love my daughter. I would *never* hurt her."

"Well, we have evidence that indicates otherwise."

"Enlighten me."

Benedict debated before deciding. "It's far too ludicrous to explain but I'll give you the short of it. I am the victim of the 1873 Nightmare Curse and I escaped it to come back in time to stop—"

Benedict froze, his eyes widening.

"To stop what?" Luther was leaning in and it seemed he was believing Benedict's every word.

"Lucia's death," he breathed.

"Lucia *dies*?" Luther's voice cracked. "When?"

"What time is it?"

Luther grasped Benedict by the shoulders. "When does she die?"

"Today."

Luther stumbled back, horror flooding his face. "What time?"

Benedict ducked his head down. "Just after ten o'clock tonight."

Luther whipped out his pocket watch and looked at the time. "That's less than eighteen hours from now. Who did it?"

"I don't know. I was framed for it."

Luther stared in repulsion. "That's unthinkable."

"Glad you think so."

"What can we do to keep her safe?"

Benedict thought. "Keep the Brotherhood as far from her as possible."

"I'll see it done."

Luther flipped the watch thrice before pocketing it and a realization plowed into Benedict with all the force of a speeding train.

He'd seen that habitual trick before.

On the ghost who'd warned him about the approaching demons.

The ghost who'd pleaded for him to save Lucia's life.

The ghost who was surrounded by various sigils. Violet ones. One that meant illusion. The one that was forced upon him.

Benedict's entire world upended. He swayed on his feet.

Luther Turner was his Jacob Marley.

Not Nicholas.

Which meant Nicholas was probably still alive in 1873. Which meant he was fully capable of casting the Nightmare Curse.

Everything fell into place.

Nicholas was on the board.

Nicholas had investments in the research.

Nicholas fought with his cousin about fabricating evidence for stock purposes.

Everything started changing after they told Nicholas—after they cured him. They were attacked by the Brotherhood only after the fact. Nicholas manipulated them. He was the one who'd suggested they hide Huffam's death. Nicholas was probably the one who reported Huffam's body. It's the only thing that made sense. Benedict also bet it all that he was responsible for his death too.

Nicholas was the one who killed Lucia.

Nicholas was the one who framed him.

Nicholas was the one who cursed him.

"*Angels fucking demons*," Benedict gasped. "Where did you say Lucia was?"

"With your friends. Miss Sabine and that Nicholas Whitehill fellow. What's going on?"

"He's going to kill her."

Benedict raced for the door.

Police were milling about outside his house when he arrived. Benedict's front step was cordoned off as an active crime scene. Two officers were standing guard, another patrolling. His front door was wide open, an inspector standing in it. He was sure there were others. His heart sank.

"Excuse me!" he shouted up from the road. The officers turned to him, seemingly annoyed at being bothered—

especially at such a late, or rather early hour. "My companions were supposed to be here, do you know where they were off to?"

The inspector tipped his hat. "I encouraged them to go elsewhere for the rest of the night. I believe they were heading to a Whitehill's residence."

"Fuck," Benedict muttered and took off, slipping and sliding on the snow and ice.

He wasn't sure how long he ran for, but he was casting spells and protections every step of the way. None of the demons were attacking. He didn't know if that was a good or bad thing.

At Nicholas's home, Benedict rushed the steps and hammered on the door. Dickens, Nicholas's butler answered the door, unimpressed. Then light lit his eyes in familiarity.

"Lord Edwards—"

Benedict pushed past him and rushed through the entryway. "Where is he?" he demanded, flinging open every door he came across. All were empty.

"He is not here, sir. I've been under the impression he has been staying with you of late."

Benedict whirled in shock. Not here? Where was he? Where was Lucia? Where was Sabine?

"No, he was until tonight and I was framed for a murder I didn't commit. Has he been here at all?"

"Not since he picked up his clothing for the Whittaker Ball."

Benedict threw open Nicholas's office and a thought struck him. He went in and immediately went to Nicholas's finance book. Dickens had followed him in.

"Sir, you shouldn't be in here."

Benedict found the leather book and slammed it on the desk, his palm pushing it into the wood as he beheld Dickens's gaze. Fury was emanating from his every pore.

"Nicholas has put a hit on my fiancée and plans to afflict me with the Nightmare Curse come Christmas Eve. Now I discover he is nowhere to be found. This—" he held up the ledger— "will give me damning proof. Now, do you want to be an accomplice to his crimes? Or do you wish to assist me?"

Dickens paled but rushed into the room. "What are we looking for?"

"His financials. Anything that determines he benefits from the immortal diseases remaining uncured."

It was minutes later and both Benedict and Dickens found damning evidence. His stocks and investments both showed he had a vested interest in the long-term treatment of diseases. He also had a secret research team, funded by the stocks he had artificially inflated to find a cure, but were paid handsomely for silence. Guidelines indicated he wanted any cure discovery kept to specific individuals. Worst of all, Dickens found a contract in a secret compartment for the Brotherhood. They were to kill Lucia this night. There was also a second one, amended for the fourteenth. The day they'd cured him. The day of the new attack.

Benedict felt ill. He was going to be sick. He let out a broken sound and Dickens clapped him on the shoulder and held it through his pain.

"I am so sorry, Lord Edwards."

Benedict nodded. He'd never felt such betrayal. Nicholas had been his friend—his mentor. But he wasn't any of that. He was…

His rival.

His Antithesis.

"I have to go." Benedict pocketed the evidence and darted out into the exceedingly early morning.

He had a horrible feeling that he knew exactly where they were.

As he ran out into the street to hail a hackney, he felt a sudden blow to the back of his head and everything went black.

LUCIA TURNER

DECEMBER 21, 1866

Lucia was absolutely terrified. Her blood turned to ice as her hair was gripped in the hands of the Brotherhood, and her face was hovering over the basin of a fountain. She was shaking with cold and fear, every inch of her trembling. Hands bound behind her back.

Sabine was sobbing nearby, bound and gagged, her beautiful olive gown ruined. Rose bushes and thorns were creeping along the walls of the broken solarium courtyard, following cracks in the flagstones. Nicholas was unconscious by the staircase that led to the main house—and had been for some time. Lucia worried he was dead.

The three of them had been on their way to Nicholas's home after being turned away by both the police station and the inspector outside Benedict's residence. On the carriage ride over, a brigand posed as an injured woman in the street, and their driver—soft-hearted fool he was—was duped and killed before a dozen Brotherhood members descended upon them. They'd been no match for their numbers. The three of them were tied, abducted, and their magic suppressed by various sigils, while Nicholas's carriage was commandeered.

Hours later, they'd arrived at an abandoned estate, red glass windows casting a bloody glow on the snow, rose crests wrought in iron and tapestry, and overgrown gardens hanging on with fingers from winter's onslaught. They'd been led through the halls, everything covered in a thick layer of dust, wind howling through broken walls and roofs. As if they only had one destination in mind, they were brought to a courtyard and more magic suppressing sigils were layered upon them.

Lucia knew whose estate it was.

Ten Brotherhood members watched over them, playing guard, arms crossed. Nicholas had tried to fight them hours ago, but he was gifted with a needle to his neck that immediately dropped him. He'd been unconscious ever since.

Now, Lucia was faced with her reflection and the threat of impending death. Night falling behind her.

She knew this was what had happened to her before. This was what Benedict had been framed and sentenced for. He'd told her stabbing and drowning. But seeing it, about to experience it? That was a whole new beast.

Her question was, why hadn't they done it yet?

Just then, a frenzy suddenly stirred up in the Brotherhood milling about. Lucia managed to look up in time to see Benedict shoved down the stairs, groaning. Blood dripped down his temple.

"Welcome!" the presumed leader announced. He had dark hair, mutton chops, and a flashy suit. "Our employer requested your witness for the contract completion, so here we are. Enjoy the show, boy."

The man holding Lucia suddenly fixed his grip and began pushing her down to the water.

"STOP!" Benedict screamed. "You hurt her and I will kill him, and you can say goodbye to your precious fucking payday."

Lucia was yanked up and greeted to the sight of Benedict crouching, hauling Nicholas by his hair against his person. There was a silver knife to his throat. To Lucia's surprise Nicholas was very awake, very alert, and very afraid.

"Benny, what are you—"

"Shut the fuck up," Benedict hissed.

A flash of shock struck Lucia.

"Why would I care if you kill your little friend?" the leader asked—but to Lucia's dismay, there was a thread of uncertainty.

"*Friend,*" Benedict scoffed with disgust. "Yes, such a beautiful deception he played." Benedict nicked Nicholas with the blade and a thin trail of blood slipped down his neck. "I think you should care very much if I kill your employer."

The leader's lips tightened and a challenge entered his pale eyes. "You don't have it in you. In your heart he is still your friend."

Dread coursed through Lucia as she saw the words strike their mark, making Benedict flinch. Was Nicholas—? No. No, he couldn't have. He couldn't be.

"Are you willing to bet all he still owes you on my heart? Because I'm not a betting man, but if I were, I'd know those are shit odds."

"Listen," the leader stepped forward, hands raised, the façade breaking. "Maybe we can work something out."

Realization hit Lucia like a carriage. It was Nicholas. Nicholas did it all. Had her killed, had Benedict framed, had him *cursed*. All for money—for fucking *money*.

Sabine made a sound of despair as she came to the same conclusion.

"Yes, maybe we can."

The leader's eyes flickered to Benedict and Nicholas— Nicholas who was very clearly not drugged. Then to Lucia. "What do you want?"

"Let her go," Benedict said viciously.

The leader looked to Nicholas, back to Benedict, then to the man holding Lucia hostage. He nodded and suddenly Lucia was released. She fell to her side, her shoulder stinging. She wriggled until she could get to her feet and stumbled to Sabine, her red dress just as ruined. As she managed to get Sabine's gag off with her hands behind her, she heard Benedict shout.

"If you let the women go, I will ensure you are paid for the completion of the contract without finishing it. I will deal with *him*."

"Benny, you can't really think—"

"I want to hear nothing from you. You are *nothing* to me."

Sabine hissed. "I'll fucking deal with him myself. That bloody fucking *traitor*."

"I don't want our names brought into this mess," the leader said.

"I will make sure of it. Just release them."

There was a hesitation. "Fine." The leader nodded again and two men came to their aid, removing their bindings.

Lucia and Sabine clung to each other as they crossed to Benedict. As they made it to his side, relief coursed through her. Just being out of their reach gave her hope.

Suddenly, Nicholas threw a violet sigil back in Benedict's face—stunning him. Benedict stumbled back, inadvertently releasing him. In response, Nicholas grabbed Sabine and hauled her against him, an incendiary spell in his hand.

"Or I can pay you triple and you can kill all three of them," Nicholas wagered.

"You bastard!" Sabine snapped, driving her elbow into his gut. His incendiary spell slipped from his hand, catching the edge of her gown. She frantically patted it out.

"You decide! In the meantime, I think I'll pay the Turners a visit—give them my condolences." With that, Nicholas stole from the courtyard solarium and out into the night.

"Sabine go!" Benedict yelled. "We've got this handled, you go get Nicholas!"

Sabine grinned wickedly, eager for revenge. "I'll make him rue the day."

Sabine took off after Nicholas, Lucia and Benedict holding the line. The Brotherhood hesitated, watching them with uncertainty.

"Choose wisely," Benedict warned. "You're playing with your lives here."

The Brotherhood members all glanced at each other, all of them clearly wanting different things.

Several cast spells and they engaged in battle. Benedict threw power spells and incendiary spells, pushing Lucia behind him. She saw a blade strapped to his side and took it. Her magic was still blocked and all she had was her hands. She felt helpless.

One warlock attempted to rush Benedict, but Lucia stepped out and slashed with the blade. She sliced along his forearm, and he hissed. Benedict caught him with a cleaving spell, and a cross opened on the man's chest before he dropped.

The fight continued, Benedict protecting Lucia while she begged her magic to return.

All the while, Benedict was quickly twisting his fingers—casting. He pocketed these spells as he tossed out others. He casted illusion and then under it, Lucia noted several incendiary spells, a summoning circle, a demonic warding, and longevity. He blasted the Brotherhood with another cerulean sigil. Finally, he tied all the hidden spells together, and threw it out at the Brotherhood.

Cerulean flames erupted in a circle, encompassing all the remaining members, the fire burning white-hot. The inferno was ten feet tall, reaching for the broken glass ceiling. Lucia couldn't be sure, but she thought the circle was slowly closing in.

Benedict grabbed Lucia by the hand and tugged her out. They began to run together, out of the courtyard, down the halls.

They dashed across the front drive where several horses were tied. Two ropes hung empty, evidence of Nicholas's and Sabine's departure. They were probably miles ahead, and they had no hope of catching up in time to help Sabine. Benedict untied every horse and urged them away—they all took off. On the far side of the drive were two carriages, Nicholas's and a plain black one. Furiously, Benedict released the horses attached to Nicholas's carriage and then set several incendiary spells to it.

The once silvery carriage erupted in blue flame, tongues of it licking up the sides, eating and destroying every inch in its path. The wheels crumpled and the body came smashing down.

"Fucker," he spit.

Benedict grinned, feral, and then hoisted Lucia into the black carriage, climbing in after her. He closed the door and then he was casting guidance sigils on the two horses. They immediately took off down the snowy road. As they did, she felt the block on her magic dissolve.

Benedict collapsed against the bench then filled her in on what he'd learned in his absence. That her father was really his Enabler—his Jacob Marley—and that he'd been trying to protect them. He'd been the one who'd implored him to save her. He told her he broke into Nicholas's office and found all the evidence that solidified his guilt—the contract, the finances, the ledger.

She'd never felt a betrayal cut her so deep.

As the carriage negotiated over the countryside terrain, Lucia hoped Sabine was okay, and she hoped they made the right call by taking a carriage.

Benedict dropped to his knees before Lucia, clasping her hands.

"I was so scared," he admitted. Tears brimmed in his eyes. "It was almost the exact same as last time. Only this time I had no time—I wasn't running only to be too late. I'd arrived and I nearly had to witness it all. It nearly broke me, and I knew I would do anything to save you this time." He cupped her cheek. "I cannot live without you. I cannot breathe without you. You are my soul, my very essence."

Without waiting for her response, he pushed her against the bench and kissed her. It was deep, desperate, and wild. It was teeth and tongues and hands and nails. She moaned beneath his glorious assault, reaching and clawing for his clothes.

"I need you. I need you," he whispered like a chant.

"You have me. Take me."

With those words, Benedict tore the once beautiful velvet dress right down the center. The ruined and already torn dress parted like wet paper, exposing her breasts. Benedict's hands and mouth went to them, his tongue flicking against her hardened peaks. Her desire had her aching between her legs, growing wet and wanting. She arched into him, moaning as her hands stole across him, ripping the buttons from their stitching. The metal plinks of them sounded on the carriage floor as she ravaged him, shoving his coat and shirt from his shoulders.

"Love," he mouthed across her chest. "I can't wait, I need you."

With her hands in his hair, her mouth at his ear, she nipped his lobe. "Then fuck me."

Shock jolted through Benedict's body before he put his hands on her waist and spun her around, facing the bench. He discarded the rest of her bodice, leaving her utterly exposed. Hiking up her skirts, his hand found the slit of her gown, palm sliding against her knee, her inner thigh. His finger slipped to the tiny undergarments she was wearing and pulled them down, then, he pushed the skirt up over her bare bottom.

Two of his fingers slipped between her legs, pumping in and out of her wetness, sliding her arousal down her legs. She trembled as he curled them in a come-hither motion, her eyes rolling back in her head as she rocked against his working fingers.

"So wet," he purred.

She heard the sound of fabric sliding and suddenly she felt the head of his cock pressing into her drenched core. She was practically dripping for him already. Without any warning, he removed his fingers and pushed into her. She felt it sing through her blood. Arching with a wanton moan, feeling him sink to the hilt deep within her center, she was in bliss.

He pumped in and out of her harshly, the need between them pulled so taut from her near death. They needed to solidify the bond between them, the lovemaking so primal and claiming. It was as if by fucking so desperately he could dissolve the trauma of the night.

The carriage was filled with the sound of their flesh meeting, the slick sound of his cock thrusting into her. It was dim but moonlight caught them, limning them in sensual shadows. She could smell the musk of his perspiration, the heady scent of bergamot and sandalwood, flowing over the slight notes of blood and magic.

His hands were on her hips, guiding his pounding, drawing her to him. He deepened his pumping and she arched deeper. He leaned down over her and kissed down her spine, mouth ghosting and pressing every knob and notch.

An orgasm began coiling through her and her moans turned into mewls. Benedict's movements began to grow wild and she knew he was going to lose control soon. One of his hands slipped between her legs and played with her clit, circling it firmly. Her legs began to shake and that climax started hurtling towards her. She trembled, her toes curled, her channel clenched.

"Oh fuck, Benedict. I'm almost there."

He toyed with that bundle of nerves like a master violinist played his strings. She bit her lip as Benedict's mouth found the juncture of her shoulder, teeth sinking in as his pleasure ratcheted up. Suddenly, her orgasm tore through her and she keened a moan as his pleasure roared through him. His cock throbbed within her, pulsing his spend inside her. She rode the waves of her bliss as he slowed his thrusts, submitting to their finishing.

Together they collapsed against the bench, sliding to the floor. Benedict was still buried within her, his arms wrapping around her waist. With his mouth on her neck, he kissed her there and then nuzzled into her thick black hair.

"Citrus and clove," he murmured. "It's divine."

She smiled and stretched, feeling quite a lovely soreness between her legs. The rocking of the carriage had his still sheathed length stimulating her into wanting more. She shimmied and began to feel him grow hard in her again. The Staying certainly had its benefits.

Moments later they went for another round on the floor of the carriage, Lucia on top this time. She rode him with the motions of the road, her breasts bouncing in Benedict's palms. He flicked her nipples as she ground down onto him, the friction hitting her clit just right. It all sent her soaring into another climax where Benedict quickly followed her over the edge.

She laid atop him, soaking in their sex and sweat, absorbing all the desire and love swirling between them. Leaning down, she kissed him, touching his tongue with hers, letting it evolve into a languorous dance.

Eventually, Benedict pulled on his ruined shirtsleeves and handed her his coat—seeing as the top half of her dress was utterly ruined. The two of them leaned against each other, exhaustion claiming them as they cantered on the ride home.

Idly, she wondered if Sabine had caught up to Nicholas yet, and if she had made his ass sorry it was ever born.

DECEMBER 22, 1866

Partway through the journey a thump sounded on the carriage door. Lucia jumped and immediately formed a defensive spell.

"It's me," Sabine's voice came through the carriage walls. "Slow down and let me in—I'm fucking freezing. And I hope you're both fully dressed in there."

Lucia's face flushed hot as Benedict scrubbed a hand through his hair. He undid the sigils of guidance and the horses slowed. When they stopped, the door swung open and they were greeted to Sabine's wind-blown visage.

"Fucking angels, it smells like debauchery in here. But fuck it, it's warm." She climbed in. "Benedict, care to actually drive this carriage? Your horses look utterly lost. We're not far from your townhouse, if that's any consolation."

Benedict sighed, but climbed out. The carriage shifted as he climbed up onto the driver's bench. They began moving.

Sabine shut the door and then sat opposite Lucia, crossing her legs with a smirk.

"What?" Lucia demanded.

"Your cleavage looks lovely."

Lucia looked down and realized that the one button she hadn't shredded in her lustful haze had finally let go and the curves of her breasts were fully exposed, the coat hardly covering her nipples. Quickly, she wrapped the coat around herself and Sabine laughed.

"Here," Sabine said, plucking out a pearl hairpin that had miraculously survived her chase, and pushed it through the hole of Lucia's borrowed coat. It managed to hold it closed. For an extra measure she charmed it with a locking sigil.

Lucia flushed and tucked her sex-tousled hair behind her ears.

"The motherfucker got away," Sabine said bitterly.

"Nicholas?"

"Yes, like I said—the motherfucker."

"What happened?"

Sabine sighed and leaned back, tugging on her hair. "I chased him for a good two hours, casting back and forth, but he got me with an illusion spell—he's always been stupid good at those—and when I finally broke out of it, he was gone. No hoof prints in the snow, no sound in the distance, nothing. It was like he vanished."

Lucia sat back and processed this. After a moment she asked. "Are you okay?"

"I'm fine. He didn't actually get any hits on me."

"No, are you *okay*?"

Sabine stiffened and then shrugged. She twisted her lips and her chin trembled. "I just feel so stupid. I thought I knew him…that we had a connection. But now I come to learn all this…" She inhaled and tears lined her eyes. "I feel so betrayed."

Lucia touched her hand and Sabine took it, looking away shamefully. "We'd even slept together. I thought it was love, I thought we were finally going to make it work. Now I just feel used and dirty."

"Don't," Lucia whispered. "You are not dirty. Or damaged or fallen or any other adjectives that are dancing around in your mind. He tricked *you*. He manipulated *you*. The fault is on him."

Sabine nodded, her dark eyes swimming. "I'm so angry."

"I am too."

"I want to kill him."

"He would deserve it."

Sabine let out a choked laugh, but finally smiled.

They came to an abrupt halt with the sound of Benedict's surprised yell.

Lucia and Sabine shared one single horrified look before both bolting from the carriage. There, they bore witness to Azenor dropping Benedict into a snowbank, her Achilles tendon bleeding as she squawked in pain and fury. Benedict tumbled down the bank, a cerulean spell in his palm. Sabine immediately blasted off several incendiary spells as Lucia wrought protections around them, tying them into a shield.

They were in a park, pathways cleared of snow where mounds bordered either side in a mockery of mountains. Lampposts dotted the way, red ribbons hanging from them. Shadows stretched with the trees that surrounded them, park grounds extending around them with an expanse of untouched snow.

The three of them prepared a battle against Azenor, taking a pummeling. One of her runes broke through Lucia's guard and knocked her flying onto the slick pathway. Her hands were skinned, blood stinging, and the sight gave her a horrible idea.

Just then, they heard the bay of hellhounds. Beyond the perimeter of the park, hellhounds galloped towards them. Hollis followed them, ghosting across the snow.

Panic laced through Lucia as she dove into the carriage, digging around beneath the seats—they were no match for two demons and hellhounds, especially on their own with their limited magic. Under the seat she found a compartment and within which she found several vials of holy water and a thin silver blade. She uncorked one vial and dipped the blade in before dousing her injured hands.

Then, she did the unimaginable.

Hauling in a deep breath, she placed the knife tip to her breastbone and slowly carved. She winced and gritted her teeth through the pain, but she did not stop. After she finished, she took the blade to her palm, blood and holy water blending together. She could swear she heard her teeth cracking as she clenched, hissing through the pain. She repeated this on the other hand.

Once finished, she pocketed the blade and remaining vials before stepping out of the carriage and began to cast.

Benedict was exchanging casts with Azenor, the demon diving at him on unholy white wings. She tossed him up and he attacked her wing, damaging it to the point she had to throw him. He rolled down another snowbank. Sabine was frantically summoning sigils of protection and deflection as the hounds' pounding footsteps and hellish howls filled the night. Her dark red hair was a snarl about her face, dark-golden skin flushed with fear and cold.

Their time was ticking. The hounds were the tipping of the scales. They could not fight two demons and the beasts without irrevocable loss.

The squall of energy Lucia summoned was immense and it took her breath away. She felt a rush of adrenaline as the spell that took form was not solely the viridian of her magic, but divine white and chthonic black. As she wove, blood began to mix through the spell, sigils and runes forming in the air.

"*Lucia,*" Benedict gasped, eyes wide.

She had been taught how to combine like spells into one larger spell, but one inherent ability she possessed was utilizing infernal and seraphic runes. It was a rare ability and frequently dangerous, as some warlocks played with arts they were not supposed to. It was her best kept secret. No one knew about it except her father who had sworn her to secrecy. She hadn't told a soul, not even Benedict—until now.

Benedict grappled with Azenor, swatting away her claws and shrieking face.

She was nearing the end of her casting when the hellhounds arrived. They beat upon the protections Sabine had erected, red sparks shooting as they damaged her magic—though, they'd hold for a while yet. A few moments later Hollis arrived, hooded with his cosmic visage, driving his beasts harder at Sabine. Azenor was increasing the wildness of her attacks on Benedict, and was commencing with an aerial assault that had her arrowing, spearing him into the snow. Hollis turned his eerie attentions toward Lucia, gliding across the ground.

"*STOP*," Lucia shouted as she held an orb of undulating magic. Striations of crimson and viridian writhed within the globe of black and white. As she spoke, the magic in her palms flared.

On her right she had carved the seraphic rune for binding. On her left was the infernal rune for the very same command. Then, upon her chest was the warlock sigil for binding, as well as command, and oath. Together, with this amalgamation of magic she could force the demons to submit to her.

Hollis hissed but stopped. Azenor's claws were wrapped around Benedict's throat, frozen with Lucia's shout.

"Let him go," Lucia demanded.

Azenor sneered. "I cannot, little warlock, I am bound to take him as the curse dictates."

"Then I want to negotiate."

"No," Hollis intoned.

Fury propelled her. She stepped forward. "I command you both to negotiate with me."

Azenor stiffened. "I must take him to his time and let the curse play out. It's what it wants. If I defy it, I begin to die."

The Demons of Cronus and Christmas were sometimes coined Ghosts of Christmas, as they were not active outside of the eve. But as proven by Azenor and Hollis, they were living. And as evidenced by Calanthe, they could certainly die.

"You can take the caster."

"Not until the dawn of the curse's commencement."

Lucia deliberated, shaping her will. "I command you to kill—"

"Do not waste your breath, warlock. The same curse prevents the Demons of Cronus and Christmas from attacking one another."

"I could make you hold still while we kill you," she challenged.

"You could try," Azenor offered, a wicked glint of delight in her eyes.

Lucia imagined it was a trick. Perhaps if they attacked, the binding would break and the demons would be free to wreak havoc on them. Perhaps she wouldn't be able to reinstate it. Perhaps nothing would happen. Regardless, Lucia wasn't willing to risk their lives on it.

Lucia's will on the magic was crumbling. It was an unexercised power and she didn't have the strength to hold it so long and so tight. She had never attempted this feat, let alone with it over two demons at once.

"Then hold him," Lucia spit. While she could force them to act against their wishes, she could not overpower a curse. "Hold him here in this time until the night of Christmas Eve, just before the morning of Christmas Day. Keep him unharmed and in the city until then and we will bring you the caster for dawn."

Azenor contemplated, fiery eyes eager, greedy, ravenous. "It is a deal."

"Swear it."

Ire flashed in Azenor's flaming eyes.

"Both of you; swear it."

They both bit out the oaths that didn't want to slip past their lips.

Slowly, Lucia crossed the space between them, her flimsy protections in place, coming before Benedict. He stared at her with awestruck jade eyes, his mouth slack, Azenor's hand at his throat, her blazing eyes on her. Balancing the power of runes and sigils in one hand, she swiped some of her blood and then with it on her index finger, painted a tracking spell on Benedict's forehead. It would last seven days and seven nights—an amount of time that she prayed would be a surplus. Faintly, it glowed viridian before fading away, the magic burrowing into him.

Benedict stared at her, light green eyes piercing in the night. He was staring at her as if he wanted to drown in her. As if he'd never seen anyone quite so clever. She met his eyes, letting a trickle of warmth into them.

Then she turned, and that warmth faded into ice and a mask of apathy.

Boldly, with fear and determination boiling in her blood, she met Azenor's brimstone eyes. "Anywhere you take him now, I will know. So do not try to hide."

Azenor's teeth pulled back over her lips. "Resourceful little wretch, aren't you?"

Lucia copied the look. "Count your fucking days."

Azenor hissed but began dragging Benedict away, her fiancé gazing at her desperately.

"I love you," he said, all the faith in the world suffusing his voice.

"I love you, too. I'll come for you," she swore. "I promise."

The words still lingered on her tongue when Azenor took to the skies, taking Lucia's heart with her.

STAVE SIX

DECEMBER 22, 1866

Hollis called off the hounds when Lucia commanded him. When he too disappeared, Lucia held her breath and the spell until she was sure he was well and truly gone. She finally let it go, and when she did, she deflated, falling to the ground. Sabine caught her and helped her back into the carriage.

"Let's get back and we'll discuss things further. After a rest," Sabine said, casting guidance sigils on the horses.

They were moving and grief struck Lucia raw. She could feel the tether of Benedict's location, but even so, she felt intense regret at letting the demons take him—even with the precautions she'd stated.

"We should start looking for Nicholas immediately."

"No," Sabine said firmly. "We are not making rash decisions when Benedict's life is on the line. We rest, wash, eat, and then figure out what the fuck to do moving forward."

"We need to find out where he is—"

"Yes, but not when your mind is addled and you're acting impulsively. Trust me, darling. I want Nicholas found just as much as you do—more so to give him a piece of my mind, and a well-placed kick, but that's beside the point." Sabine grasped Lucia's hands and stared intently in her eyes. Sabine's were so dark. So pretty. "We do this with the utmost preparedness and we can put this whole demonic business behind us."

"And the Brotherhood?"

Sabine swore under her breath. "A problem for another day. Though, I think we know someone with connections that can hold them off, even with Nicholas's bribery."

"Who?"

Sabine looked at her sideways. "Your father."

Lucia shouldn't have been surprised, but a flash of it went through her. Of course, her father had dealings and connections with the Brotherhood. It was a welcome relief that he was associated with them, rather than behind her murder and Benedict's cursing, but she still didn't like it.

They trundled to a stop outside of Benedict's townhouse—*her* townhouse—and hustled their way inside. Without a butler, the house was chilled with a lack of heat, the cold seeping into her bones. With no one to greet them, the house felt too big and empty. Locking the door behind them, Lucia and Sabine quickly washed up and met up in the kitchen to scavenge for food. They found some bread and hard cheese, nibbling on both when Lucia found a bar of chocolate and Sabine gathered some jam and biscuits. Together, both with dripping hair, they went to the drawing room and closed themselves in it, dragging blankets and pillows in front of the hearth—creating a nest.

Sabine lit the fire with an incendiary spell, the fire blazing red. She pulled the white nightgown over her knees and hugged them, toes buried beneath a blanket. She stared into the flames and Lucia saw the pain in her eyes, the ache she couldn't fix.

Lucia braided her long black locks, the ends of her hair creating splotches on Benedict's borrowed shirt. She could feel the distance between her and him, pulling taut as he grew further every second. They were traveling and Lucia had a pretty keen idea as to where they were going.

The abandoned Edwards estate.

Finishing the braid, Lucia popped a square of chocolate into her mouth and then huddled closer to Sabine.

"I'm glad I have you," Lucia whispered, gazing into the flames. "I don't know where I'd be without you."

"Sorely living a much-dulled life, I'm sure," she teased then softened. Sabine tipped her head to rest against Lucia's. "I am glad for you, too."

"Did you ever think this is where we'd end up when we took that terrible anatomy course?"

Lucia and Sabine had met at eighteen after registering for a six-week anatomy and physiology course. Lucia had signed up for biology purposes, to see the structure of the body and how it might be afflicted by the immortal diseases. Sabine had taken it to better understand the human form and to have a deeper understanding on the moving parts to better portray figures in her art. They'd sat next to each other and both had the sinking realization that the teacher was woefully inept and they would be learning very little from the class. Regardless, they had stuck it out, if only to bond together and point out when something was egregiously wrong with the material.

Sabine groaned. "Don't remind me. The fact I had to inform the instructor that the mannequin was disproportional and that unless the first sketch was afflicted with a condition, all the organs were drawn on the wrong side of the body."

"Don't forget the female diagram that was missing half of its reproductive tract."

"I despair to think of the budding physicians who took that course."

"I'm sure they're practicing and charging top dollar to unassuming board members."

"Lucia!" Sabine chastised.

The two of them dissolved in fits of giggles, Lucia shocked that she'd managed to take her mind off Benedict—albeit as temporary as it was. Her heart sank and she cuddled into Sabine more for comfort. Her dearest friend, reading her mood, wrapped her up.

"Did you want to talk about how you can use infernal and seraphic runes?"

Lucia shook her head.

"Okay."

Together, the two of them huddled in the nest of blankets before the fire, slipping into sleep and preparing to seize the next day, hunting down Nicholas and rescuing her fiancé. Her last conscious thought with her head pillowed on Sabine's shoulder was a sharp blade of a thing.

I can't wait to see the chains of Nicholas's sins drag him to Hell.

DECEMBER 22, 1866

Benedict was bound to an old chair in the courtyard of his family's crumbling estate. His wrists were raw from him trying to work the ropes loose, the friction stinging his flesh.

He'd let it fall into disrepair after his parents alienated themselves from his life with their heinous acts of soul selling, murder, and vice. The estate held only stained memories of all the worst kinds now.

In front of him prowled hellhounds, Hollis sitting cross-legged on the stone fountain, robes draping, Azenor lounging in a window sill, the flesh on her red rune-covered leg exposed by a thigh slit. It seemed fundamentally wrong for demons and hounds to exist in the daylight, but here they did. Faint winter sun gilded Azenor's feathered wings, while Hollis was basking in it like a cat, cosmic face turned towards the burning star.

"I understand the need for the muting spells, but why the bindings?" Benedict asked.

Azenor raised a black brow. "Because you have arms and legs and access to holy water and silver? I am not stupid, boy."

"I do have to relieve myself though."

Azenor stared him down. "That does not sound like a problem that concerns me."

Benedict gritted his teeth. "And food?"

"You won't starve being deprived of sustenance for a single day. I have seen tortures in Hell, and it takes much longer than that to kill you."

"Water then."

Azenor didn't respond. Benedict sighed and tipped his head back, staring at the watery sun. He didn't desperately need to relieve himself, but he would soon. On top of being uncomfortable, he was cold, the bitter chill of winter seeping into his bones. The solstice had taken place last night, with it bringing them ever closer to Yuletide and gloom.

They were silent a long while, Benedict growing anxious and bored. Finally, a thought struck him.

"It's unlikely that we'll be completing the curse the traditional way, so would you be interested in informing me who the players in my story were?"

Azenor stared at him drolly then glanced at Hollis. He did not respond.

"I suppose it would do no harm at this point." She was still lounging. "Who do you still wonder about? Your Lucia is the Lost, her father your Marley—the Enabler. Mister Christopher Taylor was to be your Discarded, that Sabine was the Believer, Klaus your Undervalued. Who else? Oh, your Antithesis—Nicholas."

Benedict gritted his teeth. Of course, all the players made sense. It was horrible, the realization that Clarence was right.

Oftentimes our caster is one of our characters.

His fucking Antithesis. Nicholas was supposed to be his foil. His Fezziwig to Scrooge's—well, Scrooge. He was supposed to be good. Everything Benedict wasn't.

But he was greedy, wretched, corrupt. Seeking money over friendship, suffering over investments. Did that make Benedict the good one? The true positive parallel to Nicholas's inhumane actions and depravity? Had the Nightmare Curse's terms been egregiously mistaken?

Benedict hung his head and despaired. He may have saved Lucia, but he lost Nicholas—again—and that heartbreak, while not as devastating as his fiancée's, was still acute. Knowing his value was deemed so far less than money in Nicholas's eyes hurt.

Watching the sun move across the horizon, Benedict was painfully aware of the passage of time and the proverbial guillotine that hung over his head. He prayed whatever Lucia was doing would be enough to save them all.

DECEMBER 22, 1866

Lucia and Sabine were on a mission. They'd begun their day, rousing from the nest of blankets before the dying embers of the fire. Energized, Lucia had gathered a small assortment of ingredients from the kitchen and spread them out on a tray at the hearth. Immediately, Sabine still rubbing her eyes, Lucia demanded they begin the locating of Nicholas and his impending downfall.

"We need to find out where he's hiding, and then we have to gather all the evidence we have of his crimes and present them to the constabulary if this ends less than favorably."

"Less than favorably?" Sabine asked, sleepy eyes critical.

"If we have to kill him ourselves."

Their brainstorming brought them to plead their case to Nicholas's butler who had surprisingly acquiesced to their requests and brought over all pertinent information from the Whitehill Traitor's study. Some of his investments were well hidden within shell corporations, but he had the paperwork that damned him. They discovered more than one contract for Lucia's assassination, as well as a spell book containing marked pages for the Nightmare Curse. Folded within the page detailing the Scrooge Curse was an ingredient list attached to a "to get" list to perform the curse.

Lucia's heart ached for Benedict. She had cared for Nicholas, too. But he was Benedict's closest confidant and mentor. This sort of deceit would have lasting consequences upon his trust and psyche.

Reaching out to her father rather reluctantly proved successful, and Luther Turner was practically tripping over himself to prove himself to her. He arrived at the townhouse upon her request with some questionable looking men. The two men flanking him were both scarred, with eyes battle heavy, and hard faces.

Sabine was penning a letter to the constabulary about Nicholas's intentions—with the spell book as evidence—and Benedict's recounting of information from 1873. They were both hoping Luther would provide a written statement about the Brotherhood's involvement and threats on her from the board. Lucia hoped it would be enough to completely clear their names should the need arise.

"Do you have any ideas of where Nicholas might be?" Luther asked after Lucia explained everything—Nicholas's betrayal, the truth about the curse and how Nicholas had manipulated it all. Luther had balked upon hearing about his recent death in Benedict's timeline, but composed himself swiftly.

"I have a list." Lucia handed over a sheet of paper with locations listed, likeliest at the top. "But if he flees the country, I have no way to determine his whereabouts."

"Don't worry, wherever he is, he's still on this side. The Watch hasn't reported any Travel."

The Watch acted as a guardian over the five portals that allowed entry and exit between London and Vonor. All Travel must be reported and documented and evidently, Luther had ins within that reporting. Wherever Nicholas was, it was still within this plane, and there was only so far he went until he met the crumbling fringes of this world. Of course, their world was still expanding outward with every new influx and charge of magic, but regardless, there was still an end.

"That is good news, I suppose." Lucia still felt overwhelmed.

"Lucia," Luther said firmly, clamping his hands on her upper arms to reassure. "We will find him and make sure Benedict returns safely."

Lucia nodded, tears choking her throat.

Luther turned and handed off the list to the two unsettling men. "Search these places and keep me informed if you find anything."

They departed without a word, leaving Lucia and Luther standing in the entryway. She fidgeted awkwardly.

"Do you want some tea?"

"No, I wouldn't want to impose."

Lucia knew how badly Luther wanted to say yes, but he knew he shouldn't because she was just being polite and he wanted her offer to be a genuine one.

"I do have a favor to ask of you, though."

Luther perked. "Anything."

And so, she asked him for the letter and he immediately accepted. She watched him pen it and then hand it off to Sabine for her perusal.

Lucia stared at the letter that would clear Benedict's name of any wrongdoing should Nicholas have any secret safeguards. It was odd how things had seemingly changed thus.

Once they had a clock counting down on her head, and now there was one on his.

DECEMBER 23, 1866

It was evening and Benedict was cold and exhausted. He couldn't get a comfortable sleep bound to the chair and his stomach was gnawing on itself. The only consolation was that water had been provided and Hollis had finally allowed him reprieve from the excruciating pain from his bladder.

Azenor had disappeared a few hours before, Hollis acting like the proverbial guard dog with his hounds, prowling and watching. He stared at Benedict with sightless eyes.

There was something about the third demon that unsettled Benedict deeply. Perhaps it was his aura. Or perhaps it was what he represented—the unknown. He kept an eerie silence, and Benedict didn't know how to broach it. He didn't know if he wanted to.

"My hounds tell me your women have been busy," Hollis said in his abyssal voice. "Recruiting strange men to hunt down your Antithesis, imploring your law force to investigate, pleading your innocence. It's admirable, their dedication. Tell me, how did you capture such devotion?"

"I would do the same for them."

Hollis tilted his head to the side curiously. "Why?"

"They're dear to me. In different ways."

"Interesting."

They lapsed into silence and hours passed, eventually, Azenor returned—and not alone. Benedict's stomach sank when he saw who arrived, looking disturbingly the same as ever. He couldn't contain his shock as his jaw dropped.

"How is this possible?"

"We're the Demons of Cronus and Christmas, boy," Hollis intoned, a hint of humor to his cryptic presence. "Are you so surprised?"

DECEMBER 24, 1866

It was just after the witching hour—three bells after midnight—when the two suspicious men returned with Nicholas in tow.

The fair-haired traitor was bloodied, cradling an injured arm, and sporting a black eye. Lucia couldn't find any sympathy in her heart. When the men threw Nicholas into a kitchen chair, he grunted, but was smart enough not to get up. As he was sat, one of the men twisted a sigil of lemon-yellow magic and shoved it at Nicholas. The muting spell rocked him back and he stiffened.

"Ow," he said dryly.

"Suck it up," the caster said, then bound his wrists to the arms with more yellow magic.

Nicholas twisted his mouth in a mockery of a cruel smile, a split in his lip only adding to the ridicule.

How had they been so wrong about him? He'd once been so soft, those gray eyes like cashmere, his smile always gentle. Now, he was carved of granite and cruelty.

Nicholas swiveled his attention to Lucia, then Sabine. "So."

Lucia crossed her arms over her chest and stared him down. She was in shirtsleeves and pants, as was Sabine, the two of them having decided to be dressed and ready should need warrant it.

"So, should we spare the villainous monologue or would you like to tell us what motivated you to have me killed, and Benedict blamed for it? Then to add insult to injury, curse him seven years later?"

"It wasn't seven years later."

"What?"

"It wasn't seven years later," he repeated.

"I assure you; Benedict gave us the date."

Nicholas inclined his chin, dried blood trailing down it. "The eighth time is when it finally worked."

The reality struck Lucia like a brick. Her eyes flew wide. "You've been trying to curse Benedict for eight years? Why?"

"He was getting too close to the cure." He shrugged.

"Why the curse then? Why not just outright kill him or have someone do it like you'd done to me?"

"For the social black mark. Anything Benedict touched would have been deemed corrupted by the masses. No one would want any part of his research if he were such a villain."

"And you were so sure the curse would take him? Out of all the terrible people that exist, you think he was worthy of the curse?"

"The prerequisites are quite specific. I thought I'd take the chance. I made sure I stayed close to him because I saw the people that could be his players, and I knew if anyone would find out a cure it would be him. Until you."

"Until me."

His eyes grew heated. "I thought maybe I could convince you to keep it a secret, but you'd already reported your findings. Then by that point I realized too late you'd never bend to me, you were too…Samaritan. Too good. You'd never see things my way. You'd never see me like I see you."

"And how is that?" she bit out.

"Come now Lucia, don't be stupid. You're smarter than this."

"Luce…" Sabine warned, a note of realization in her voice. And with it anger.

Nicholas laughed darkly, throwing back his head. "I thought myself in love with you, you foolish dolt." He scoffed. "But you never once looked from Good Ol' Benny Boy." He shrugged. "So, I realized you were a problem—you had to go. You'd never be mine, and you were too soft-hearted to keep the cure to the worthy. You want so desperately for anyone to access such scientific discovery. As if it is their right."

"It *is* their right!" she fired back hotly, striding forward. Everything in her wanted to slap him. "How dare you imply otherwise?"

"I do more than imply, I announce."

"Why are you being like this?" Sabine hissed. Lucia could see the broken pieces of her being held together by sheer force of will.

Nicholas rolled his head towards her mockingly, endearingly. "Because you two furious ladies want to see my demise, and I have nothing to lose. It's cathartic to have it all out now."

"You are a despicable human being," Sabine growled.

"Oh darling, you're only put out because you found out you were second best—again."

A twinge filtered through Lucia at the allusion to Sabine's and Benedict's past—however amicably it ended.

Ire bloomed in Sabine's eyes and in a rage, she lunged at him, cuffing him by the throat, wrapping her long slender fingers around it. In her other hand she grew an incendiary spell. She glowed red with molten rage, hand held aloft behind her.

"I could incinerate you right here, right now, and there's not a single thing you could do about it."

"True," Nicholas conceded. "But you need me to get precious Benny Boy back. Don't you?"

Sabine was still as stone, her wrath frozen as if with Medusa's stare, but Lucia flinched.

"Sab…" Lucia murmured warningly.

"I thought as much," he said, leaning back—relaxing. He inclined his chin, exposing his throat more beneath Sabine's iron grip. "Go on, kitten, sheath those claws."

True fury erupted on her face and Sabine's knuckles whitened. She dissipated the spell and then, once the fire guttered out, she took that hand and slammed her fist into Nicholas's face.

New blood splattered and Nicholas yelped.

"Fuck!"

"I hope you enjoy the sunrise," Sabine growled, leaning in, digging her nails into his neck. "Because it's the last one you're ever going to see."

"Is that a promise?" he taunted.

"I swear it."

Cold shot through Lucia. Warlocks didn't swear promises for good reason. This didn't feel right.

He grinned devilishly. "Good."

And then suddenly his hands were unbound and the caster with the yellow magic disappeared out of thin air. The second warlock bore a violet silence sigil over his mouth, another purple sigil—binding—hovered over his chest. And there, glimmering like a fucking sugarplum, was an ornate spell for illusion.

Nicholas's specialty.

He'd tricked them.

"Oh fuck," Sabine cursed, covering her mouth and backing away. Then she whispered. "You bastard."

Because there, Lucia realized, between Nicholas's unbound hands was an oath sigil and connected to it was a thread of violet that met Sabine.

Oh fuck.

Sabine had just sworn an oath. It was inadvertently, but that mattered none. What mattered was that she had sworn that the sunrise of Christmas Eve was to be his last. Should the sun rise Christmas Day and Nicholas see it…

"If your threat isn't fulfilled, kitten, you forfeit your life."

Sabine—a caster with unparalleled speed—formed a binding spell and threw the red magic at Nicholas. Then she punched him again for good measure.

All the while Lucia was unraveling Nicholas's spells on the silent warlock. When the last filament disappeared on the first sigil she spoke firmly while dismantling the binding spell.

"Where is the other warlock? Your accomplice?"

"Outside," he answered, anger coating his tone. "This little wretch tricked us with an illusion and then knocked out Rudolphus. Before I even realized what had happened, he was casting and acting as if we were hauling him in here."

Lucia cursed, tugging the threads of the spell. "Is Rudolphus still alive?"

"I think so."

The last of the spell vanished. "Go check. Once he's settled, contact my father. We can deal with Nicholas."

The scarred warlock slipped outside. Lucia returned her attention to Sabine and Nicholas.

"How long will it take us to get to the Edwards's Estate?" Lucia asked, sensing Benedict's location. "It's normally four or five hours."

Sabine pulled her attention from her ex-lover and crept to a window, parting the drapes. "With the roads in this condition? Optimistically—eight."

Eight hours.

Lucia did the math mentally. They could leave within two hours which put them at noon. Barring obstacles and accident, that left plenty of time until the dawn of Christmas Day.

"Let's go then."

It did not take eight hours.

Between the treacherous roads and Nicholas's treachery—casting illusions that sent them in the wrong direction, made false demons appear in their path, attempts of sabotaging the carriage, throwing himself at the door and half out of the vehicle—it was turning into twelve hours. The roads were a whiteout, the carriage wheels and horses struggling through it, even with Lucia and Sabine casting spells to clear the snow.

The sun was beginning to set and with it their energies. They had been expending so much magic on the journey, and it was only going to be more when they needed to cast for light as well.

The girls were taking turns, one supervising Nicholas, the other driving and clearing the blizzard. When it was time for Lucia to switch off, it came as no surprise that the traitor was unconscious during Sabine's supervision. The warlock was sporting a lump on his forehead while Sabine maintained the picture of innocence.

"He fell," Sabine lied.

"Hmm, it's probably for the best."

"It is, isn't it?"

When Sabine went out for her turn in the cold, Sabine watched Nicholas, ensuring she casted the magic muting spell at regular intervals. When he began to stir, she struck him.

Thirty minutes into her Nicholas monitoring shift, the carriage wobbled before listing to the side, and dropping abruptly.

"Fuck!" Sabine shouted outside.

When Lucia poked her head out into the dense white, she groaned seeing Sabine in the snow, kneeling before a broken axle.

"How bad is it?" Lucia called out.

Sabine swiped the dark red hair out of her face. "Beyond my skill set for a full fix. I can do a temporary repair, but there's no promise the spell won't break before we get there. If it does, I might not be able to catch the carriage in time again."

Lucia went over and studied the break beneath the carriage. She cringed at the shattered wood—they'd likely hit a rut and stressed it. This kind of damage was also beyond her. She didn't have an affinity for repairs that some warlocks did. Her skill sets lay within infernal and seraphic runes as well as the learned ability to link several like spells into one larger one.

Lucia looked over at their surroundings and noticed they were unsettlingly close to a bridge, and had the axle given out even a few yards later, they could've been careening off the edge. She felt her stomach roil while simultaneous relief coursed through her. Sabine's skill in speed was what saved them.

Lucia looked around and weighed all their risks, then looked at her timepiece. They didn't have time to spare.

"We'll have to take the horses."

"Are you mad?" Sabine asked, aghast. "Did you fail to notice that there are only two horses and three of us?"

"It did not escape my notice, no."

Sabine cocked a brow. "You want us to share? Without saddles?"

Lucia hesitated. She didn't know what to do. The timeline she'd bartered for was giving her anxiety, and with it, thought processes that reflected it. She was muddled, panicked, not thinking clearly.

"Our options are severely limited," she finally said.

"We could always drag him behind the horses."

"Sab!"

Sabine just looked at her, snowflakes catching her long lashes. "Let's try the repair on the carriage first and just slow down our speed. If it breaks, we'll be able to react in time and then we can revisit the horse situation and the dragging of Nicholas."

Lucia deliberated then nodded.

"Do it."

"We'll have to make more frequent stops to ensure it holds." She glanced at the blur of the sky. "It could be near midnight when we get there."

Anxiety struck through Lucia. "Then we better get on it."

Sabine set to work. Lucia returned to the carriage. Nicholas remained unconscious.

Lucia spelled him to blocked again—just to be safe.

DECEMBER 24, 1866

"You killed Lucia."

That had been the first thing Benedict had said when Azenor brought the betrayer forward.

Nicholas of the present was standing in the abandoned courtyard of the Edwards's Estate in the past. Azenor had evidently retrieved Nicholas from 1873, but for what purpose, he did not know. This entire situation was peculiar, indeed. Never had the curser been pulled to the past, but also never had anyone broken the spell.

What was unsettling though, was that Nicholas was not cured. He was still afflicted with the Wasting, cheeks gaunt, skeletal form, weak muscle tone. He was colorless, his eyes watery. Leaning on his owl head cane, and coughing into a handkerchief, he appeared *old*.

"You killed Lucia," Benedict repeated, anger flooding him. "And you framed me for it and then cursed me."

Nicholas looked around, confused. "Where are we?"

"The Edwards's Estate—1866."

"How?"

"After you so rudely cursed me, I broke out of the spell and went back to fix everything."

"*When* is it?"

"Depending on the hour…almost Christmas Eve or the actual eve."

"Ah, so Lucia is gone then."

"No, you fucking asshole. I saved her this time. She is alive and well."

"That's not possible."

"All the Demons of Cronus and Christmas would have agreed with you," Azenor answered. "But he does not lie." The winged demon strode up to Benedict. "But have you noticed? Nothing you've done here changes the future." She falsely pouted and tutted.

Despair clawed through Benedict. He'd cured Nicholas here, yet before him stood a sickened Nicholas. He turned to Azenor warily.

"What does this mean? For when it's all over?"

Azenor contemplated. "You've branched a new timeline. This one will continue on the predestined path you've now curated. The other—yours—will continue as it has been for the last seven years, with or without you."

Benedict's heart sank. "And Lucia?"

"She is dead in your true time, no?" When Benedict nodded, she continued. "Then if you live to see the dawn you'll return to your time and she will still be gone. If you don't, well you'll be dead and it won't matter."

"No. I'm staying here. I'm not going back."

Azenor cackled. "You think you have a choice, boy? The magic of the curse only lasts till dawn. Once it approaches, you'll be pulled back."

"No…" Benedict breathed despairingly. "No one has ever broken from the curse before. You can't know that for certain."

"It may have never happened, but I know this magic, and I know I'm right."

Benedict didn't want to go back to a life—a world—without Lucia in it. He didn't want to go back to that cell and spend another ninety-three years in misery and squalor. He'd rather die than return to that. He'd just gotten her back, just had a glimpse of her, a taste on his tongue…he couldn't let her go. He refused.

"Perhaps I can find a way to subvert that as I did the original curse."

"Not while I live," Azenor replied.

"Then perhaps you need to die."

Azenor slapped him and his head jerked to the side. He felt blood bloom in his mouth, the taste of copper spreading over his tongue. The pain developed delayed and then hit him in a rush. Slowly, he turned his face towards the demon, stared her down hard, and spat the blood at her bare feet.

"Careful, Lucia's oath might strike you down if you're not gentle enough."

Azenor growled, and Benedict bared his teeth in response.

"Why did you even bring me here?" Nicholas snapped.

"Because the curse you casted will end here, and one way or another we'll get a soul."

"And if they kill me?"

"Well, luckily Hell is my home and I'll devour your soul there."

"What makes you so certain I'd go to Hell?"

Azenor gazed at him dolefully. "You cannot be this dense Mister Whitehill. Murder—hired or by your own hand—and cursing and framing are all bad deeds, and they do indeed go punished." Azenor went over and patted his cheek. "The angels wouldn't want you anyway. They ask you not to be afraid, but when you are the unworthy soul in their presence you have every reason to think their celestial holiness would incinerate rather than cleanse you."

"That wasn't the deal!" Nicholas yelled.

"It's in the fine print, sick boy."

Nicholas fumed and Benedict found himself amused by the other warlock's outrage. All things considered it was the only thing he could find joy in. Nicholas continued his raging.

"We have him tied up," Nicholas stated, pointing to Benedict. "Why is he still alive?"

"Because we can't touch him. Not until the night of Christmas Eve before the dawn of Christmas Day. It was an oath."

"I swore no such oath," Nicholas sneered. "I can kill him and end all this."

"Alas, we did and we swore he would be unharmed, which would mean I would have to prevent you from touching him."

Benedict stared at Nicholas, penetrating him with all the hatred he could summon. How could he speak of his death so flippantly when they'd been friends for so long? It was a dagger to Benedict's heart and he felt all the love he held for Nicholas blacken and decay beneath it.

Nicholas swore and hobbled over to the fountain's edge with the help of his cane. When he sat, her glared at Benedict, too.

Eventually, Benedict tired of the staring match and ignored Nicholas. Tipping his head back—knowing he'd have the worst crick in his neck—he slipped off to sleep. When he did wake, he was correct in predicting a sore neck. He was stiff in the chair and roused with a groan, looking around bleary eyed, and cold. Hollis and Azenor were both nearby, conversing heatedly by the chill light of winter sun, light filtering through the broken panes of a window. Nicholas was on a wooden bench, curled up beneath a wool blanket. Benedict felt a surge of jealousy at his nemesis's blanket possession.

The whole of the day passed uncomfortably. Benedict stuck to the chair, shifting around with a countdown on his head. Nicholas pacing on his cane, muttering bitterly to himself. Azenor taunting the both of them. Hollis remaining stoic.

As the light began to fade outside Benedict's heartbeat sped up. His hope was dwindling. He didn't know where Lucia and Sabine were, but his life was quite literally in their hands. And those hands were the only things stopping those around him from ending his existence. He felt as if they were circling like hawks, waiting for their opening—and such an opening was coming soon.

"One of us will be dead by dawn," Nicholas started as the last vestiges of sunlight began to disappear. "I may as well ask this burning question."

"I doubt I'll answer it," Benedict returned.

Nicholas cocked a mocking smile. "I wouldn't be so certain."

Hesitation stilled Benedict. "All right, ask away."

"We met Lucia the same night, what did she see in you that she didn't see in me?"

"*What?*"

"She chose you before even considering me, despite all the more I could offer her."

Shock coursed through Benedict, his brows rising high. "Are you saying you fancied *my fiancée*?"

"The entire time you were with her, yes, I desired her. And I waited for her to realize you were a paltry man, and I could provide her with more luxury than she could imagine. She would never have to work again."

Benedict was stunned, Clarence's words coming back to haunt him again. How his brother was in love with his husband. How he cursed him for it. "Yet you had the Wasting. What could you have given her—ten years?" He was struggling to wrap his head around it all.

"She would have created a cure for me and we'd have kept it to ourselves."

"Yet you killed her."

"If I couldn't have her, then why should you? I knew what was best for her."

"You're delusional. Did you ever really know her at all?"

"I knew her enough. I wanted her. She was so perfect, so untouched—" Nicholas leaned in conspiratorially. "Did you even get a chance to fuck her before she died? I would've taken that sweet—"

Nicholas didn't get a chance to finish as Benedict finally broke free of his restraints and hurled a power sigil-enhanced punch straight into his face. Nicholas went stumbling back, clutching his face and groaning.

Benedict was relentless with his next blows, throwing spells at Nicholas that he couldn't dodge due to his diminished health. He let the magic course through him, a river of his anger and hatred for his once best friend and mentor. It rushed out of him in volleys of cerulean that beat down Nicholas till he was a pitiful mess.

Azenor and Hollis were stood still, caught by their oath. They had to let it happen.

Nicholas managed to twist a spell beneath Benedict's assault—illusion—and the violet magic struck Benedict.

Benedict froze, assaulted by images of Lucia's death replaying over and over. Drowned. Stabbed. Kicking and screaming. Thrashing beneath the water. Twisting in agony as the knife went in. Over and over, it looped, tormenting him. Terror grasped him, twisting him into panicked knots. His heart raced, his eyes flew wide, mouth parting.

Like a terrified rabbit he was paralyzed. The feelings, the visions, they were overwhelming. He felt his lungs burning as he struggling for breath.

Lucia drowning.

Lucia stabbed.

Lucia dying.

It replayed.

Until suddenly he remembered—this was an illusion. None of it was real.

Without seeing what he was doing, he wove a sigil to break Nicholas's illusion. Suddenly, the blue spell took form and he shoved it through the terrifying images. It shattered like a stone through a window, all the pieces raining down.

When he regained his true sight, Nicholas was nursing his wounds from Benedict's magical assault. He wasn't strong enough to endure it all and his breath was reed thin, blood dribbling down his chin. He leaned heavily on his cane, bracing against the fountain.

Furiously, Benedict began assembling spells.

"You ruined my life," he said, forming an incendiary sigil. "You killed my fiancée." A power spell. "You framed me." Destruction. "You took everything from me, cursed me, betrayed me—and for something as fucking stupid and selfish as *money*. And obsession." The three spells twisted into a monstrous creation. "And for it all, I will kill you."

"Ben—" Nicholas said, raising his hands in surrender. He was white as a ghost, blood speckling his face from the blows. "Please."

"Where was 'please' when Lucia begged for her life?" He hardened his stare. "Nothing will save you now."

And then he aimed the spell, and let it engulf Nicholas.

Nicholas screamed as the blue fire took him, consuming him. The power sigil made the flames from the incendiary spell more aggressive—larger, hotter—and the destruction one made sure it all ended him.

It took minutes for Nicholas to die.

Benedict watched over his karmic funeral pyre, the azure tearing into the warlock, turning him black, devouring his fine clothes, his fair hair, his pale eyes. None of it was spared beneath the flame's wrath.

When it was over and Nicholas stopped screaming and twitching, he looked over at Azenor and Hollis, both of them standing still.

"Is it over?" he asked them. "The caster is dead—you get his soul."

Azenor shook her head. "No. We did not reap the soul—you took it from us."

Horror threaded through Benedict.

"Now the soul we'll take is yours. At dawn this ends as Hollis drags your soul by the chains of its sins to Hell."

He'd fucked up.

He hadn't realized.

If he hadn't killed Nicholas, he would've had a chance to finish this without battling the demons. Now, the demons had to die for him to live.

"Count your moments, boy," Azenor said, sitting on the edge of the fountain with crossed legs. Red light shined on half her face, casting the other side in shadow. "This is it."

Benedict stood in silent horror, but inside he was readying for the battle of his life. It was nearly nightfall and it would all end here.

Just then, the double doors of the courtyard burst open and with it came all the blazing fury of Lucia and Sabine.

DECEMBER 24, 1866

"Here's your fucking curser," Lucia said as her viridian wreathed hand threw Nicholas through the doors, and down the steps.

Nicholas tumbled down the steps, bloodied, windblown, and wholly pale. He moaned in pain as his elbows and knees and head knocked against the stone. He sprawled on the ground as Lucia and Sabine stared imperiously from the top step.

All eyes were on them. Azenor and Hollis were on the edges, gazes—even non-visible ones—were trained on them, Azenor quirking her brow and twisting her smile into a grimace. Benedict stood near the fountain with a look of devastation on his features, and there at his feet was a blackened husk.

"Ah, but he is the wrong one," Azenor said stepping forward.

"What?" Lucia asked in disbelief. "No, this is Nicholas Whitehill."

"But not the Nicholas Whitehill who has cursed Benedict Edwards. He is from an alternate timeline."

"It's still the same fucking person."

"Is he?" Azenor's eyes slid to the still smoking body by Benedict. "Because I'm sure he'd beg to differ."

"We had a deal."

"But you brought the wrong caster. Technically, this Nicholas has done no wrong."

"He tried to have me killed! Twice!"

"But you live."

"That's not the point!"

Azenor shrugged. "Demons aren't honest beings. You should know this when making deals with them."

Fury raged through Lucia and boiled her blood. Her hands turned to claws at her sides as she began twisting fingers. She slowly descended the steps, eyes she knew were blazing with frost, stared down the demons.

"I used infernal and seraphic runes," she enunciated clearly. "And I will use them again. You really want to refuse this soul I bring you, and risk destruction? Oblivion?"

She continued crossing the threshold that held the tide of her violence. A silver blade slipped into her hand and she held it between her fingertips. Lucia approached, smelling the charred scent of flesh and hair. Her hand went to Benedict, eyes flickering to him heatedly while she caressed his shoulder, squeezing, before smoothing that hand over his chest and guiding him backward as she took the lead.

Nicholas was dragging himself across the flagstones, over to the side of the courtyard with demons.

"We can make this trade," Lucia offered. "And all this will be over between us."

Azenor shook her head. "That's not how the curse works."

"Then *make* it work."

"We are contained by the parameters of it. We cannot act out of our own will accordingly. You seem to think we have powers beyond the will of the universe."

"This seems an unorthodox situation, surely an exception could be made?"

"No."

The word struck Lucia in the chest. "No? *No?* So, Benedict must repent then to be free?"

"Yes, but your boy will not."

"Why do you say that?"

Azenor cocked her head and laughed. "Because he feels justified in his miserly hoarding of knowledge. Of keeping his research secret. Especially now that he's aware that its existence is the reason for your death, and his curse. He will have felt he made the correct decision, therefore the reason for the curse cannot be forgiven."

"So, this is it? Death?" Her eyes slid to Benedict who had depression roiling off him in waves.

Red light of the windowpanes cut across Azenor's face from the dying light, casting the other half in ebony shadow. She smiled at Lucia devilishly, the scarlet light making her teeth bloody, every one of them turned into a ruby.

"Death for you all," Azenor returned, lunging as night fell and the oath was null.

Lucia threw a blocking spell out and Azenor smashed into it. She yowled and then carved her arm, forming bloody runes in the air. The two of them entered into battle.

Nearby, Nicholas was trying to stand, but Sabine was on a rampage. She thundered down the steps on high leather boots, her fists turned to claws as she rapidly casted against her betrayer ex-lover.

Benedict was engaged in combat with Hollis, the demon attempting to summon the Hounds of Hell, but Benedict kept destroying them before they rose from the flagstones. Even so, Hollis kept those raising hands.

Lucia channeled shield spells so she could carve her runes. The shields held over Azenor's assault of infernal runes, while Lucia cut her flesh and painted seraphic runes. Her skin was stained red and angelic symbols began appearing before her eyes. For every rune she made, she had to cast a sigil to strengthen her shield. Each time the shield was weaker and uglier, like coats of paint on a wall. But she was building an army of her runes, and when she released them, it would be a slaughter.

Sabine screeched as she fought against Nicholas's sugarplum illusions. She used destruction sigils on every one, but each breaking of a vision was taking longer than the last. Sabine only had a moment to throw an incendiary or power spell at Nicholas before another illusion was consuming her. Through sheer force of will and magnified by her quick casting, she was holding her own—and perhaps the only one of them who could, considering the speed required.

"You are scum of the earth," Sabine snarled at Nicholas, dark eyes blazing. "After you said you loved me too, I learn you just wanted fuck someone else, and I was the closest thing."

An incendiary spell caught Nicholas's dirty sleeve.

"I hate you, you insufferable fuck," she continued. "You are poison to everything you touch. You've corrupted the affection of everyone around you."

Nicholas cocked his head, an epiphany lighting his eyes. "Is that what you think? Or is that your fear? Do you think *you* are the poison? That *you* are the rotten one?"

Another illusion shot into Sabine's face.

The three of them maneuvered about the space with their battle partners, sliding into garnet light and shadows, cracks of moonlight limning profiles and curves from broken panes. The sounds were shouts and insults, taunts and groans, the shuffle of feet, the crackle of magic, the susurrus of fabric, the keening howls of hounds, thuds and blows, cries and moans.

A hellhound tore through the stone floor, lunging at Benedict. He yelled in surprise and dropped with a power spell half-finished in his hand. The hound pinned him to the ground and he grappled with it, one hand against the beast's throat as its jaws snapped at Benedict's face. He screamed as smoke rose from his fingers, his hand burning. With the other hand, he completed the spell and then blasted the hellhound off of him.

The beast flew backwards and hit the stone wall wrong, neck snapping as it was crushed against its own body. Its flames extinguished; ember eyes gone dark.

The air was filled with the scents of blood and brimstone, sweat and smoke. Everything was painted red from the broken windows of scarlet stained glass. Lucia could taste copper in her mouth.

Behind her shield that was bubbling and cracking, the viridian magic looking venomous and sickly, Lucia had an arsenal of seraphic runes that she was organizing into an Elven Star. At each of the seven points were the elements: earth, air, water, fire, spirit, light, and magic.

There existed a spell with sigils of the seven elements that could potentially kill and grievously harm a demon. Lucia was casting the seraphic equivalent where such divinity would be a veritable explosion against a demon.

She threw another bandage over her shield and finally painted the lines connecting each of the runes together in her blood.

"What you do to that timeline no longer matters, what you do here changes nothing," Hollis taunted Benedict as a hellhound half emerged from the courtyard ground.

That must have been the trigger for Benedict because the rage that entered his eyes was unparalleled. With an amalgamation of spells, even more than Lucia could count, Benedict twisted them all into a knot. When he released them, Lucia caught sight of the devouring sigil. She watched as the spell crashed into the demon's chest and tore Hollis apart.

The spell ate at him, burrowing between his ribs and carving out his heart, his lungs, eviscerating him before it ripped through him. Blood and stars rained around them, the loose robes of Hollis's garb shredded in the air and fluttered to the floor among the gore. He began to crumble to ash.

Azenor screamed.

All that was left of the Demons of Cronus and Christmas was Azenor. All that was left was the present—the now.

The Ghost of Christmas Past had been beheaded.

The Ghost of Christmas-Yet-To-Come had been torn.

And now the Ghost of Christmas Present was destined for a fate among her brethren.

The hellhounds bayed mournfully before slipping beneath the earth to return to the underworld. Sparks danced on the stones before they completely disappeared.

With the Elven Star finished, Lucia let Azenor shatter her patched shield. She readied the spell and took aim. When she released it, there was a sudden, violent flash of blinding white light. Lucia winced and covered her eyes, ducking beneath her hand.

It didn't even have to touch Azenor to be successful. Just being in the mere presence of divine light was annihilation for the demon. Azenor froze, hung in the air, suspended by seraphic light. It shone through her skin, her white wings. Her mouth and nose and eyes were filled with this potent white light.

It was seconds before the light consumed Azenor, turning her into a winged pillar of momentary divinity. Her mouth was open in a silent scream as it took her, the purity of the light boiling the infernal runes from her flesh. She turned supernova before she shattered into a thousand stars with a silent scream.

Ash rained down as snow began to fall from the broken glass ceiling. Wind whispered through the cracks, keening with the echoes of demon's death knells.

All that remained was Nicholas.

Lucia and Benedict were both breathing heavy after the destruction of two demons, but they both turned their attentions to Nicholas and Sabine. Sabine was clawing her way out of an illusion, snarling insults at her once lover.

"Useless fiend! Vile cockroach! Impotent bastard!"

Nicholas batted away her spells until she suddenly charged him, dodging an illusion. Sabine summoned a cleaving sigil and with that bloody red light she arced the magic downward and severed both of Nicholas's hands at the wrist.

He screamed as both his hands thumped to the flagstones, never to cast again. He whipped his gaze up to Sabine, panic lighting his gray eyes while she looked at him with all the viciousness of a wild beast.

Slowly, and with a flare of dramatics, Sabine began casting and grinned devilishly. Lucia knew the spell Sabine was casting would have normally taken mere seconds to draw, but she knew Sabine wanted him to suffer. To feel the impending doom and death. Sabine was the fastest caster Lucia had ever known, but this drawn-out spell was for show. When Sabine drew the last line of cleaving, she held it aloft for a moment.

"If there was a god he would forsake you, if there was a devil he would pity you," Sabine enunciated slowly. "But there is not. There is only me and I am your ruin."

With that, Sabine cut her magic down and split Nicholas down the middle—from skull to groin. Blood flooded out, splattering noisily on the stone before his body crumpled in a messy heap. Viscera and gore were violently showing, organs spilling out, heart letting out a few struggled beats. A single gray eye stared out from the remains.

Sabine's chest was heaving, silent tears coasting down her cheeks. Her arms hung limply at her sides while she took it all in, or maybe even drew into herself and away from it all.

The demons were annihilated.

The caster was dead.

The Nightmare Curse ended there.

"It's over," Lucia breathed, turning to Benedict in disbelief. "We did it. You're free."

Benedict looked between Lucia and his hands in terror. His green eyes met her, filled with all the despair she felt thundering towards her heart.

"I'm fading away."

DECEMBER 24, 1866

He felt the previously untouchable curse threads snap in his chest. As soon as all the demons and Nicholas were eliminated, whatever bond they held over him broke away, the edges crumbling. As the curse hold fell away, Benedict began to feel light—airy, intangible. He realized that with the curse officially ended time was pulling him back to his own.

The tug was insistent and inescapable. He met Lucia's eyes with the barest despair he owned. He would never see her again.

He tried to commit her to memory. Her long black hair, the waves windblown and tangled. Her eyes, like two sapphires, thick lashes framing them. Her beautiful sculpted face, the high cheekbones, the slope of her nose, her pillowy lips.

He'd never touch her again, kiss her again, make love to her again. She was slipping through his fingers all over again. Tears brimmed in his eyes, stinging, blurring her visage.

"I love you," he choked out, fading.

"No!" Lucia despaired, racing over to him. She grasped his hands and though he could feel it, it felt like if she squeezed too hard, her hands would go through.

"I'm so sorry love, but you get to live. You get to save people."

"Not without you."

"We don't know for certain what happens to this body," Benedict said ruefully. "Maybe my past's consciousness will return." Though he wasn't certain, because not only was his spirit fading, this body was too.

"I'm not taking that risk," Lucia said determinedly. "You're not going anywhere."

Benedict's mind was floating, he was ceasing to be.

A flash of emerald and white light pricked his consciousness. He caught sight of a seraphic rune, but he wasn't well educated enough in the celestial sorts to know what it was. A flicker of black magic came next and Benedict recognized the infernal binding rune. Ebony and ivory and viridian danced between Lucia's fingers, a furrow in her brow, fire in her eyes. Blood painted her skin as she carved runes, sigils hung in the air, runes floated between.

Benedict felt himself sway, his mind muddled and splitting in two. He felt pulled in two different directions, like opposing magnets. Until finally he felt something spear his chest, like a harpoon locking him in place. He was no longer fading. He was firmly on the ground. He gasped and then his mind cleared with startling, sparkling clarity.

Lucia's blue eyes were filled with angry tears, black and white and green magic wreathing her, blood marring her golden skin. She was shaking and Benedict went to her. He was sure on his feet as he captured her up.

"What did you do?"

"What I had to."

He pulled back and cupped her cheeks. "Am I truly here?"

She nodded, tears coasting down her cheeks. "I bound us together. Blood by blood, soul by soul."

Benedict gave a start. "So, if I die…?"

"Then I die, too."

"*Lucia,*" he said with dismay. "How could you risk yourself like that?"

"I don't want this life without you. I love you; I *need* you."

Emotion surged in Benedict and burned in his chest. His eyes watered and he clutched her tighter. Without conscious thought his lips were crashing down on hers. They were so soft, sweet, and decadent—he could get drunk on it. Her lips moved against his, pouring passion and devastation into the kiss, so potent he could taste it. He knew she was just as intoxicated as he.

Lucia let out a soft moan, almost a whine against his mouth. He smiled in turn against hers, his hands roving up her sides, along her spine, and into her hair at the nape of her neck.

They were sweaty and messy and bloody, but it was evident that neither of them seemed to mind. Benedict had injuries and they sparked pain at every touch—even so, he never voiced it for fear Lucia would stop. He needed her touch branded into his skin.

The sound of a door opening startled them and Benedict chanced a look at the reasoning. Sabine was striding out of the broken courtyard, back held painfully straight, head high. Benedict realized with a pang of self-loathing that Sabine just witnessed their rejoicing moment when she was just forced to slay her own lover. Guilt struck him, but he couldn't quash the relief and disbelief of what Lucia had done for him—for them.

He was looking at Sabine's disappearing form with a mixture of emotions when Lucia's hands came to his jaw and cupped him. Gently, she turned his gaze to hers.

"She will be okay. We will be here for her. But right now, can we have this moment?"

"Of course," he whispered, and bent down slowly to kiss her again.

It was more chaste this time, but that made it all the more meaningful. It was measured but that didn't mean it wasn't loving. It was a reassurance and a confirmation.

They broke apart and then tipped their foreheads together.

"Think we can get back by Christmas morning?"

Lucia laughed. "Perhaps with all three of us and some magic? Yes, I think a Christmas miracle is possible."

Together, hand in hand, they left behind the massacre they'd rent. Forevermore, the abandoned Edwards estate would be sullied by the culmination of the Nightmare Curse—of the final Nightmare Curse. And despite it never coming to pass in this timeline, Lucia's death would forever stain that fountain's edge. This place would be the product of ghost stories and sordid tales of woe and misery. Benedict didn't mind, the place should be demolished anyhow, there was nothing but bad memories here for all those involved.

They found Sabine and wrapped her up. They didn't say anything as she cried.

STAVE SEVEN

DECEMBER 25, 1866

Everyone woke up surprised when no death occurred from the Nightmare Curse Christmas morning. The church bells chiming the hour did not toll a demise. Instead, it heralded a new era free of the Demons of Cronus and Christmas.

But no one knew that. Not right away. It was only Lucia and the few surrounding her that had participated in the destruction of the curse, and the killing of the demons, who did.

Surprisingly enough, despite the horrid conditions of the road and the whiteout from the snow, they did indeed make it back for Christmas morning. They'd ridden the horses hard through the snow, strengthening them with sigils, keeping the riders warm with more magic. No one said anything about the conspicuous presence of only two mounts. Lucia didn't mention how Sabine had been forced to ride with Nicholas on the journey to the estate. He'd been bound and gagged, but even so, she knew Sabine hated it, but perhaps she hated his absence even more. Lucia riding with Benedict this time felt like some sort of cosmic juxtaposition she didn't want to ponder.

Immediately upon arriving at Benedict's townhouse, they took note of the cleared police presence and the complete lack of heat. The home had been plunged into winter's chill and it was dark. Without a word, Sabine set off with an incendiary spell in hand to all the hearths in the home and lit them all.

Baths were drawn and they all bathed. It was the wee hours in the morning when the three of them sat before the drawing room fire, once again in the nest of blankets Sabine and Lucia had slept in last time. They were exhausted, but sleep didn't claim them like one would expect. Instead, they sat there together, Lucia in the middle, sharing a plate of cookies, commiserating in the pain of Nicholas's loss and betrayal—and how it had hurt them all in different ways. Yet each was just as potent as the last.

Come the morning as the bells tolled, a knock sounded at the door. Benedict went to receive it, dressed in sleep clothes and a dressing gown. Lucia followed, dressed similarly, her ebony locks still damp and freely cascading down her back.

"Merry Christmas," a messenger greeted brightly upon the opened door. "This is for a Lord Edwards from a Lord Turner. Is this the right address?"

"It is," Benedict confirmed.

"All right then." The messenger handed over a thick envelope and in exchange Benedict dropped a couple coins in the messenger's hand. He tipped his hat in thanks as he scurried down the steps.

Benedict called a Merry Christmas as well, and then he returned inside to the much warmer house, and opened the letter. The contents spilled out and Benedict read it all eagerly. After a moment he chuckled a laugh and shook his head, pleasantly surprised.

"What?" Lucia asked from behind him, wrapping her arms around his waist.

"Look," Benedict said, handing her the letter.

Luther had been working around the clock the past few days—all last night included—to dismantle the corruption of the board and Nicholas's wrongdoings. It wasn't over, nor would it be for a very long time, but he'd made significant strides.

This was the report of his success.

Unofficially, the Brotherhood admitted all of Nicholas's involvement and employing of them; on the record, an undisclosed organization was contracted by the traitor. With all the evidence Lucia and Sabine had gathered, Luther was able to take one copy of it to the boards, and one copy to each of the editors in chief of all of Vonor's newspapers, plus an additional copy to the dean of the university. They were forced to change their self-interested and selfish goals of money on the board, or face a reckoning when the Herald, Tribune, and Gazette all tore apart their reputations. Many members had now stepped or were stepping down from their positions, while a few had attempted threats. Which were met by a visit from the Brotherhood—on behalf of Lord Turner.

Luther had also organized and paid for any funeral costs for Huffam once the investigation was closed—with a small bribe to keep their non-reporting of the crime to a small slap on the wrist of "don't do that again" rather than an obstruction of justice or accomplice. There was also a note offering sincere condolences for Benedict's loss from his soon to be father-in-law.

It wasn't all going to be undone in one night, but they'd done some significant damage to the board's reputation and made some progression towards ensuring the proper use of the board and its seats—and it wasn't to fill pockets with coin.

"My father came through for us," she said softly. She paused, twisting her lips in thought. "Isn't it odd," she continued, "that we thought he was the one behind it all—to kill me and curse you—and he ends up not being the villain, but the person who sorts the mess behind the scenes?"

"It is, but I rather prefer this outcome—you being able to keep your father—even if we had to lose Nicholas instead."

Lucia placed a hand on his breast, over his heart. She knew a piece of it was broken, and she wanted to fix it. His parents would've never done the same for him. His dearest friend had led the ultimate betrayal against him and now the love he'd held for him was wholly corrupted.

"It is not so simple as a trade."

"No, it is not," he agreed.

She pressed a kiss behind his ear. "We'll move past this. One day this will be but a memory, but you and I will both be here still."

"Promise?"

"Promise."

Benedict covered the hand that was on his chest and turned slightly to kiss her. Their lips met slowly and Benedict lightly traced her bottom lip with the tip of his tongue. She was just about ready to deepen the kiss when he pulled back.

"We have a wedding to get to."

Lucia's eyes flew wide. "We what?"

"Don't you remember? You agreed to marry me today."

Lucia was dumbstruck. "You wish to marry today? After everything?"

"It'll be all the more reason to. We don't need an extravagant event. Just a small intimate thing. For us."

Lucia inhaled and blinked, mulling over his words. She considered and then sighed. "All right. But only if I get to wear my dress—I had it custom made, I'll have you know."

"Of course, my love."

Hasty invitations were sent to Lucia's parents, requesting their presence before the poison garden for the marriage of their daughter. Sabine had taken the reins on the event, quickly fashioning an arch decorated with swaths of evergreen boughs, red velvet ribbons, and mistletoe. A sprig hung directly in the center, perfect for encouraging the pronouncement kiss. In addition to Sabine's arbor skills, she pulled Lucia's hair in a loose chignon, tucking holly and mistletoe into the waves.

When Lucia came into view, she did so on the arm of her father under the watchful gaze of her maid of honor— Sabine, dressed in deepest wintergreen—Lucia's mother, and Benedict. Benedict was standing on one side of the arch, clad in a black and crimson suit. Lucia's red lips curved in a smile as she looked down.

Benedict couldn't take his eyes off of her and she watched those jade eyes darken as he drank her in.

Her dress was form-hugging, lace over satin, the sleeves coming to a point over the back of her hands, her shoulders bare. The skirt flared over her hips, but kept a slit up the thigh, allowing a glimpse of the scarlet garter above her knee. Angry and bloody marks were still carved into her flesh, evidence of her affinity for infernal and seraphic runes, but Benedict didn't seem to mind.

It was cold, but the clouds had parted to reveal the sun. Creamy gold light sprinkled across the snow, lending a soft buttery haze to the scene. The pathway they walked on had been cleared and it glittered beneath the sunshine and the warmth of the fires provided by the present warlocks. Flames of viridian, cerulean, crimson, and jade licked the winter air, swallowing the faint snowflakes that began to fall.

It was painfully noted that Benedict had no best man, and Nicholas's absence was like a physical thing.

As Lucia made her way to the end of the path, Benedict stood there with a halo of snowflakes on his brow. Luther handed Lucia off to Benedict with a clap on the shoulder and a smile. Benedict returned it. A snowflake melted on his lashes, but it was clear he didn't care. He only had eyes for her.

"You and I are here," Benedict whispered.

"And it's just the beginning."

They joined hands and their officiant began.

DECEMBER 25, 1866

They were married in the garden and they made love in their home. This merging of their bodies was an intimacy like no other—their souls bonded in blood, their hearts linked through vows; a binding they never wished to break.

Benedict and Lucia were scarred many times over from the ordeal. Physical ones like the runes Lucia had carved into her arms and chest, and internal ones like a traitor's mark. But Benedict would take these wounds a thousand times over the life he'd been forced to endure before the curse.

Once upon a time this was the worst Christmas of his life—imprisoned, alone, shattered, and the love of his life murdered. Now, his love was wrapped in his arms, her golden flesh bare beneath his hands, free for him to touch as he pleased—and oh he touched, and oh he pleased.

"I love you," he whispered against the soft skin of her ribs, lips coasting over the underside of her breast.

She arched, running her hands through his chestnut locks. "I'll never get sick of hearing that."

"Good, because I don't plan on stopping."

She giggled. "Speaking of stopping, I think we have dinner to get to. My parents will only wait so long."

Benedict groaned against her. "Don't they understand what day this is?"

"It was Christmas first, darling."

"Bah humbug," he joked.

Lucia arched a brow. "Do you wish to tempt fate?"

"I wish to tempt you," he flirted, his voice sultry.

"Cad," she teased.

"Vixen," he returned, pinning her down into the bed as he slowly entered her.

She sighed, hips undulating with his rhythm, feeling exquisite pleasure build between them. Their movements danced together until the crescendo built and they crashed against each other, climaxes taking them as they shuddered and pulsed through the final waves.

When they finished, Benedict simply held her realizing she was his and he was never letting her go again. Because he would let nothing—not even space or time or death—take her.

EPILOGUE

DECEMBER 25, 1873

This Christmas had been the one to change it all seven years ago. Seven years ago, Lucia's husband was cursed and broke time to save her. In doing so, he'd saved countless lives—those who were victim to the Nightmare Curse and those afflicted by the Wasting.

The cure was quickly dispensed to those who'd needed it, and now no one had to die of the Wasting or Ember Fever if they sought the treatment. But first, Benedict had specifically called upon Christopher Taylor to have him be the first recipient. Mister Taylor was more than overcome with emotion and begged to repay Benedict in some way, but her husband would not have it. Since then, the two had struck up a friendship. It was not enough to heal the wound Nicholas had left, but it helped.

Lucia sighed happily and watched her two children chase each other around the Christmas tree while she placed a hand to her swollen belly. She had fallen pregnant with their first, Stella, just a month after they'd married. It had been perfect timing to get the cure for Ember Fever released before she settled in for the duration of pregnancy. Born right as summer was giving way to autumn, Stella was a beautiful babe with wide eyes that stayed doll blue, and her father's chestnut hair. Her brother, Eric, two years her junior, had his father's jade eyes and his mother's black locks.

The room was alight with a golden glow from the candles and tree, the heavy red drapes parted to reveal as much sunlight as possible. Their family dog, a golden retriever fondly called Goldie, was sprawled on a pillow before the crackling fire—a red ribbon tied in place of a collar.

Lucia smiled as Stella caught Eric, the two of them tumbling to the floor, laughing. Turquoise light wreathed Eric's fingers, powder-blue magic dancing between Stella's. The two of them were coming into their magic slowly and moments of high emotion—happiness included—brought out sparks of it. Lucia knew it would soon to be time to teach them.

They would have time soon. Lucia's studies were mostly conducted from the home now with the children. She had given up her office placement years ago, but still came in if they were in a pinch. She missed teaching sometimes, and she went in when the desire struck her, but she loved being with her children more.

"Merry Christmas and Happy Anniversary, my wife," Benedict said, coming up behind her. He placed a hand on her belly and kissed her throat just as their third baby kicked at his touch.

Lucia leaned into his affections as she felt their child move within her. This was everything she had ever wanted. How had she gotten so lucky?

"Happy Anniversary, husband," she murmured as he bent down for a kiss.

She pressed her lips to his. A slide of his tongue against the seam of her lips had her opening for him and she positively melted for his touch even after seven years of marriage.

"And a very Merry Christmas," she finished against his mouth.

Suddenly, the front door opened and a very familiar voice called out.

"Everyone better be in their Christmas best—or at the very least, clothed in here!"

Stella and Eric gasped in unison and scrambled to their feet. "Auntie Sabine!"

The two of them—in their Christmas best of evergreen velvet—took off to greet their aunt just as she came around, arms laden with parcels and gifts for the children. Stella and Eric wound themselves around Sabine's material clad legs— she had sworn off dresses unless the occasion truly warranted it—and made her carry them into the drawing room with peals of laughter.

Dickens, their butler, had taken over duties after Huffam's and Nicholas's deaths. Seeing Sabine struggle with the children and presents, he went to assist with the parcels.

Sabine, too, had healed since that arduous Christmas. No longer did her dark eyes hold the pain of betrayal. It only came in flashes now—as it did for all of them—but there were new people in their lives, and those people were the balm to that particular burn.

"Mama!" Eric called from Sabine's left leg. "Will you tell us the Christmas Story?"

Lucia smiled. "Oh, I think your father tells it much better."

Eric turned his hopeful gaze on Benedict, who positively melted under his son's innocent green gaze.

"All right, come sit by the fire."

The children disengaged from Sabine and scurried over, sharing the large pillow with each other and Goldie. They settled in, and before Benedict went over to their babies, he kissed Lucia one more time. When he crossed to them, Sabine came to stand beside Lucia, locking arms, just as another guest arrived, leaning against a doorframe and staring adoringly at Sabine. Then, Benedict crouched before their children and recited the tale.

"It all began, once upon a nightmare curse."

AUTHOR'S NOTE

The Nightmare Curse draws inspiration from both Charles Dickens's "A Christmas Carol" and Dante's "Inferno", and while I used their imagery to support the narrative of the world of Infernal Curses, I do not believe in the Christian faith. I especially do not believe that certain people are damned. Therefore, while Heaven and Hell do exist in The Nightmare Curse, they do not appear as they do in scripture.

I also want to speak on two other modern inspirations for The Nightmare Curse. Those two are Rebecca F. Kenney's "A Court of Sugar and Spice" and the film Scrooge: A Christmas Carol (2022).

Last year, Rebecca and I spoke about both wanting to write Christmas Carol retellings for the holiday season of 2023, I was very clear about my inspirations and we decided we should both write our stories. Even though our books came from the same source material, they are wildly different.

Scrooge: A Christmas Carol (2022) is what sparked the entire concept of the time travel and staying in the past portion. I watched it on repeat last Christmas with my first daughter and I kept getting drawn into the moment with the song "Later Never Comes" and I wondered what could have happened if

Scrooge were allowed to go back in time. If he could mend his mistakes. If he could be with his Isabel/Belle. I decided I wanted to find out.
And thus, with those four pieces of media I was inspired to write the world of Infernal Curses.

ACKNOWLEDGEMENTS

It's always surreal writing these. To be wrapping up my third published book is so unbelievable—especially on the heels of my trilogy wrapping up. There's always so many people to thank and I'm always so worried I'll forget someone, so, in no particular order…

As always, Michael, thank you for everything you are, everything you do, and everything you will be. You are my unwavering support in this life; you push me, guide me, motivate me, and applaud me. I could not have pursued this journey without you. I love you.

Thank you, times one thousand to Kaja McDonald/Averil the Artist (@bookishaveril) for designing this stunning cover and for constantly going above and beyond for me. Your support and enthusiasm means the world to me. You are so wonderfully talented and sweet, and I can't wait to continue working together on future projects.

Rebecca F. Kenney, without you this book legitimately wouldn't exist. Your book was one of the biggest inspirations to start this novel—and truth be told, you are one of my biggest inspirations. Thank you for supporting me in this indie author journey, answering all my silly questions, beta reading for me, sharing my posts, checking in this summer about the progress on the retelling, and for being you. I know you're busy, but you're incredible.

The Last Wyrd, you ladies give me life. Thank you for being there when I need to vent or need writing advice. I can't wait to see what you all put out next.

To my beta readers, (Julie, Josette, Marcella, Ashley, Logan, Gabriela, Nirav, and Kennedy) thank you so much for taking a chance on me and my little dark Christmas book—especially with such short notice and turnaround. Producing creative content is my biggest dream, but often it feels like screaming into the void, and just you showing interest was enough to reassure me and your enthusiasm for this story made my heart so warm. Thank you for believing in me.

Thank you to Cydney Daemon (@cydneydaemon) for your ceaseless love for my writing. Your DMs always brighten my day and you are quite possibly one of the sweetest people I've ever encountered on Instagram. Thank you for liking and sharing all my posts, and showing such excitement for my upcoming projects.

To Vivienne and Rosalie, my daughters, my sweet baby girls. Neither of you two know it yet, but you are what makes it all worth it, and you are what gives me the balance I need in this life. Thank you for existing, I love you both more than words can explain.

Thank you to Maria and Sierra who both showed endless enthusiasm and support for this book and me, even though it may not be your cup of tea. Y'all are the best and I'm so lucky to have you both in my life.

Mom, thank you so much for everything you've done, especially helping me with the girls so I can keep being an author and a mom. Thank you for sharing my books and being so proud of me. I love you.

Dad, Jenna, and Brandon, thank you for being there for me—but maybe don't read this one, or my others. (Okay, Jenna can, but that's it.)

And finally, thank YOU as always, dear reader. For taking this chance on me and this little book. I hope you enjoyed it and if you did, I'd greatly appreciate it if you left a review. I hope you stick around to see what I come up with next!

ABOUT THE AUTHOR

Kayla McGrath has been writing since the age of thirteen out of spite, having read a book with a love triangle that didn't go her way. After that, it became a passion. If she's not writing, then she's reading, or drinking endless cups of chai. Kayla lives on Vancouver Island with her husband, two daughters, and two boxers.

She is the author of the Cold as Iron trilogy and the Infernal Curses series. The Nightmare Curse is her third book.

You can find her on Twitter (@KaylaMcGrath_), TikTok (@kaylamcgrath_), and on Instagram/Threads (@kaylamcgrathbooks).

THE COLD AS IRON TRILOGY
This Broken Memory
These Ruined Dreams
Our Shattered Fates (Coming Soon!)

INFERNAL CURSES
The Nightmare Curse

"He isn't who he says he is, but more importantly, she isn't who she thought she was."

Book one in the Cold as Iron trilogy, available in paperback, e-book, and on Kindle Unlimited.
Turn the page for the first chapter!

CHAPTER 1

There are monsters in the north and one is dead at my feet.

I didn't kill it. I'm not sure I'm capable but given the circumstances and opportunity I would. I absolutely would. The iridescent wings allow a false sense of whimsy, but I know their jagged edges are a more reliable indicator of their nature. What I know is that they hunt for pleasure, and they kill for more.

Whatever got to this one was no gentle beast, rounds of torment haunt this corpse, varying levels of healing wounds scatter its form. Missing nails and teeth, gashes in delicate flesh, burns upon limbs. Its face is a ruin, its eyes flat and white. It's as if it were tortured.

This is the second one I've found.

It had been only three days ago and I'd mistaken the last one for human. It was after a closer look I noticed its pupils were cat eye slits and patches of its skin were lilac-scaled, glimmering in the catching light like a fish.

With a start, I notice the soundlessness of the air. There's the easy quiet of almost silence—of breath and birdsong—and then there's the eerie silence before their arrival. It twists up and out, blanketing the world beneath a heavy cloak, as if even the river cowers in its bed.

I pause in my investigating, listening. Springy boughs of the evergreens above sway in the wind, whistling through. The permafrost layering the vast Yukon muffles sound and bites into my knees through the leather, nipping into my toes. My eyes survey the silvery sky, noting the likelihood of snow on the horizon—another sound dampener. Snow, in this northernmost hell can be the difference between life and death. It's the difference between exposure from the elements and exposure to them.

Dread sinks low in my gut, an oppressive haze of malicious sick. The foul aura scrapes at the edges of my consciousness, the malevolent presence closing in. Dark. Wrong. Sinister. Deadly.

Finally, there's a definitive rustle and I'm on my feet, alert.

It isn't one of them, but they're coming.

Palming a blade I'd stolen years ago, I shoulder my backpack encumbered by venison and a strapped compound bow, and begin hastily backing up. Keeping my eyes trained upon the direction of the sound, I feel behind me for the rough bark of a climbable tree, sweat beading upon my brow. Through the thicket and beyond the bushes, the sharp, steady crunch of twigs sets my fight or flight alive.

A creature launches forth from the woods and my heart lunges in my chest. I curse and stumble, realizing with an exhalation that the beast is not a bear with salivating black jaws or worse, but a terrified deer. It's hardly a blink before it's gone. Fear-induced adrenaline sets my heart thundering only for reality to strike it still. The stag is scared, and the apex predator it's outrunning is drawing straight for me.

I turn and climb. Despite the plenty of handholds I claw into, I do not find myself grateful. My hitched breathing is marred by frequent swearing as I haul myself and my bag up the tree, each branch becoming more and more precarious. It's when a rotted branch snaps, where I slip down the trunk, that my mortality hits me. A fall will kill me just as easily as they can.

The bark rips into my palms as I scrabble and gasp, but with bleeding fingers I manage a last reach and find myself blessedly on a sturdy branch. My feet are supple and sure upon the last couple limbs, the final ascension to moderate safety. Seconds later I lean back against the evergreen, chest heaving and sweat burning my eyes. Gazing down through the needles, I spot the dead monster below—which might be a shining beacon on my location. I pray that they pass me over, that they stumble across the body without searching for foul play. Or even, that they find a new thrill before that ominous and ever creeping presence discovers me.

I pray it goes away.

I breathe.

The sickness crawls over me, telling me that they're here, and then there's a vibrant spot of color in the clearing. I clasp a bloody hand over my mouth, knowing exactly what the bright bit of blue and ill sensation means.

Them.

White flesh melds with a shock of cobalt blue scales upon forearms to razor-tipped claws that spread down forelegs into the talons of a dragon. It's humanoid, with a beautiful face and midnight eyes. Long silver hair flows like a banner, a crown of antlers settling on its brow. It is garbed in little more than a draped sheet, dingy and dirty but once white.

Unsheathing the blade I'd managed to wedge into my boot during the climb, I grip it in a fist like a talisman and hold my breath. My heart crashes in its cage, frantic as a bird.

The creatures have a wicked presence about them. It is an aura, penetrating like smoke and darkness, a sticky haze that becomes progressively more oppressive until you feel as if you'll never take a breath again. I've had this sixth sense of detection as far back as I can remember. Ever since I became trapped in this wasteland and waking without a flicker of memories.

I watch in horror as the creature stands next to the slain beast. The monster stops and ponders, prodding the corpse with a toe. A second figure, small horns coiling from its brow, a lion-like tail swishing from the base of its spine, steps from the shadows uttering a chiming, masculine chuckle, while the first lets out a snort of disdain. As nausea threatens to lodge in my throat, the horned-and-tailed figure hauls off the butchered thing without a word. I hold my breath, an anxiety-riddled scream threatening to burst as they depart, moving with animal grace and the surety of being completely unrivalled.

I wait, watching the evening light fade fast and burn into the deep purple of night. I wait, clutching the knife. I wait longer than I must. I wait until the anxiety quells and my heart slows to a natural rhythm.

When I eventually deem it safe to descend, I wince from my stiff neck and aching muscles. Rubbing my pains away, I search the vicinity, probing with that innate sense and finding no creatures roaming or lingering.

Returning my weapon to my boot, I clamber down from the tree, stewing in resentment. Try as I might, I cannot escape the forest. I have no long-term means to defend myself and I have little to show for my extended survival here. I don't even know who I am. I have no idea where I'm supposed to be or what to do. Was I truly the only survivor of the crash with Jacob? I've only been able to bring myself to venture that way once, unable to stomach the massacre that Jacob had painted before me. I've never investigated for evidence of survivors, but the frenetic energy of the creatures surrounding the site has been enough to keep me at bay.

Halfway down the tree an explosion rings out and I jump in surprise, nearly plummeting the remaining distance. Far to the east is a large fire, orange and yellow flames licking up the sides of something considerable, smoke pluming into the air aggressively like a locomotive train. It isn't so unusual for the monsters to create unnecessary destruction.

Exhausted from day's events, I drop the remaining feet and pull out a small flashlight, anxious to navigate the long stretch of forest to my cabin. My home base used to be a cabin for a well-off—if not particularly wealthy—family, but aside from my stay, has remained vacant. The building is entirely self-sufficient with solar panels, generators, personal well, and every system required to manage a household. There's a semblance of safety to it, a presence of protection in addition to its natural warmth. There's something about the place that naturally deters the monsters—something about it so repellent that they refuse to come near.

Within hours the sky permeates into solid ebony—midnight—and only the thin beam of my light cuts the dark. It's when I find myself at home, I can breathe a sigh of relief.

The cabin stands sturdy and grand, from the preciously chosen logs, to the immaculately maintained tin roof. It welcomes me with a solid door made from cedar and iron, its black shutters hammered into the same metal that flank the windows. The structure spans an acceptable two floors, boasting a single furnished bedroom and another smaller bedroom, sans mattress, as well as a lavish but entirely unused study. The slate steps leading up to the porch before the front door are comfortably worn with age and unknown footsteps.

I know this place's secrets like an old friend. I know that the shutters on the bathroom window have rusted out and now rattle in the wind, that the second step on the inside staircase creaks, and that the kettle on the kitchen stove has a heart-shaped dent in the bottom edge.

As I begin up the stone path, watching my feet on the uneven pavers, a sense of something wrong bleeds into my awareness. I pause. It isn't them, but I take in the home. It takes exactly seven seconds before I realize.

The lights are on and smoke is curling out of the chimney.

"Everyone has secrets, and they are unravelling the very fabric of fate itself."

Book two in the Cold as Iron trilogy, out now! Available in paperback, e-book, and on Kindle Unlimited.

"It's time to play Lady Fate's Game."

The final book in the Cold as Iron trilogy, coming this winter! Soon to be available in paperback, e-book, and on Kindle Unlimited.

Kayla McGrath